More Than Halfway There

David Hartshorn

ISBN: 978-0-578-55504-1

For Bev. Always Bev.

Prologue

Two moments cause a queasiness in the belly of a weary hiker who's been laboring through the woods too long: when everything looks the same, or when nothing seems familiar. Like the subtle onset of a head cold – a sniffle here, a rogue cough there – the realization creeps steadily up on him until he's forced to concede he is lost, and hopelessly so. Either he's wandering without bearings beneath a suffocating canopy of trees and clambering over the same mossy rocks from hours before, or he's encountering, with flagging spirit, unrecognizable terrain, where even the strongest sunlight is serrated by dense foliage overhead into jagged shafts of pale yellow on the forest floor. As afternoon's shadows lengthen and merge into the gloom of twilight, panic pushes its way into his throat and lodges there. Uneasiness turns to dread. No longer in search of adventure, he simply wants out of this inscrutable landscape. I know this because I've been that hiker, though I'm jumping way ahead of myself in the story's telling. Before losing direction in the Great North Woods of New Hampshire, once my home, I had to cram what remained of an abandoned life into some suitcases and a few trash bags and go searching for a new one.

Hunkering down in my former hometown marked the latest tally in a lengthening loss column. Like an animal with an instinct for the underbrush, I needed a place to lick my wounds in private. Years earlier, before my world exploded, when I was certain I was busting out of this town for good, I'd barely glanced in the rear view mirror as my tires clawed at the gravel beneath them, spewing dust and pebbles into the collective faces of everyone I was leaving behind. Now, almost thirty years removed from my grand escape and parked in a scenic rest area on the hilltop overlooking Jackson Meadows, I shook my head like a punch drunk fighter about to force his body through one more round, even when he understands that the blows to follow are likely to send him crashing to the canvas. In the distance below, the sleepy village beckoned like a Rockwell postcard. Church spires rose in homage to an unresponsive Almighty, and giant trees, outlasting generations of families, lined streets with homes sagging and listing beneath the weight of their years. But I knew different. And I hadn't forgotten why I'd left. It was all I could do to turn the key in the ignition and point my car toward a town that had always discouraged its inhabitants from dreaming or deserting.

CHAPTER ONE

"Well glory be, look what the dog's dragged home. If it isn't Jacob Taylor." As I rumble up my father's rutted gravel driveway and hoist open the trunk of my car, freshly coated with road dust and dead bugs, the voice now hailing me from the direction of the house next door is a familiar one. It belongs to John Caldwell. Nearly half a lifetime ago he was my closest friend and co-conspirator in the petty offenses of our youth. Nowadays John lives with his wife and children in his boyhood home, a rambling structure of steep, pointed gables and brown paint flaking away like pencil shavings. John's ancestral roots burrow deep into the fertile history of Jackson Meadows, and there's no question he's a lifer here. The month is May, so John is clean shaven, his habit being to forgo his razor once the average daily temperature nears the freezing mark and allow his beard to flourish until Groundhog Day. Never in any particular hurry, he ambles out from behind a woodpile stacked with architectural precision and crosses the patchwork of dirt and grass which passes for his lawn, approaching with an easy familiarity, as if we've spoken only yesterday. In truth, I've taken pains to avoid him during my recent trips back here, a thought that stabs at my already bruised conscience.

No one properly indoctrinated in the customs of Jackson Meadows, New Hampshire has ever placed much stock in social niceties, and thus John and I make quick work of the obligatory handshake and "how ya doin's," successfully conveying affability without divulging any sensitive information. John then lingers beside me at the rear of the car, sizing up my trunk load of sad belongings. To say he is at a loss for words would imply that he is searching for them. Which he is not. He is perfectly comfortable standing there, more or less in silence, letting one unexpressed thought cascade into another. From years of experience interpreting the empty spaces in our conversations, I know John's going to think this unexpected encounter through before committing to any communication beyond the obligatory, even when it's as obvious as a missing front tooth that my car is down one occupant. Knowing John like I know myself, I also know he's not going there, not yet anyway.

Despite the distance that time and circumstance have wedged between us, John still feels like a brother to me, though there's no denying we shoulder the weighty history of contradictory emotions which often accompany such a kinship. Two years my senior, John matured half as fast. As kids we were inseparable, and I lived to emulate him. The way he dressed or walked or combed his hair – I plagiarized it all. If John liked a song, it became my favorite too, and I naturally fell into his habit of composing songs, always silly, about characters who lived in our village tucked snugly into the White Mountains.

There was, for instance, Percy Wright – pencil thin and ragged – who squatted in a tar paper shack near a sandpit in Reverend Hollow, the saddest part of our poor town. With shoulders permanently stooped, he'd scuffle past mismatched wooden storefronts which ran the length of Main Street, his sunken eyes fixed on the sidewalks and gutters in search of currency and cigarette butts. *(Watch out, I'm stinky Percy/ Touch me and you're gonna need a nursey.)* We took care to hold our breath as we passed through his airspace. And then there was Betty "Sandbags" Rollins, another street dweller, with ginormous breasts apparently no bra could accommodate. She fascinated two wide-eyed, pubescent boys. *(Call me big Betty Rollins/Giant jugs I be a haulin'.)*

"Need a hand?" John offers, interrupting my musings. Obviously he's deduced from the luggage that I'm going to be bunking next door to him.

"Pretty light load," I reply. "But sure. Appreciate it." Ten minutes in town and already I've reverted to the terse vernacular still in fashion around here. Closed mouths, closed minds: the Jackson Meadows prescription for living. Yet even as our spare conversation crawls turtle-like below the customary social speed limit, I can barely summon the energy to keep pace; and like an actor in a theater with lousy acoustics, I find myself straining to project my voice.

"No problem there," John assures me. "Looks like you've only packed for one. Me, I'm just building up the old woodpile. Months to go till lockin' up time." By which, of course, he means winter. It's an expression I've not heard in years, and a bleak reminder of where I've ended up.

"Still feeding that outdoor wood furnace when the weather turns?" I already know the answer, and toss this out in part to keep the conversation going, but mostly to deflect his reference to my solo status.

"It's a good system," he responds with a solemn nod. "I keep the fire going while the chopping and splitting keep the old ticker . . ." He pauses to search for just the right cliché.

"Ticking?" I suggest, ending the suspense.

"You said it."

When I was growing up, the Caldwell family, large and industrious, labored almost daily over their backyard mountain of wood, which expanded and contracted according to temperature and season. It was a matter of family pride never to hand over good money for heat when, with the help of sturdy backs and an abundance of trees, they could produce it practically for free. During the warmer months, the sharp, cracking sound of splitting and stacking, accompanied by an occasional curse prompted by the wayward arc of a sledgehammer or splitting maul, beat like an erratic pulse throughout the neighborhood, and from mid-October until the spreading warmth of April, the Caldwells saturated the air with smoke from seasoned hardwood thick enough to taste. To me, it all seemed vaguely reassuring, as if someone were tending to a welcoming hearth during winter's inhospitable days and nights. In fact, I kind of admired the family's single-minded resoluteness, even when all it entailed was feeding a fire.

"You run on ahead and unlock the door," John suggests, as he easily yanks two bulging suitcases from the cluttered trunk. "I'll catch up."

Although thus far John has rarely broken eye contact, I can see that from the corners of his eyes he's been taking inventory of the contents of my car, scanning for clues to explain the reason for my arrival. A more impetuous conversationalist might come right out and ask. Not John. He keeps his cards well-hidden and waits for the tell.

With my days of confiding in him long ago abandoned, I opt for more banality as we pause in awkward silence on my father's small side porch next to the driveway. Awkward for me at least. I ask him, "How are Meg and the kids? Still got all seven under the same roof?" Then, rather than dig into my pocket for the house key, I instinctively pluck the spare one off a nail hanging behind the paint-starved shutter of the window nearby.

John chooses not to reciprocate by inquiring about persons conspicuously absent from my life, nor does he answer my question about his family. True to form, he responds to a direct question with something other than a direct answer, remarking instead, "That nail's probably older than you. Key too, I'd imagine."

He's right. For all the good the key did us, we might just as well have left the door unlocked when I was growing up. Almost everyone who knew the Taylor family also knew of the key's location, and would routinely help themselves to it when we weren't home. It was not at all unusual to open the kitchen door and find a note on the counter, often commencing with, "You weren't home but . . . ." Sometimes there'd be a postscript to the note informing us that its author had watered the plants, which had looked mighty parched, or had folded some towels in the kitchen laundry basket while awaiting our return. Occasionally there'd be no note, just food left on the counter or in the fridge.

"I seem to recall that little bit of rusty metal causing you some big trouble back in the day," John remarks, nodding with a mischievous grin in the direction of the kitchen. Stealing a page from his playbook I offer no reply, though I do understand exactly what he's referring to. I never considered the key much of a security risk until Pearl Whitney, an elderly church lady bent on taking the express lane to sainthood, utilized it to drop off some homemade cookies for my mother, who was running a bake sale for the ladies' guild at All Saints parish. When old Pearl tottered into our kitchen clutching her decorative tin of cookies – ginger snaps as I recall – she discovered me helping myself to a heavenly confection named Susie Farrell. Barely into our freshman year of high school, Susie and I were compensating with enthusiasm for what we lacked in experience. We hadn't made it out of the kitchen before the frenzied groping and fumbling with buttons and zippers had commenced.

The response to my "How the heck do you unhook this thing?" came not from Susie, but instead from a horrified Pearl, who dropped her cookies where she stood, crossed her hands over her ample bosom and exclaimed, "Sweet Jesus, have mercy!" At the time, I guess Pearl and I were both sending up prayers of a sort, hers being the only one petitioning for spiritual relief.

"The kids are healthy. When you're one of seven you learn pretty quick how to carve out your own private space in life. Meg's good too, or good enough, I suppose." John has answered my question about his family only after I've forgotten asking it, and before I can follow up on his cryptic remark about Meg, he adds, "She still enjoys running the emporium, but good help's hard to come by, even harder to keep." In spite of my dismal circumstances, I smile inwardly to hear John pronounce "harder" as "hahdah." Technology may have shoved our noses into everybody's dirty laundry as the world shrinks to an uncomfortable intimacy, yet the edges of the accents up here in these mountains have been buffed and smoothed only slightly by such encroachments.

John's always referred to Meg's retail business as an "emporium," endeavoring, I assume, to make the place sound more sophisticated than it really is. As animated and enthusiastic as John is reserved, Meg has worked her darnedest to make her customers feel as though they're leaving her cluttered store with a sampling of pastoral New England tucked into their one hundred percent recycled paper bags. And while "Meg's Shop in the Barn" does have its rustic charm, it's largely a run of the mill gift store stuffed with moose and bear figurines, wind chimes, tee shirts, and all things "Robert Frosty," as she likes to put it. Previously, Meg called her establishment "The Old Woman in the Shoe," and even hung a clever, hand-painted sign out front depicting unruly children spilling out the doors and windows of a giant, partially laced boot. Eventually, when one customer after another began reciting for her the abusive and manifestly unlawful ending to that particular nursery rhyme, she wisely junked the sign and changed the name.

With John tarrying behind me on the porch, I wrestle with the key in the stubborn lock until, abruptly, here we stand, just the two of us, true friends in memory only, together in this musty kitchen for the first time in years. Stealing a look around, I sense John eyeing me for a reaction. Unlike the old days, we've not been greeted by any brownies or pies baking in the oven. There's nothing scrumptious warming on the stovetop, no notes from helpful neighbors, and poor, horrified Pearl Whitney shuffled off her mortal coil years ago. These days, empty tin canisters, once stuffed to the brim with flour and sugar, tea bags and homemade cookies, sit uselessly on the dull countertop. The tired wallpaper, faded and stained, separates in spots at the seams and curls back on itself like tiny waves. "Feels a little close in here," I remark, mostly to break the silence which is sitting like an anvil on my chest.

"Let's see, by my calculations your dad's been up there at Meadows Retreat three, nearly four months now. That about right? An empty house'll turn stale in no time." On its surface John's remark sounds innocuous enough. Just the same, I detect reproach beneath it. Choosing not to wait for a response, he strikes off toward the car for more of my stuff, leaving me alone in the lifeless kitchen of a house I own but in no way want.

CHAPTER TWO

As uncomfortable as I might have been with John lurking about, I'm surprisingly more so after he plops the last of my belongings on the yellowed kitchen linoleum, lightly punches my shoulder, and announces his departure. "I'll leave you to get settled in. Gotta get back to work. See you later, maybe."

I catch the "maybe" and interpret it as a dig at my propensity for sidestepping contact with almost everyone in Jackson Meadows. For as long as I can recall the town's weekly newspaper, *The Jackson Meadows Reporter*, has run a "locals" column penned by a succession of gossipy old ladies with little to do other than gather news about who has visited whom, who's been admitted to or discharged from the hospital, and what family has added or subtracted members. Not exactly Pulitzer material. Nevertheless, people here seem to gobble it up. My own mother would never fail to ring up the column's author to report that her son had returned for a short stay, which she'd always describe as "wonderful." After she was gone my father continued the tradition, reluctantly I'd assume, until he pretty much forgot who I was. Despite the occasional publicity, those who knew I'd been returning home rarely spotted me. I was just a name buried in a column or a set of out of state plates parked in the driveway.

With John having taken his leave, my remaining companion is a weariness which long ago burrowed its way into my bones. Standing mute and motionless as a stone in the dining room of the nearly empty house, I close my aching eyes to a silence so deafening it seemingly has the power to rouse the dead. In no time I'm hearing voices of people who once swapped stories over heaping plates of food, people whose love of eating was exceeded only by their appetite for living. From the direction of the kitchen, I swear I detect the sound of running water and the noisy clatter of dishes being dried, then stored in cupboards by wives who are now free to chatter about topics previously off limits around their husbands. And from just beyond the dirty windows comes the discordant clang of metal against metal as burly, red-faced men, sleeves rolled to the elbows and sweat soaking their shirts, pitch horseshoes and boisterous stories back and forth in the twilight of a buggy summer evening. Shutting my eyes like fists, I resolve to ignore these ghosts, to grant them their space in the hope they'll afford me the same courtesy.

No such luck. As I lug my belongings up the narrow staircase toward my old bedroom, my weight on the creaky wooden steps mimics the sound of rusty nails being pried from stubborn wood, rousing memories nearly forgotten. These stairs haunted my childhood nights. With my bedroom awash in spooky shadows and my heart thumping in my ears, I'd lie motionless beneath the covers and wait for their awful moaning to alert me that a monster was coming for me. On my worst nights, when I couldn't contain my terror, I'd cry out for help. That's when my mother, perched at my bedside and stroking my flushed cheek with her cool, slender fingers, would try to allay my fears. "Jacob," she'd coo to me, "there's no need to be afraid. Remember, God has assigned a guardian angel to protect every little boy and girl from bad things." It made for a good story – and I appreciated her efforts – but never spotting so much as a feather, I always concluded my winged protector had flown off for safer haven.

Having nothing better to do and nowhere to go, I begin nosing around the house, randomly opening doors to closets with bare hangers, peering into mostly empty drawers, musing how this must be what a place looks like after thieves have made off with all the good stuff. The few remaining upholstered chairs, threadbare from age, beckon to me with empty arms, and now and then I slump into them to reflect upon my new surroundings.

Homes, if they last long enough, narrate their own histories, and like an archaeologist I lightly run my fingertips over the imperfections in the interior walls and woodwork, tracing the pocks and gouges, the nicks and scrapes, trying to recall how they were inflicted. Scratches run where chairs have been carelessly raked along hardwood floors, and muted stains linger in portions of the carpeting where food and drinks were spilled and haphazardly blotted up. A circular portion of hardwood floor in the living room remains blackish and marred by water stains from the leaky Christmas tree stand my father Archie refused to junk, until my mother uncharacteristically put her foot down and ordered its retirement.

Putty framing the edges of one dining room window is clumped and irregular. It's the window Archie made me replace after I'd overthrown John's outstretched mitt one spring afternoon and sent a baseball smashing through it. A section of molding along the nearby door frame remains gouged from the night I engaged in combat with a dive-bombing bat, finally dispatching it by means of a wild forehand with a tennis racquet.

And once a glossy white, paint on the front room window seat has been dirtied and chipped by those who perched here to read or simply to bask in the sunlight. It's also where my beloved grandfather, a fastidious dresser and station master for the old Boston and Maine Railroad, would place his grey fedora whenever he'd visit. As a child, I could not resist the feel of its cool, silky lining on my buzz cut noggin. I'd pull his hat down over my eyes and ears until I'd forced its perfectly creased top to pop outward, transforming a fedora into a Stetson. After he died I used to see a lot of him in my mother. Now she's disappeared too. So in a way I lost him twice.

I stop to study Archie's outdated calendar dangling uselessly from a slender nail near the kitchen window, outside of which his ancient mercury thermometer remains fastened to the porch's support post by a rusted screw. My father faithfully recorded each day's weather on his calendar, along with details of current events he deemed noteworthy. The calendars always came free from our local oil service. Incongruously, some of their most stunning nature photos managed to include an oil delivery truck, as if customers were to believe that an oil truck would actually be parked next to a stand of majestic redwood trees or at the ocean's scenic edge.

I could understand why Archie maintained a diary of sorts on his calendar, and I was quietly proud to discover he'd jotted down an accomplishment by the son he couldn't risk spoiling with direct praise. What I could never fathom was his curious habit of recording the weather. After all, he was an accountant, not a farmer. Neither his life nor his livelihood depended upon barometric pressure, temperature patterns, or precipitation. And besides, television and radio told us more about the weather than he could possibly observe from a front porch or a window. Nevertheless, with the dedication of a monk transcribing scripture, my father faithfully recorded his daily meteorological data.

As a kid, when I'd question my mother about this peculiar habit, her response never varied. She'd smile at me and say, "If you write things down, Jake, then you never entirely lose them." I failed to grasp how the permanency of the written word had anything to do with the transience of the weather, and eventually gave up asking. Predictably, John and I composed a song about my father's quirky behavior. *(I'm Archie Taylor the weather recorder/Watchin' the sky, that's my disorder.)* These recollections float like ghosts through my head as I trudge back up the creaky stairs, drop onto the bare mattress in my old bedroom, and wait for sleep to carry me somewhere better than where I'll be tomorrow, which is visiting one Archibald C. Taylor.

CHAPTER THREE

The first assault to the senses is the color of the walls, best described as institutional pastel, a faded shade of green that reminds me of the unwrapped mints which sat like dusty buttons for weeks at a time in the candy dish on my grandparents' coffee table. The second wave of attack arrives by air, specifically the place's stench, which would have to improve considerably before one could charitably label it disagreeable. With no other ventilation in sight, the sodden air being pushed impotently about by tall floor fans in the lobby and narrow hallways reeks with the smell of antiseptics and cleaning agents, a unique brand of nursing home perfume. It's all I can do to keep my breakfast down, particularly when I spot staff workers, obviously desensitized to the pollution, washing down their morning pastries with hearty gulps from coffee mugs.

Prudently resisting the impulse to take a calming breath in the pungent air, I cross the tiled lobby, sticky with whatever has been mopped onto it, and stop at the receptionist's desk. The white-haired woman with a fifties' beehive hairdo manning her post glances up at me, blinks twice, but says nothing, reminding me how people around here, habitually suspicious of strangers, wait for their conversational opponent to make the first move.

"Jake Taylor," I tell her, breaking our silence. "Here to see Archie Taylor. Is he still in the same room?" I notice that this woman's bony, bird-like face is caked with make-up, as if she's attempted to spackle the cracks and wrinkles which spread throughout it like a spider's web. Yet what really attracts my attention are the long black brows she has drawn above her eyes. They are so thick and extend so far she has essentially underlined her forehead.

"Might I ask if you are related to Mr. Taylor?" she inquires with frosty efficiency. I am certain she has demanded I further identify myself simply to demonstrate that henceforth only one of us will be steering this conversation to its conclusion.

"Yes, I'm indeed related," I respond, disinclined to conceal my irritation.

"And would you be so kind as to tell me in what way you are related?" she counters.

"By blood," I say, childishly pleased with myself for being so evasive.

My sarcasm immediately causes her spine to straighten and her lips to purse as though I've just jammed a lemon slice into her mouth. Taking a moment to compose herself, she studies the computer screen to her right, then curtly informs me that she will need to see my driver's license, if indeed I hold a valid license from any state in our fine union.

"You're kidding me, right?" I say.

No response.

Having regained the upper hand in this power struggle, Miss Makeup locks her steely eyes on mine like a gunfighter at high noon, a sour expression still puckering her cracked lips, which by the way are smothered in gobs of cherry red lipstick.

Heaving an overly dramatic sigh of displeasure, I begin digging into my hip pocket for my wallet, until it dawns on me that my father has no restrictions on visitors. As a matter of fact, while I've been standing here wasting my time with this miserable old crow, at least a half-dozen visitors have crossed the lobby and sauntered down the halls without so much as a glance at me or my nemesis. Something doesn't add . . . .

"Harriet!" Startled by a voice booming like a cannon shot from our flank, both of us snap to like well-trained soldiers. From my left, a burly, crimson-faced woman in a navy blue pants suit is lumbering furiously toward us like a rampaging mother bear bent on defending her cubs. Unlike my wrinkled adversary, whom I now presume to be Harriet, this navy blue she-bear has a large plastic name tag affixed to the broad lapel of her jacket.

"I'm through warning you to stay away from this desk!" she roars angrily. I swear Harriet's hairsprayed beehive is blown backwards by the verbal explosion. "The next time this happens, Harriet, I'm calling your daughter. Do you understand me? Now you skedaddle back to the day room. No more wandering around. Do I make myself clear?"

Cowering from eye contact, the previously feisty Harriet rises creakily from her chair and totters off in a crooked path down the nearest hallway. Although Harriet's jewelry, makeup and bright pink dress appear much too formal for this place, the fuzzy yellow slippers she's sporting on her feet comport perfectly with the footwear of others who, like her, reside here. Sheepishly assessing my mistake, I track Harriet's unsteady progress until she pauses to steal a look backwards, possibly to make sure no attack is being mounted from the rear, then slinks around a corner. Only then do I turn to face my beefy rescuer, who has assumed Harriet's former position at the desk.

"I'm terribly sorry, sir. My name is Joy Foster. I'm the supervisor here. May I assist you?"

"No, but thanks anyway," I reply, not at all prepared for another encounter. "Just here to visit Archie Taylor. Oh, wait, could you confirm his room number, please?"

"Certainly," she replies with military crispness. All business, this woman. Hammering her thick fingers on the keyboard, she snaps her head sideways at ninety degrees to check the screen, then reports, "You will find him in room 14. That's room 1 - 4," clearly proud of her efficiency. Mumbling a thank you, I sidle away, thinking as I leave how I may have actually preferred the company of Harriet and her fuzzy slippers to the inaptly named Joy.

Walking down the hallway to my father's room is much like navigating an obstacle course. Wheelchairs carrying stick figures of skin and bone are scattered in pell-mell fashion like bumper cars after the ride has ended. Other residents of Meadows Retreat, worn to the nub by age and disease, shuffle with stooped, bony shoulders and flagging effort through the drab corridors. Whatever their mode of transportation, everyone here wears the same vacant expression. Twice I'm startled by keening cries emanating from darkened rooms. They sound more like the wailing of wounded animals than humans in distress. Life, I am again reminded, can drag out too long.

But the most heart wrenching sight thus far greets me just outside room 14, where I happen upon Lillian McGinley, once the principal of Jackson Meadows Junior High, now a resident till death at Meadows Retreat. Old age has claimed another prisoner, and in her debased captivity she's shrunk to skin and bones. Some aide on the home's staff has artlessly raked a brush through her stone gray hair. The front has been pulled back and then teased upward as if she's been facing a stiff wind; the back remains tangled in messy swirls like a bird's nest.

As if it were yesterday, I can still see Mrs. McGinley, impeccably dressed and with ramrod straight posture, pulling students aside in the hall to scold them about their comportment. It was irrelevant to her that these same students were good kids, children of hard-working farmers who'd already milked cows and fed livestock before their school day had even begun. No matter. She demanded they behave like proper ladies and gentlemen. Today, on the tail end of life's timeline, she sits belted into a wheelchair with a small tray attached to it, repeatedly shuffling a deck of playing cards. I'm certain she does so simply from habit, as the vacuous look in her eyes informs me she has no clue where or who she is, or why her life once mattered. It could be Archie was right after all to keep his calendar diary. He might've been on to something. Maybe the things we do have meaning only for as long as we can remember them.

Encountering Lillian does not exactly fill me with optimism as I steel myself to enter room 1 - 4, as Joy would say. I've been here only once before. That was about four months ago to drop off my father ("dump" might be a better word) together with some belongings I'd hoped would make him feel more at home. At the time I scattered some photographs around the room, some on his dresser, one or two on the stand next to his bed, a few on the wall. They captured happier moments, which seem longer ago now than they actually were. One frame held a photo of my parents on the couch with their bloodhound Otis, who would've made a truly great hunting dog if only one were hunting for crotches and ass cracks. Otis's real specialties were sleeping and depositing drool that spread like oil slicks on the floor. Other photos had been snapped at the beach or on birthdays or other family occasions, when Archie and my mother were young and vigorous and life stretched out promisingly before them.

Shortly before his admission to Meadows Retreat, as he was sinking deeper into dementia, I used to fantasize that a photograph, or maybe a name or a face, or perhaps one of his favorite movies, would temporarily jump start the old man's memory, magically enhancing the cocktail of drugs meant to retard the progression of his insidious disease. Inexorably, however, the fog settled thicker and thicker around him until he was often invisible to me, and I to him. Yes, there would be breaks of lucidity when the old Archie, feisty and involved as ever, would reemerge for several days, but over time such appearances became briefer and less frequent. When the inevitable moment arrived for me to leave him on his first night at Meadows Retreat he seemed right at home, as if he belonged there. Which he did. "Go tell Mary it's time for bed," he instructed me. "Been a long day." Mary. My mother. My late mother. Gone nearly five years now. Mercifully spared the sadness of that awful moment. All that is left of her now is whatever exists in the memory of her only child, the son who remembers too much.

Despite my misgivings about air quality, I do pause for a deep breath before knocking on the door to room 14. I've been dreading this visit. As a kid, even though I could barely swim, I was always the one to leap without hesitation into the icy waters of the town's swimming hole at the old quarry on its outskirts, jeering at those of my friends who would sit dangling their legs over the edge of the rocks, refusing to jump for fear of the bone-chilling rush that would steal their breath away. Now, like the most craven of my childhood companions, I dawdle at the entrance to my father's room, afraid, as were they, of the consequences of a sudden plunge.

Rather than walk right in I give a half-hearted rap at the partially closed door, hoping to hear a voice, any voice, ordering me to turn around and walk away. Or better yet, no voice at all. Surprisingly, what I hear is Archie Taylor himself. A frailer sounding Archie Taylor, but still my father, the only blood relative left to me in this world. “Come in,” he calls weakly. I have nowhere else to go. And so I do.

CHAPTER FOUR

Wrapped in a plaid bathrobe that looks big as a blanket on him, he is sitting next to his bed in the brown recliner I purchased for him, his thin frame nearly swallowed up in its rich, leathery expanse. The recliner is tilted so far back that what I mostly see are the scuffed soles of his slippers. They are the hard type, like slip-on dress shoes, the old-fashioned kind he's always preferred. "Who's there?" ask the talking feet.

"Hi, Archie, it's me," I say, warily edging closer to him. "It's Jake. It's your son."

"Who'd ya say? Speak up. That you, Jasper? Didn't you see the flag? No need to come traipsin' in here asking me if it's open today," he responds with annoyance.

"No, Archie, it's not Jasper. It's me. It's Jake, your son."

"You deaf, or just plain stupid? I said the flag is green. Whole damn town knows what that means. Don't know why *you* can't figure it out."

By now I have made it to my father's side, a child still drawn by a parent's gravity. Despite my earlier trepidation, now combined with my utter confusion as to what the hell he's talking about, I want to touch him, possibly even give him a quick hug. Although he's no longer the father I once knew, he could still pull off the part if only he had the mind for it. His white hair has retained its thick wave in front, the one he used to comb so precisely off his forehead. And even as his eyes see what his brain mostly fails to register, they remain a deep blue, no sign of cataracts. Mottled by patches of white stubble, the skin hangs off his jaw line and neck more loosely now than it once did. These days there's no calendar hanging nearby. No need for one when time is fixed and measured only by whatever disjointed thoughts happen to meander in and out of his brain.

"Goddamnit, Jasper. You still hanging 'round? It's no mystery. Green flag. Tow's running. Slopes are open. Got it?" he squawks in agitation.

Then it clicks for me. He's talking about the Mt. Prospect ski slope just outside of town, a small mountain attractive only to kids, novices and old timers. Of course today is May 15th, but what difference does that make to Archie? For a number of years the tradition in Jackson Meadows was to hang a green flag outside Freeman Dexter's pharmacy on Main Street whenever the snow conditions were deemed suitable to fire up the local rope tow. Back then, long before cell phones and personal computers, that simple flag was the most effective way to let people in the village know if conditions were suitable and the slopes were open for the weekend.

Each winter, one member of the Jackson Meadows Ski Club would be charged with making that critical determination. He or she would place the necessary calls to the ski patrol and tow operators, and would also put the flag up and take it down. "Keeper of the Flag" was the not especially creative title for the honorary position, whose holder knew all too well that parents burning with cabin fever were desperate to shoo their kids out the door on a wintry afternoon. One could make a fair number of friends, or conversely enemies, while holding down that job.

Of course, that was about thirty five years ago and Jasper Hogan, who always wore a woolen black and red checked hat with earflaps a la Elmer Fudd, is dead and gone. These details do not matter one whit to Archie. As for me, the urge to hug him has been supplanted by a sad distance I cannot cross. It was a silly dream, I know. Nevertheless, I'd hoped he'd make a little more sense this time, that at least a few rays of recollection might break through his cloud cover, allowing him to recognize the son with whom he once fished and threw a baseball, and whom he hugged with all his might when the woman who meant the world to both of them departed it unexpectedly. I now understand with the brutal clarity he'll never again enjoy, that he's irretrievably consigned to the same fate as everyone else in Meadows Retreat, this state-approved dumping ground for walking corpses.

Trying to engage him will be useless. In fact, he's already begun muttering into his sternum and shaking his head vigorously from side to side, as if embroiled in some heated dispute. Rather than try to coax him into substituting me for Jasper I take the coward's way out and breezily exclaim, "Ok, Arch, thanks for letting me know. Gorgeous day to hit the slopes. Maybe I'll grab my skis and meet you there." Without another word or even a farewell glance, I turn and make my escape. My stay, heartlessly brief, has already been more than my own heart can bear.

CHAPTER FIVE

Over the next couple of days I patronize the town's only grocery store worthy of the title at off hours in order to avoid bumping into anyone I know, or even worse, someone I've forgotten who recognizes me. Sewn into the hem of the mountains that surround it, the village of Jackson Meadows has always dawdled behind the times like a distracted child, habitually out of step with the faster-paced world beyond its rugged borders. The locals up here steadfastly embrace their isolation and geographical hardships. They have no quarrel with inclement weather trapped by jagged mountain peaks rising blue-tipped in the distance, as if portions of the sky passing overhead have been scraped onto them: *Foot of snow today, heard tell there's more comin' tomorrow . . . River froze mighty early this year, what with all them below zero days . . . Cows was up to their knees and hocks in mud, had to pull 'em outta the field with the tractor. Almost got that son of a bitch stuck too*. In retrospect, that could've been part of what Archie was doing with his calendar: documenting his mettle, and his family's success, in the face of the elements. He obviously couldn't control the extreme weather that beset the North Country, but goddamnit he could declare victory nonetheless by refusing to let it diminish his spirit or curtail his happiness. And thumbing his nose at Mother Nature, well, that would have been just like Archie Taylor who, at his pugnacious best, could have passed for a young James Cagney: *You coppers will never take me alive.*

In my brief forays about town during my first days back here I see that the expansive wooden porches of the older homes still hold wicker chairs, or swings suspended from hooks in the ceilings, even as the sagging roof lines of some of these porches bow in defeat to the weight of accumulating years. Many of the homes have been handed down from one generation to the next, with the sorrier looking ones evidently having passed to those who can ill afford the upkeep. Regardless, it seems when the weather turns warm, as it has this month of May, porch sitting remains a favorite activity. It calls to mind how years ago, Jonas Conway, the brim of his green John Deere hat pulled characteristically low over his eyes, sat upright in his porch rocking chair for the better portion of a day before anyone realized he'd died there. At least the news of his untimely passing quelled the indignation of those who'd not been extended the courtesy of a return wave.

Even those lacking porches are undeterred in their resolve to sit and watch the world pass by, and so they set up lawn chairs in their driveways, usually at the edges of their garages for a little shade or protection from the wind. Whatever their vantage point, or for that matter their degree of safety, those who sit and watch are content to observe whatever happens to travel past them while they chew over and digest the news of the day.

Speaking of news, one upcoming event, much anticipated I'm sure, is currently being advertised on a large portable sign located on the town green. With a few exclamation marks tossed in for good measure, the sign alerts all those hungering for an evening of entertainment and education that the topic of this month's lecture series at the town hall is "The Art of Composting!!!" How much artistry, I wonder, is required to create a heap of rotting garbage. And in an ironic bit of juxtaposition, the daily outdoor classes of Senior Zumba are conducted on the green right next to the enthusiastic compost sign. While women teetering at the precipice of elderly and adorned in brightly colored workout attire struggle to preserve their youth, their big-bellied husbands, now retired and with little else to do, congregate nearby to wolf down coffee and sticky pastries and watch their wives gingerly wage battle against Father Time.

Not all the sights in Jackson Meadows are so amusing, however. As I drive up Mechanic Street toward the covered bridge where I garnered my first awkward kiss on a frosty October evening, I spy a young man, but still a boy really, cinched at the waist to a long tether snaking back to a porch railing. Standing next to him is a folding chair with a built-in cup holder for his water bottle. Physically, this kid looks as robust as a plow horse, yet even from afar it's obvious he's profoundly challenged. Stumbling upon a human being leashed like the family dog truly startles me, and unwilling to believe what I think I've just seen, I execute a sharp turnaround in the muddy parking area next to the bridge and head back up the street.

Only upon my return, as I park my car to study him awhile from across the street, do I realize that this poor kid has been tied out there to partake of his own version of porch sitting. Whenever a car approaches, his previously expressionless face erupts into a goofy jack o' lantern grin, and he waves with manic delight. Invariably the car returns a honk or two his way, provoking yet another animated how do you do. Far too preoccupied and excited to make use of his plastic chair, he remains standing and vigilant for the next motorist.

I did not cry when I returned to the barren home on High Street, nor did I shed any tears when I abandoned the imposter who's now playing the role of my father at Meadows Retreat. Yet right now, inexplicably, my eyes moisten at the sight of this stranger who has found a simple joy merely by waving to people driving by, people who, in their lifetimes, will experience opportunities unimaginable to someone whose dreams may never travel farther than the stretch of roadway just beyond his driveway.

But then again, who am I to judge the quality of someone else's happiness? Must happiness be parsed? Should we be happy only for the right reasons? And, in one fashion or another, aren't we all standing in our own driveways, straining our eyes and our ears while we wait for something pleasing to appear?

CHAPTER SIX

Life goes on and lawns need mowing. I've always rather enjoyed cutting a lawn, and so I've informed Albert Drew, who said little, yet made it clear by the stormy look on his face he wasn't much pleased with the news, that I will not require his landscaping services for the time being. The cut of the sharp, whirring blade is clean and satisfying; it tidies up one's yard and, superficially at least, one's life as well. Even more satisfying is the mental solitude mowing a lawn affords. It is not a social activity. Thus engaged, the best I can offer the world is a brisk wave or some improvised, one-handed sign language and a smile.

I've done some of my best thinking behind the encompassing drone of an engine, and on this bright Sunday afternoon, craving escape after my recent ordeal with Archie, I'm pushing his old mower in long, precise passes up and down a front lawn whose late springtime green is more attributable to weeds and clover than actual grass. At the moment, I'm actually thinking more about John's life than mine, probably because he is perched on a ladder two stories up on his house, scraping off years' worth of old paint in preparation for a fresh coat. I'm silently rooting for a different color this time, although I'm sure if uninspiring brown is again on sale John will scoop it up. John has always maintained that brown is practical; it covers well and doesn't show the dirt. All very true. I'm convinced, however, that he buys it only for the bargain price, even when he can surely afford more expensive paint, along with someone to apply it. For years he's worked at Burton's Supermarket, which has in turn furnished him with the longstanding quip that he'll never lose his job, given his position there as "Nonperishable Manager" which means, I think, that he's in charge of canned goods and, well, nonperishables. It's a cornball line which he never fails to deliver with the same straight face. I think he enjoys the grimaces it produces. From time to time today I've glanced up to discover John eyeing me as well, and I wonder what he's thinking as he turns slightly on his ladder and squints into the sun. Having exchanged waves an hour or so ago, we've been freed to eyeball each other without the obligation of further social interaction

Having no desire to consider what new assessments John might be making of me, I revert to my thoughts of him. Though he'd never whine about it, John's life hasn't always been easy. Bringing up the rear as a "late in life baby" in a large family, he was pretty much left to fend for himself while growing up. By the time he hit grade school, his parents were considerably older than those of the other kids, and they'd had it up to here with the rigors of child rearing. Thus, coming and going almost as he pleased, John became the stray dog of the neighborhood, with most everyone warming to him and including him in family activities whenever possible. I recall how one parched summer when he was about ten, John misplaced his sneakers. Making do with the only footwear he could locate, he clumped around in green, gum-rubber boots for nearly a week until my mother, swearing him to secrecy, purchased a new pair of sneakers for him. I'm sure his parents never noticed.

Which is not to say they deliberately neglected him, or that they didn't love and care for John in their own distracted manner. It's just that at their age the demands of parenthood had them overwhelmed. For instance, when John entered kindergarten and the Caldwells were asked to provide a copy of his birth certificate, only then did they discover they'd been celebrating his birthday on the wrong date. Certain he'd been born on an important day in March, they'd mixed up St. Patrick's Day with his actual date of birth, the first day of spring. Or maybe it was the other way around.

As my gaze oscillates from the pattern of my cut to John on his ladder, I spot one of his younger daughters, the one with strawberry blond hair and freckles whose name I can never remember. She's enjoying a book on a sunny window seat behind a large bay window, once the favorite perch of Meg's cat, Lilly. Even though John has always taken practically everything thrown his way in easy stride, he absolutely could not tolerate Lilly or any other member of her ungrateful species. Dogs, parakeets, guinea pigs, rabbits – the Caldwells have owned and responsibly cared for them all. But no cats, no way, not on John's watch. That was, until Meg happened upon Lilly foraging in the dumpster behind her store and promptly adopted her. John tried reasoning with Meg, who only pulled the squirming feline closer to her bosom when he suggested alternative housing arrangements.

"She told me the damn cat would starve if we didn't take it in," John once groused to me. "Said its death would weigh heavy on my conscience. Well, mister, I would've rolled the dice on that one. Damn thing's more bear than cat. Hell, it could hibernate all winter and still wake up fat."

Although John lost the war with Meg, he claimed victory in a lesser skirmish with his furry, obese nemesis. Knowing that out of physical exigency the portly Lilly was more or less confined to her fluffy silk pillow beside the bay window, John spent the better part of one afternoon erecting an elaborate bird feeder directly outside that window, situating it so the cat could not gaze outdoors without being tantalized by the sight of birds fluttering and landing, all seemingly within the reach of poor pillow bound Lilly, who could only paw anemically at the pane. John's scheme was transparent to everyone except Meg: drive the corpulent pussycat crazy. Any satisfaction derived from his plan was fleeting, however, as a month or so later Lilly was found dead, face first in her food bowl. Before she died John had taken to calling her Elvis.

When we were kids, painting the house was a task that fell to John's father Leland who, with baby-fine white hair circling the fringes of his otherwise shiny pate, always looked old to me. Or maybe it was because of his pipe, which he spent more time cleaning, filling and attempting to light than actually smoking. I always found it ironic that even when he was able to leave the demands of the family's prized woodpile and outdoor furnace behind him, Leland would still tend to a portable fire.

Perpetually inquisitive and routinely distracted by his cogitations, Leland would entirely disengage from conversations whenever an idea he'd been mulling over, or the topic of the discussion itself, especially absorbed him. Without warning or apology he'd simply clam up, often in mid-sentence, while he wordlessly followed the meandering path of his curiosity. Recognizing from experience what was occurring, everyone who knew Leland would wait patiently in church-like silence for him to rejoin the conversation. It was therefore not the least bit unusual to spot Leland, still as a statue on the sidewalk, staring eyeball to eyeball with a neighbor, neither of them uttering a word. Much like his father, John is inclined to chew things over before committing to speech, and despite inheriting Leland's tendency to turn a little prickly, overall he possesses an even disposition and a generous heart, notwithstanding his fiendish plot against the now departed Lilly.

CHAPTER SEVEN

There's counterfeit reassurance in daily routines. By keeping our days regimented, all the while pretending this brief candle of ours will not be snuffed out by an unexpected breeze or an unhappily directed drop of rain – at least not yet – we seek peace of mind and a good night's rest. Even in the wreckage which has become my own life I've taken solace in the predictability of the daily regimen I've adopted since retreating to Jackson Meadows. Lacking shades in my bedroom, I've been rising as soon as the sun hits my eyes, forcing me to acknowledge the arrival of another empty morning.

Good or bad, therapeutic or merely palliative, my lifelong remedy for distress has always been physical exercise, the kind that leaves one doubled over, hands on knees and gulping for air. The more troubling the problem, the more I've tried to sweat my way through it. It's hardly surprising, therefore, that I've begun taking early morning runs through the sleepy streets of Jackson Meadows past homes with bedroom shades still partially lowered like drooping eyelids. Each morning I see housewives in bathrobes and curlers carrying baskets of wet laundry to clotheslines, and burly men in work boots and jeans, still dirty from the day before, gripping large mugs of coffee as they walk stiff-legged to their pickup trucks, often parked on patches of dirt next to the houses. And because I've been following the same route for a few weeks, dogs of uncertain ancestry tied to trees or rusty iron stakes, who at first strained against their tethers to snarl at me in choking, wheezing coughs, now eye me with grudging familiarity and silent mistrust. I also believe I've memorized the mowing schedules of the town's maintenance workers.

Frequently during my runs I pass a bony little man with a mop of tangled white hair. Habitually dressed in baggy corduroys and a jean shirt with cut off sleeves, he slavishly pushes a scruffy brown dog in a metal shopping cart. This perky canine, clearly the alpha male in the relationship, is always nattily attired with a bright orange bandana around his neck. Sitting tall in his movable throne and surrounded by bottles and cans salvaged for redemption, Captain Jack, as I have named the little mutt, regally surveys the landscape and passersby. Meanwhile his feeble servant, head bowed and arms straining to full extension, struggles like Sisyphus to push his precious cargo over the uneven pavement. It's easy to identify the benefit Captain Jack derives from this arrangement. As for his hard-working owner, I confess I haven't entirely figured that part out yet.

On many mornings I also spot Jackson Meadows' only apparent panhandler, who reports for duty early. Most likely in his early seventies, he looks a good decade older. Ensconced in a plastic patio chair near the entrance to a modest war memorial park containing a solitary granite monument not much higher than your standard gravestone, he's awfully difficult to ignore, especially after he's detached his prosthetic left leg and propped it next to him. Shiny pins adorning this guy's ratty jean jacket, complemented by a black hat with large gold lettering, announce to the townsfolk, as if they didn't already know, that he's a Vietnam veteran. The unpublished subtitle to his proclamation is that life has not been kind to him since returning home so many years ago. In an effort to stir up some patriotism and (more importantly) charitable inclinations in those who pass by, he's placed a little American flag near a plastic army helmet resting upside down on the sidewalk, while on the other side of his chair an old boom box blares Sousa-like marches and patriotic songs non-stop. When the skeptical part of me wonders if he even served his country, my conclusion is always the same: If it's a scam it's not working very well; I can usually count the donations in his upturned helmet without ever slowing down.

It's much the same each morning as everyone eases his or her way into another day, reminding me that Jackson Meadows is a town of crooked people, and by that description I do not mean criminals. It's just that by the time people around here have toiled and scratched their way to middle age, a considerable number of them have literally developed arthritic postures. Life up here in the North Country can do that to a body, what with the failing mills and factories, logging mishaps, a tourist-driven economy which demands grueling hours, the meager return from hardscrabble farming, and bitter winters which seize the landscape in early November and refuse to relinquish their icy grip until mud season arrives in April. Although we never exchange waves, I've begun to take an interest in my new neighbors, and I find myself ruminating about their lives, much as John and I did decades ago when we composed our juvenile songs. I wonder if they envy the apparent freedom of my days as much as I yearn for the direction and purpose I've imputed to theirs.

As my stamina improves and my daily runs carry me to the outskirts of town, I pass a number of old farms marked by collapsing barns and rusted machinery lying scattered about like lost toys. A few of the acreages contain graveyards dating back more than a century, when it remained common practice to bury family members on one's property, and here and there blackish stone memorials protrude above the dewy springtime green like oblong rocks. Meanwhile, logging trucks with oversized loads and groaning engines rumble past me on the undulating roads, and out here where no one cares a whit about leash laws, my fear of untethered farm dogs escalates.

My expanded route also leads me past a phone booth on the rocky shoulder of Route 2 near the Connecticut River, the watery border dividing Vermont from New Hampshire. The phone is missing, the booth's plexiglass has disappeared, and its frame is bent and rusty. There was a time, long before the advent of mobile phones, when I'd drive to this spot to place calls not intended for parental earshot. I heaped fistfuls of change into the coin slot while laying the groundwork for another night of fun. Running by it these days, I fantasize about hearing a familiar voice over the wire and recapturing the excitement of my youthful adventures. Of course, the phone is long since gone, as are all the friends I once dialed up. I can dream all I want, but there's no magic waiting for me here by this silent river. And when you come right down to it, it's not that I'm looking for an answer to a phone call, or to life for that matter, merely the peace to live without one.

****

Typically, after each day's run, I cool down by walking a short distance up North Main Street to The Gas Mart, where I grab a copy of the *Boston Globe* and, if I'm in a decadent mood, the *New York Post*. When I was a kid this place was a two-pump filling station, full service of course. The owner and seemingly only attendant back then was a crusty old geezer named Vern, etched into my memory because he possessed only a right arm. I never learned what happened to its left-sided partner. I would sit mesmerized while I watched him, with impressive dexterity, top off the gas tank, check the oil, wash the windshield, dispense change, and hand out whatever that month's promotional gift happened to be. During summer it was usually cheap glassware or an inflatable beach ball. Winter's offering always seemed limited to an ice scraper with the name of a local bank or insurance company on it.

The secret to Vern's ability to function as a full service attendant was his left armpit. Sooner or later, everything seemed to end up tucked between the often sweaty stub of his missing left arm and the side of his chest, where his work shirt would be blotched with oil and gasoline stains. The left stub was where Vern held the nozzle while his right hand removed the gas cap. It was where he clutched the paper towels for the dip stick and the windshield, as well as the bills coming back in change. And to the hygienic discomfort of his customers, Vern would frequently wedge the station's promotional gift up there as well. On such occasions, my mother would accept the proffered item with exquisite courtesy and then whisper sternly to me, "Don't you dare touch it!" To this day, whenever I hear someone boast that he or she can "do that with one hand tied behind their back," I think of Vern and his multi-purpose stub.

This morning it's an entirely different world at The Gas Mart, where I am smartly greeted by Edward, who mans the front counter with military efficiency. "Morning, Jake," he exclaims brightly, offering up a half salute. "Going to be a warm one for sure." Like so many others born and raised up here, Edward transforms a one syllable word into two. Thus, "sure" becomes "shu-weh" and what is pumped for free into a customer's tires is "ay-yah." Edward is sporting his customary bow tie clipped to the collar of his carefully pressed robin's egg blue Gas Mart dress shirt; and once again this morning he has greased and parted his dark, stringy hair into a style which I suspect he believes emulates George

Clooney or perhaps, from his elderly mother's epoch, Cary Grant. Sadly, it looks more like a dead-on imitation of Adolph Hitler. Straight, limp and lacquered.

"Same to you, Edward. No doubt about it," I reply, forking over a ten. I've been trained not to shorten Edward's given name in any fashion. As he politely but quite sternly corrected me at the outset of our business relationship, he is neither Ed nor Eddie nor Ted – only and always Edward, hoping, I've concluded, that his insistence on formality might elevate his occupational status. Edward and I actually attended high school together, although my hello to him at the Gas Mart several weeks ago was definitely the first time I'd ever spoken to him.

If a daily paper were conveniently available at any other location in town I might take my business there instead, since it takes only momentary eye contact with Edward to launch him into his personal publication, opinion and analysis of events worldwide and local. From last night's bonehead move by the manager of the Red Sox to terrorist attacks around the globe, from titillating Hollywood gossip to who got himself good and liquored up and then jailed overnight for fighting in Blacksmith's Tavern, Jackson Meadows's self-appointed town crier enthusiastically dispenses it all, with just a smidge of holier-than-thou mixed in for good measure.

Like the rest of us, Edward comes by the bulk of his news from television, newspapers, and the internet. I'm certain, however, that he acquires a fair number of his hometown headlines by osmosis, his mother Edna being the latest incarnation of the "locals" columnist in the *Jackson Meadows Reporter*, a position once held by Pearl Whitney. Edna's business is the business of others: Who's feeling better and – even juicier – who's not going to make it? Who's visiting whom and for how long? (And what could they possibly be doing for all that time?) Edna exists to uncover and disseminate this stuff. Manning the phone lines, pumping everyone she meets for info, and surfing social media, she's the town's news shark: perpetually circling and ravenous for new intelligence. And since, to the best of my knowledge, Edward still resides with dear old mom in their tiny Cape on Jefferson Road, well, it's easy (and a little creepy) to put one and one together.

"And how go things with your father these days, Jake?" he asks with a dramatic look of concern. As I struggle to manufacture a cheery response I note, as usual, that having placed the bills coming back to me as change for my purchase onto the counter, Edward is now hand pressing each one to smooth out the wrinkles. Once he has completed his ironing, Edward neatly stacks the bills on the counter in descending order of denomination. This is not the first time he has meticulously hand pressed my bills, nor is it the first time I have nearly apologized to him for then stuffing them into the pocket of my running shorts.

Before I can respond to his inquiry about my father Edward serves up a hot news bulletin. "I hear tell your old coach, Everett Perkins, isn't doing so well these days. Congestive heart failure, or so I understand. To be honest, Jake, I figured you'd be the one to kill him years ago, what with you firing up shots from just about anywhere on the court. Old Everett used to leap up off that bench, red as tomato soup whenever you'd take one of your crazy shots. 'Course, he'd sit right back down and act like he drew up the play when the ball went in, as it usually did. If I'm recalling it correctly, there was this one game late in the season against . . . ."

"My dad is doing ok, thanks." I have quickly learned the only hope for killing one of Edward's monologues is to interrupt it before its momentum, like a runaway train on a downhill track, becomes impossible to stop or avoid.

"You know, between you, me and those gas pumps out there I always thought Everett spent a little too much time bending the old elbow, if you know what I mean. Could be it's finally caught up with him."

Undeterred, Edward has doubled back to the topic of my former coach. My tolerance for this conversation is spent. "Always good talking with you, Edward, but my day calls. Lots to do." The little bell hanging from the push bar on the door tinkles loudly as I lean extra hard on it to make my escape.

****

Of course, what I've just represented to Edward was a convenient fabrication. Archie is not ok and never will be. I've stopped by a few more times to visit, twice when he was sleeping, and on those occasions I hovered ghoulishly over his bed to study his visage. He reminded me of a portrait attempted by an artist of mediocre talent. There was no mistaking the resemblance to Archie Taylor, yet essential details were missing, particulars that might have captured the flinty spirit which sustained him for the bulk of a lifetime, like the wrinkles that deepened around his eyes when he concentrated, or the way he tilted his jaw aggressively upwards during a conversation, as if daring you to throw a verbal punch.

On my most recent visit I did not find him in his room, and even more alarming, discovered a bed stripped to the bare mattress. With panic and rampant nausea percolating in my digestive tract, I immediately concluded he had died, and probably all alone, while searching for my face or reaching for my hand. I began racing through the cluttered hallways toward the front desk, dodging wheelchairs and walkers like a broken field ball carrier on the gridiron. Slowing for a sharp corner and a wheelchair poking along in my path, I suddenly happened upon Archie sitting all by his lonesome in the solarium, eyes closed, his face tilted upwards to catch the sun, his lips moving almost imperceptibly. My relief at finding him upright and still among the living quickly morphed to curiosity. Pausing in the doorway to recapture my breath, I wondered where his thoughts could've taken him. To me he looked almost wistful, as if waiting to be magically lifted from his plastic chair into the expansive freedom of the sky beyond the solarium's glass ceiling. And though I doubted his ability to string coherent words and thoughts together, I could've sworn that Archie Taylor, whose focus always lay squarely on the here and now, who loved to say that the hereafter, if it existed, could damn well take care of itself, was mouthing a prayer. Could it be the old Archie was still in there, gradually suffocating beneath an avalanche of confusion, still doggedly attempting to tunnel his way out? Was the last lucid vestige of him praying for escape from the imprisonment imposed upon him by his traitorous mind and, one might reasonably suggest, by the son who abandoned him to this place?

Having no solace to offer either him or me, I turned away and left him where he sat.

CHAPTER EIGHT

This morning, out of boredom and curiosity, I went rooting about in the dank cellar, where Archie stored stuff he never cared to see or use again but couldn't bring himself to throw out. Stashed behind an old, upright Victrola record player with its crank handle still attached, and a couple of antique wooden snow shovels which looked to be older than Archie himself, I found one of the folding lawn chairs he and my mother would fasten to the top of the car whenever we made our annual four hour pilgrimage to the beach in Rye, New Hampshire. Before each trip I'd lobby unsuccessfully for its close neighbor, Hampton Beach, which my parents deemed too tacky and commercial for their tastes, even though tacky was exactly what I was hoping for. In contrast to Hampton, Rye's scenic shoreline boasted more rocks than sand. Nevertheless, it was a great place for a kid from the mountains to explore.

On impulse, I carried the chair out the hatchway to the backyard, hosed off the dust and spider webs, and sat down to reflect on things. Sitting there, I recalled how, when the ocean's chilly waves had turned my skin blue, I'd retreat to where my parents sat on the beach, wrap myself in a large, colorful towel, and snuggle into a ball on this very chair while I waited for my shivering to subside. As I sit here now, the scenery I'm taking in – namely Joe Bennett's messy and overgrown back yard – is a world away from Rye's craggy shoreline. Plus, one metal leg of my chair is permanently bent to the left, and a couple of the plastic slats designed to support my backside are entirely shredded, so unless I cock my head awkwardly to the right, my view of the landscape is crooked. What I mostly see is Joe's detached garage, with its large side window broken and its roof almost entirely consumed by moss and the droppings from large oak trees overhead. Years ago, Joe used to have a pretty nice looking place, until his wife suddenly died and he stopped caring about anything except her memory.

I suppose, at one speed or another, life carries us all downstream. We float and bob with its changing currents while they spill us here and there, and along the way we do our best to maintain a weather eye for storms which roil in unexpectedly and render the waters even more treacherous. If, unlike poor Joe, we're able to withstand the sudden ferocity of such tempests, then hooray for us. Failing that, we can end up damaged and alone in places like Jackson Meadows, New Hampshire, where ironically, enduring life's travails is a matter of local pride.

Call it fortitude. Call it faith. Call it what you will. Whatever it is, either I never had it or I've now lost it, and hardly a day goes by when I'm not reminded of that bitter truth. News breaking hourly from around the globe informs me that, routinely, people's lives are shredded by unthinkable tragedy. Hearts get broken. Precious life is lost. War's collateral damages become outright carnage, as children lose parents and siblings, and mothers and fathers dig frantically through the rubble of bombed-out buildings to locate the bodies of their children, only to bury them again. Disease maims and kills the young, and from the old it steals the time they dared to hope they had left. One chilling diagnosis or medical mishap, one negligently driven vehicle, one unexpected twist of fate's cruel blade, that's all it takes to transform happiness into permanent misery.

Of what gravity and import then are my problems which, one might persuasively argue, are largely self-inflicted? I'm healthy again after my life-threatening illness, or so I've been assured. I'm young, relatively speaking, and capable of earning more money than I could ever reasonably spend, should I choose to rehang my shingle. Others, afflicted by far worse than anything I've endured, have managed to straighten their spines and soldier forward with their lives. Meanwhile, I sit in this broken old chair in my father's backyard and wonder why mine is stalled here in Jackson Meadows

****

During yesterday's visit with Archie at Meadows Retreat he startled me by inquiring, out of the blue, how Annie was doing. "Fine," I replied. "She's doing just fine and sends her love." As far as I could tell, only three living beings ever consistently teased smiles out of Archie Taylor: my mother, Mary; Otis the crotch sniffing hound; and Annie, the woman I loved with an ardor and an optimism I doubt I can recapture. The best I could elicit from Archie was a twinkle in his blue eyes or a firm squeeze of my shoulder. And by "firm" I mean it often hurt like hell, as if he needed to demonstrate both the strength of his love and his grip. On the other hand, when it came to Annie, well, she was the daughter he never had, the child he could dote upon, the one who refused to buy his tough guy persona and could unlock the sentimental side he labored so hard to conceal. Annie. Of the two remaining Taylors, I'm the only one who's lost her. For all Archie knows he might've shared breakfast with her this morning.

So much of this life is happenstance. My path first crossed Annie's during my final semester of law school. A bunch of us had cobbled together a team and joined a basketball league sponsored by the city's park and recreation department. One frigid Monday night in February a heating problem forced the relocation of our game from the local middle school to the high school, which boasted a rubberized track that encircled the basketball court. Warming up beforehand, I spotted a tall, slender girl gliding effortlessly around it, her dark hair tied into a ponytail. She had long legs and narrow hips, and was wearing red running shorts which clashed with her orange shirt, as if she might be blind to color or fashion. Her footwear was noticeably low tech for a runner who ran so lightly and gracefully that her feet barely seemed to graze the surface of the track. From a distance, her olive- skinned complexion appeared flawless, and the expression on her face could only be described as serene. More importantly, as she passed closer to me, I could see she wasn't wearing a wedding or engagement ring. Surely other runners were using the track at the time. I never noticed them. My attention attached itself to her alone, and during the first half of our game I studied her during each stoppage of play.

When the horn sounded to commence the second half, she abruptly ended her run and slid onto a spot a few rows up on the bleachers, presumably to cool down and watch for a bit. Like a schoolboy eager to show off for the prettiest girl on the playground, I was convinced that fate had delivered a perfect opportunity for me to impress her. In my jock-world fantasy, I pictured this lithe beauty swooning over my prowess and air mailing come-hither looks my way once she'd witnessed my talents.

Such was my delusional train of thought as the ball was inbounded to me near center court to commence play. With adrenalin blasting through me, I drove unimpeded to the basket, leapt skyward, and laid the ball artfully off the glass for two points, exactly as I'd scripted it in my head. Except for one minor problem: we'd switched ends of the court for the second half, something I'd totally forgotten. Consequently, I had just scored for our appreciative opponent. After pausing to allow both teams, and the refs, to finish their jeers and laughter, we resumed the game. Sadly, things only got worse for me. I became a one-man Three Stooges routine. Dribbling off my foot, throwing up air balls, failing at impossibly acrobatic layups – I committed basketball sins both venial and mortal, each bonehead play intended to atone for the previous one. The final indignity occurred during my last ill-advised foray to the hoop when I caught an elbow squarely to the nose and, with blood streaming down my face and neck, had to be helped from the floor. Someone on the sideline handed me a scratchy paper towel from the locker room, which I tore into two pieces and stuffed into my nostrils. When at last I could stop tilting my head back to stanch the bleeding, my beautiful, alluring stranger had vanished.

I was despondent. Even though I didn't know her, I was convinced I'd missed out on someone important to my life. For the next few days I brooded obsessively about her, until eventually I did what any other twenty-five year old male who had not gotten laid in several months would do: I went looking for her. Hoping she was a creature of habit and would therefore return for another workout, I blew off the following Monday's game at the middle school and drove to the high school gym instead.

To my dismay, she was not at the gym, nor did she appear the next two evenings. I knew this because I showed up each night. And once there, of course, I couldn't just hang around and stretch my hamstrings or lurk about suspiciously. I actually had to exercise. My dilemma lay in how to work out without perspiring excessively, which I've always been prone to do. At best, I figured I had one shot at speaking with her, and would hardly look my best with sweat burning my bloodshot eyes and trickling down my face like salty rainwater.

On Friday evening, after I'd been circling the track for close to half an hour, good fortune found me again, and like a heavenly apparition in sweat clothes she materialized in the doorway. Having planned for this exact contingency, I immediately ducked into the locker room where I'd stashed my duffel bag, finished a shower before the water had time to get warm, dried my hair, and reappeared on the track, fresh as the leading man in a deodorant commercial. I was feeling pretty pleased about my resourcefulness until it hit me that I still hadn't devised a workable plan for approaching her.

That's when happenstance took over again. Or maybe it was just Annie being Annie, which is to say she was always a little contrary, tending to run counter in a clockwise world. After I'd tailgated her perfect, bouncing butt for about ten minutes, Annie decided to run in the opposite direction and thus took an abrupt u-turn directly into the chest of the runner traveling no more than six feet behind her, meaning me. The first words I ever spoke to Annie, which later proved quite ironic, were "I'm sorry." The first time my skin touched hers was when I grabbed her hand to pull her slender frame up from the surface of the track.

At first she gave me a kind of puzzled, "what the heck just happened" look. Then her face brightened and she exclaimed, "I remember you. You're the funny basketball player from last week. I almost didn't recognize you without the blood on your face." Ah yes, the direct route. The only course Annie ever charted through life or a conversation.

"People have commented that red is a flattering color for me." That was it. That was the most interesting line I could come up with. My mind had gone stupidly blank, distracted by her blue eyes and a mouth that went just a little crooked on the left side when she smiled. Desperately racking my brain for something wittier to say, all I could deliver was, "I saw you last week at our game," which made me sound way too much like a stalker.

"I know," she replied, flashing that devastating smile again. "You were looking at me so often I thought maybe you knew me."

Desperate to assure her I wasn't some creep I hastily added, "No, not at all. I was just admiring your running style. Did you do track in high school or college? Because you seem very graceful."

"Thanks. I really don't know what I look like when I run and I've never been part of an organized sport. I run for the exercise and the meditation. I just let my mind drift until my legs interrupt and tell me to stop."

"Interesting." Yet another brilliant response.

"Well, it was nice bumping into you, so to speak. Good luck with your basketball."

I could see her politely edging away and slipping out of my life forever. It was time to grow a pair of onions, as Archie would say, and quit with the small talk.

"Wait, hold up just a second, please. Listen, this might sound really strange. I don't know anything about you except that you like to run, and you know nothing about me except that I play basketball and bleed quite easily. I need to tell you that every day I see people

I'll never know, and that's always been fine with me. But when I saw you – and now that we've spoken – I'm thinking it might be nice to make an exception, maybe get to know you. Believe me, I've never done or said anything like this before, but do you think you might like to have dinner sometime, or even just a cup of coffee?"

I could almost see the wheels turning in her head as she sized me up. Inwardly, I was exhorting her to conclude I might be an intriguing possibility rather than some intrusive nut job.

"Are you married?" she asked bluntly.

"No."

"In a steady relationship?"

"Not for a long time."

"Do you want to ask me the same questions?"

"No, not at the moment."

"Well, I'll tell you anyway. I'm single, which I enjoy. I'm picky when it comes to making friends and even more cautious about getting closer than that. I don't drink coffee. Be that as it may, I think I can risk a meal with you. And by the way, my name is Annie. Annie O'Rourke. Irish father, Italian mother."

"Hi, I'm Jake Taylor of no special ancestry," I said, extending my hand for her to shake.

"Hello, Jake," she said with another crooked smile that melted me down to my sneakers.

And that was how it began. Meal one led to many more. A week together became a month, and then it was a year, and somewhere in that space we plunged headlong into love like we must have sensed we would.

CHAPTER NINE

My daily runs are a pleasant enough diversion. Without question I'm in my best physical shape in years, even as I've learned that losing pounds is hardly synonymous with shedding problems. There are always newspapers and books to be read in an effort to fill up my time, and when it comes to the latter, particularly accounts of middle aged men searching for meaning and satisfaction in their drab, uninspiring lives. Unfortunately, I've found their tidy, all too predictable endings to be of no benefit. Life cannot be manipulated like fiction. And so, inevitably, when another afternoon's shadows stretch across the empty rooms here on High Street, I often find myself with little to do other than sit and think, even though I'm keenly aware that excessive rumination is a problem for me, not a remedy. Nevertheless, like a dieter of dubious resolve standing before an open refrigerator, my willpower is shot, and with barely any hesitation I abandon myself to the thoughts which haunt me. Such a life is really no life at all, and as my days plod nowhere and I pace the cage I've constructed for myself, I feel my disquiet mounting. It's the same restlessness that carried me away from my law practice and, need it even be said, from Annie. As Archie loved to say, "It all went straight to hell in a handbasket."

****

Every so often during my runs I pass an elderly woman who appears to be on the downhill side of eighty. She's shaped like and looks as sturdy as a tree stump. No matter when or where I happen upon her, she's pulling a yippy little Pomeranian the color of a fox. Interestingly, the woman's hair, which is swirled into a tight bun, is the same color as her miniature dog. I wonder which of them got the dye job. Despite their identical hue, she and the dog are of two manifestly different minds. When the old gal steers left he lists right; when she's bent on moving forward he throws it into reverse. Indeed, this obstinate canine doesn't seem to do much walking at all. Mostly he struggles to jam on the brakes and change direction by planting his tiny paws on the pavement, while his owner, yanking and tugging the leash in frustration, pulls him along the sidewalk like a mobile toy missing its wheels. Whenever their little parade passes by I often hear her remonstrating with him, as if he might be persuaded to cooperate by the inescapable logic of her words: "Now, Barry, if you'd only do as I tell you things would go much easier. Why must everything be such an ordeal with you?" And then, as if peer pressure might be the key to setting little Barry straight: "You don't see the other dogs behaving so poorly!"

Given her preoccupation with her contrary little pooch, I was certain she'd never noticed me. Yesterday, however, when I again happened upon her while walking back to High Street at the end of my run, she and Barry seemed to have reached a momentary accord regarding the direction of their constitutional. That's when she took the opportunity to speak. "You're Archie and Mary's boy." I wasn't sure if this was a question or a declaration.

"Long time since I've been a boy. But still their son, yes."

"I'm sure you don't recognize me," she said.

Instantly thrown off-balance, I offered an apology. "I'm sorry. I'm really bad at faces. You see, I haven't lived here in a long time."

"No need to apologize. Can't say we've ever met. But you must've known my husband. Joe O'Brien. And I knew your parents through church. Especially your mom. We sang in the choir together. My name's Patricia."

"Of course, Joe O'Brien," I said, happy to recognize a name at least. "He was the tailor in Hansen's, the men's clothing store, right? I remember being measured there."

"Been closed for a long while."

"Didn't Joe pass away quite suddenly years ago?"

"He sure did. Matter of fact, I killed him."

I was struck speechless. Was this woman confessing to murder, or was she just off her rocker?

"No need to look so shocked, Jake. It *is* Jake, isn't it?"

"Uh . . . yes. Correct. Jake."

"Sorry if I startled you. I assumed you knew the story. Most everyone in town does, I'd wager."

"Can't say that I have. I'm sure, of course, that you didn't actually kill your husband."

"Oh, but I did. Just not the way you're probably imagining. I was backing the car out of the driveway. In a damn fool rush for church, as usual. And Joe, well he was such a tiny little guy, he had to stand on a stepstool to measure even his shortest customers. I used to tease him that he was the runt of his momma's litter. Anyway, he was standing dead-center behind me, and to make matters worse he was bending over to pick something up. Drove right over him, head to toe. Darn near did myself in afterwards, what with the guilt and all."

Why on earth is she telling me this? I wondered. Regardless, I felt I had to be polite. "I'm really sorry to hear that story. It must have been incredibly difficult for you."

"Difficult and pretty darn lonely," she said, barreling ahead in her tale of woe. "We never had any children. All I've got is this fool dog."

"You mean Barry," I said with a nod in his direction.

"Well, you might say that. This is the latest Barry. Kind of lost track after a while. I must've had four or five of 'em."

"All the same type of dog?"

"Same dog. Same name. Life's confusing enough. Why make it more so?"

"Well, I'm sure he's good company."

"You would think so," she said slowly, eyeing the squirming little critter with disapproval.

Edging away, I told her, "It was a real pleasure meeting you. Enjoy the rest of your walk."

Although her words thus far had sounded detached from the horror of what she'd recounted, there was no missing the sadness in what she said to me before turning away to cross the street: "Kill a husband, get a dog. That's life's deal, I guess."

Possibly sensing his owner's sorrow, little Barry, for once anyway, trotted obediently along beside her.

****

Like the past several, today has turned into a real beauty. Puffy clouds float like galleons at full mast, occasionally blocking the sun, keeping the temperature comfortable and the bugs at bay. Too antsy to mope around inside, I have instead elected to mope around outside, where my wandering has taken me to the barn at the rear of the property. Unlike a traditional New England barn built for cows and poultry and farming equipment, this one's a two-story structure whose first floor served as a garage back when Archie was capable of driving. The second level, an expansive loft of high, slanted ceilings and hewn beams, was a dumping ground for all the junk that didn't fit in the basement, although once I turned eight, nothing was ever stored up there again. That's when Archie cleared it out, put up a backboard and hoop, stapled chicken wire over the dirty windows which stretched nearly to the floor, and handed me a basketball for my birthday. "Go at it, boy," he said. "More time you spend up here the less trouble you'll cause somewhere else."

And did I ever go at it. Summer's wilting heat would find me dribbling a ball for hours on end against a floor so poorly supported it bounced like a trampoline whenever I landed after a jumper or a layup. And when winter's icy winds blasted the frozen landscape and all of outdoors froze into a muted stasis, the relentless sound of my ball bouncing against barn board echoed throughout our quiet neighborhood. Often I'd use two basketballs, playing with one until the cold robbed it of its bounce, then replacing it with the other I'd left warming in the kitchen. Inventing all types of solitary games and drills to hone my talents, I spent hours in that cavernous barn, shooting until I could score with my eyes closed, dribbling until the ball felt like an extension of my hand, firing passes behind my back and between my legs against the rough surface of the walls, then catching the return bounces and leaping high for shots. Much of my time there was spent alone. That is, of course, unless John showed up, as he often did.

John's basketball talents, to put it charitably, were a little quirky. He knew how to utilize his two inch height advantage to toss in old fashioned hook shots over my outstretched arms, and he had a knack for firing up running jumpers, too quick for me to block, that seemed to leave his hand before he ever left his feet. His manic dribbling involved a great deal of circling around the court, generally taking him nowhere, until I grew bored shadowing him and he could score practically uncontested.

John fiendishly invented competitions as unconventional as his skills. We played games of one-on-one to 100 points in which neither of us was permitted to get his own rebound off a missed shot. We devised contests in which we could use only our left hand, or could take a maximum of three dribbles before shooting. One of John's favorites was "Feast or Famine," a game of one-on-one in which the shooter could call out any number of points up to a maximum of ten prior to releasing a shot. If the ball went in, then the number of points declared beforehand would be awarded. If the shot missed, the shooter would forfeit the number of points risked. Together in that barn, whose temperature extremes always seemed too hot or too cold for comfort, we laughed and argued and bumped and shoved our way through our boyhoods and into our late teens, until John met Meg and took on responsibilities. Me, I simply took off.

Parking my shadow outside, I step into the barn and climb its stairs to the second floor, where cobwebs drape the rafters like fishnets and the bright orange hoop has vanished. The large plywood backboard is still here, as am I, and there's no escaping one clear truth about this musty old place: I was happy here. What's the harm, then, in purchasing another hoop, hanging a fresh net and buying a new ball? Have I anything better to do? I've lost or abandoned too many people and too many things I once loved. Why deny myself another opportunity to feel the reassuring grain of the ball against my fingertips or hear the crisp snap of the net as a perfect jump shot, arching like a swan's neck, passes through it.

In a moment of parental weakness when I was just a kid, Archie bought me a rabbit, whom I unimaginatively named Hoppy. I was too afraid to let Hoppy run loose outdoors, and asked Archie to purchase a collar and leash so I could walk him around our yard. Archie only scoffed at my request and explained to me how, given time and opportunity, a rabbit flushed from its home and running for safety, will eventually circle back to its point of origin. I now recognize this instinct applies to people as well.

****

It takes no time to gather what I need at the hardware store, return home, secure hoop to backboard, string the net into place and inflate the ball. It's been several years since I've shot a basketball and before I toss this shiny new one up I simply stand there holding it, making its re-acquaintance, smelling it, rubbing my fingertips against its pebbly grain, closing my eyes to read its comfortably familiar message like braille. Memories, brilliant and sudden as heat lightning, suddenly flash in my brain and carry me back to games contested on gleaming hardwood. I can practically hear the harsh blare of the timekeeper's horn to commence the action and the squealing of rubber as players pivot on a dime and change direction. My body still remembers how satisfying it once felt to execute a sharp crossover dribble, separate from a defender, and release a jumper over his outstretched fingertips, knowing as the ball left my hand if the shot would be true. During high school, and then later in college, I was merely a big fish in a small pond. Nothing more than a puddle, really. Nevertheless, that couldn't diminish the satisfaction derived from the purity of a ball spinning over on itself until it settled into the net, or a move so deft it left a defender twisted and hopelessly off balance. It was bliss. It was exhilaration. It was a place where uncertainty and disappointment could be minimized by talent and hard work, a world in which outcomes were more predictable. As true and as reassuring as anything I've ever experienced, basketball was a universe away from the reality which eventually tracked me down.

Today, closing in on the wrong side of fifty, I stand alone in the slanted shadows of this old barn. No more crowds. No hapless defenders. Nothing to win or lose. No reason to be doing this at all other than to while away a drab afternoon. I take a few staccato bounces and release my first shot. Like a bird winged by a bullet in mid-flight, the ball stalls in the dusty air and barely grazes the front of the rim. A few more dribbles to get the feel of the ball, then shot number two is launched. It misses the hoop entirely. The third is a sorry repetition of the first. *Remember, it starts from the legs. Push with the legs, release with the wrist.* My fourth attempt barely ripples the net as it drops cleanly through. From then on I'm on auto-pilot, operating solely on muscle memory. It's the spin of a ball that rests in the palm of my hand before departing with a smooth flick of the fingertips. It's a spin dribble, then crossovers left to right and right to left, the brief hesitation that lulls my imaginary defender into relaxing – then a drive to the hoop. In no time I'm drenched with perspiration in the stagnant heat, lost in a dance with my younger self. I keep this up until, too drained to stand, I collapse onto the dirty floor. Body spent and mind blissfully empty, I lie on my back and stare at cobwebs clinging to the beams in the ceiling above, my only companion the labored sound of my breathing.

CHAPTER TEN

As usual, sunlight burning through the bedroom window rouses me from my bed, where all these weeks later I'm still sleeping on a bare mattress. Gimping down the hallway to the bathroom, I notice my leg muscles are protesting more than usual after yesterday's workout in the barn. Nevertheless, it's a good soreness, an old familiar one. A glass of grapefruit juice, half a granola bar, and shortly thereafter I'm out the door, down the driveway, and back into the quiet streets of Jackson Meadows for another run in the dewy coolness of this early morning. My legs feel like wood as I labor past mom and pop entrepreneurs laying out home grown fruits and vegetables for sale in rickety stands or on long folding tables in their front yards. Other industrious homeowners, anticipating the sticky afternoon heat, have already begun mowing their lawns.

Recently I've been experimenting with the Annie method of running, shutting off the music and trying to empty my mind. Sadly, I've learned that, for me, deliberately erasing one thought necessitates replacing it with another, which in turn requires erasing, and so on down the line as my brain repeatedly punches its delete and reset buttons. At serendipitous times I do enjoy fleeting moments of peace, when fixing my mind on the sound of my breathing or the rhythmic slap of my sneakers on the pavement preempts my thoughts. Invariably though, consciousness shoulders tranquility aside, leaving me no choice other than to turn the music, and my mind, back on.

Today after my run I make my usual trip to the Gas Mart for the newspaper. Hoping to shorten my interactions with Edward and avoid the tedium of his ironing, I've begun carrying the exact change. I've also taken to loitering near the back of the store and scanning the paper's headlines until Edward becomes occupied with another customer. Whereupon, with a wave and a "wish we could've chatted" smile, I spill my change on the counter and depart, much to his visible disappointment.

As I walk up my father's driveway, I spot John slathering brown paint onto a wooden shed next to his house. I send him a sturdy wave, which he returns. To my surprise, he balances his brush on the top of the can and saunters toward me. His casualness looks a little forced, and I feel myself tensing up. I really don't know what we have to talk about. The waves should've been sufficient.

"Heard somethin' yesterday," he remarks. "Sounded kinda familiar."

"Is that right," I reply. "I must have missed it. What exactly did you hear?"

"Someone, I'm not saying who, was dribbling a basketball in your barn. Any idea who that might've been?"

This is typical John, sneaking up on the subject of the conversation, refusing to come right out and ask why I was shooting around, demanding instead that I cop to my behavior. Even if I were able, I'm not about to explain why I did it. "Just looking to vary my workout routine a little bit," I lie. "All I've been doing for exercise since I got here is run."

"Well, let's see, can you dunk the ball anymore?"

"No, not even close."

"Can you touch the rim?"

"I haven't tried, but I'm guessing no."

"Well then, can you even jump anymore?"

"Not much, but I don't see what . . ."

"So all you really did then was do some more running, only this time in a smaller space and with a ball." This is a conclusion, not a question.

"To a degree, I suppose. Still, it was a decent workout."

"If you really mean to play basketball and get any benefit from it, what you need is an opponent who'll make you work even harder," he responds. He's really sunk his teeth into this topic.

"You could be right," I say, hoping my concession to his point will put an end to the interrogation.

"Well, I suppose if you're askin' I've got some time. Don't see why I can't help you out. Meg claims I could stand to drop a few pounds. So it might be a good idea for me too."

And then I grasp where this conversation has been headed from the outset. It's been John's backdoor way of asking to play. I've absolutely no clue why he wants back into that barn. Hell, I'm not entirely sure I want to venture back there myself. No matter. It's become a moot point. I've never been able to say no to John, and summoning the resolve to do so these days is out of the question.

"Well, I guess it might be good for both of us," I offer with tempered enthusiasm.

"Good enough," he says. "Shorten that run of yours tomorrow and give me a heads up when you're done. I'm on vacation this week so I'll be ready to go. Went out and bought myself some new sneakers yesterday."

As boys, John tended to plan all our adventures. I don't know where this latest one will take us. I'll leave that up to him.

CHAPTER ELEVEN

Before basketball with John tomorrow, there's a little matter of getting through another night. And tonight, like too many others, memories of the past few years are turning over in my head as if on a rotating spit. Most of them involve Annie. At times my recollections of her are so vivid, so intense, I swear I can smell the scent of her skin. She'd vary her fragrance according to the season. In summer it might be coconut from her body cream, which I think contained some sunscreen. In the winter it was usually ginger. Even now, when I wake in the middle of another empty night and fitful sleep still clouds my brain, I'll sometimes wait for the gentle puff of her breath against my cheek. Annie's gone. Gone forever. How hard it is to accept that truth. Toward the end of it all she said to me, "You can't help who you've become, Jake, just as I can't help not loving that man." Brutally frank as usual. Her love for me was immense. I should not have expected it to be unconditional.

Our first real date set the tenor for the rest of the relationship: chaos, desire, comedy, uncertainty. We took in a movie, something

French, subtitled and dreadful to follow, in one of those art house cinemas with worn seats and stale popcorn. Afterwards we stopped into a nearby bar for a drink. "Oh, let's try this place," Annie said to me as we strolled past a small, nondescript establishment. "It looks so quaint and rustic."

As it turned out, quaint and rustic were synonymous with shabby, dirty and cramped. Picking our way across a wooden floor sticky with beer, we cozied into a small booth to share a bottle of wine, a flickering candle and a narrow expanse of cheap laminate table top. How I wish the fiction that memory often becomes could transform that dive into a romantic little bistro, where we first took our yearning hearts out of our pockets and laid them bare on the table. With Annie now gone it might be more pleasant to recall it that way. This place was anything but that. While country music choking with references to pickups and girls dancing in the moonlight blasted through the bar, we dodged the erratic, backward stabs of pool cues from good ol' boys in flannel shirts and butt-sagging jeans playing eight ball nearby. Scarcely able to hear what Annie was saying, I was eager, almost feverish, to read what her lips, moist and seductively parted, might be trying to tell me.

Hour one slipped into the second as we sat drinking our wine and trying, with only partial success, to hear one another over the din. I sensed she wanted to lean across the table and touch me, maybe even lace her fingers through mine. God knows, that's what I yearned for her to do. Partway through our second bottle Annie caught the server's eye to ask for the location of the rest room. She responded by jerking her head over her right shoulder, directing Annie to the only bathroom in the bar, a single, unisex restroom roughly the size of a broom closet. Giving me her sexy, slightly crooked smile, Annie grabbed her purse, slid out of the booth and set off for the other side of the bar.

Left alone to wage battle with my thoughts, I was immediately besieged by worry about the rest of the night which might follow. My apartment was a mess. Why hadn't I cleaned it beforehand? We definitely couldn't go back there. It was much too soon for her to see how I really lived. What if she suggested another bottle of wine, or worse, a late dinner someplace else? My cash was running dry and my credit card was dangerously close to being maxed out. And supposing everything did coalesce and we ended up at her apartment, there was always the issue of performance anxiety to deal with, the excessive intake of wine and extreme nervousness being a deadly mix, even for a randy young male.

I continued torturing myself in this fashion until it dawned on me that at least four or five songs had played since Annie had left for the bathroom, meaning she'd been gone at least fifteen or twenty minutes. Like a prairie dog sensing danger, I poked my head up to look around but saw no sign of her anywhere. At first I was merely puzzled as to her whereabouts. After a few more minutes without sight of her had ticked past I became convinced that she'd called a cab and I'd been dumped in mid date.

So that's it. I can see the entire bar and she's not in it. I'm the unacceptable meal sent back to the kitchen, the movie she couldn't bear to sit through, the ordeal too painful to endure even for an evening. The clumsy metaphors kept coming, and they all meant the same thing: this was to be our only date. With a defeated sigh I signaled to the waitress for the bill, left the money on the table, and began picking my way through the rowdy patrons toward the exit which, as it turned out, was located right next to the rest room Annie had allegedly been heading for. That's when I noticed a crowd of people congregated outside the closed bathroom door parting like the Red Sea to let the bartender pass through. Arriving at the bathroom with hammer and screwdriver raised high above his head like implements of war, the bartender immediately set about prying the door's pins from their hinges. Once they'd been removed, he grabbed the edges of the door and yanked it triumphantly away from its frame as if hoisting a trophy. Seconds later, with the crowd cheering and laughing, Annie emerged from the tiny bathroom wearing a sheepish grin and turning to and fro to offer several quick waves like a bad imitation of Queen Elizabeth at a royal event.

Spotting me near the exit, Annie looked back to our table to see our former booth now occupied by another couple. Quick as a camera flash she shot me a look of confusion. I smiled back reassuringly, as if to say I had abdicated our spot in order to come to her rescue, because of course she could always count on me to be there for her. That's when the good natured cheers with which she'd been greeted began turning to a grumbling urgency, as it dawned on all the onlookers that the bar's only restroom was now minus its door. When a group chant commenced for the bartender to reattach it, and quickly, Annie and I stole away unnoticed.

Once outside, I lightly grabbed her shoulder and said, "I have to ask. What happened in there?"

"Just what it looked like," she answered, more calmly than I'd expected. "I got locked in the bathroom."

"Ok," I said, pausing to select my words tactfully, "but how exactly could – or did – it happen? Did the lock break or something?"

"No, actually there were two locks. One that slid across the top of the door and another one which was a little button on the knob. To be safe I used them both. Simple as that."

"Well, it couldn't have been too simple, right? Because you couldn't get out."

"I could have if I hadn't taken the piece of tape off the little button. I thought someone had put it on there as a joke. Ha ha. Apparently I wasn't supposed to use the button. Next time I'll know."

"Wait. Next time? Are you saying you'd consider going back there?"

"Of course, silly. Now it's our place. We have a funny story about it, a little history there together. We can't just turn our backs on history."

"Especially if one doesn't want to repeat it," I muttered. But she was already humming one of those insipid country songs and leading me by the hand down the icy darkness of a winding street.

CHAPTER TWELVE

Archie. Archibald C. Taylor. Middle name of Cleveland. What could his parents have been thinking? The name's always reminded me of a ruddy Scottish golfer walking fairways browned by salty winds from the nearby sea. Since my return to Jackson Meadows, Archie has migrated inexorably from the periphery of my brain to a position of prominence, front and center. With jutting chin and hands anchored defiantly on hips, he demands my attention. Always has, even when I failed to garner his in return. It's possible that I associate Archie with golf because one of my earliest memories is of him dragging me into the back yard to give me a lesson. I couldn't have been more than eleven. He showed me the grip, demonstrated how he swung the club, placed a plastic golf ball on a tee and said, "Ok, boy, show me what you've got."

What I had was nothing. The club was way too long for me and I found it impossible to swing without turning my left knee severely inward and hunching over at the waist. "What the hell kind of swing is that?" he barked. "You're all twisted up like you're expecting someone to kick you in the nuts! Straighten up, boy. Use your arms." The lesson only got worse from there. Although I did manage to send the ball into the air a few times, mostly I tore large, gouging divots out of the lawn. In disgust, Archie abruptly ended the lesson, and for a long time my golf career, by asking if I needed a new basketball.

Notwithstanding the checkered quality of our history, I can't help fretting that part of him is sitting up there in Meadows Retreat, staring at the empty doorway to his room and wondering why his son hasn't visited. In his clearer moments, could he be thinking, as I too often do, how sad life can become when it's defined mostly by losses? Or, mercifully perhaps, his mind has gone permanently blank and I'm simply projecting my melancholy onto him, imputing thoughts to a brain that's being ruthlessly erased like a chalkboard. Wherever the truth lies, I'm haunted by a crazy impulse to save him from that nursing home. Ironic, really, since I retreated to Jackson Meadows in a last-ditch effort to save myself from myself, if that even makes sense.

Killing empty hours with him in Room 14 cannot be the solution. He has no dignity there, none of his spark. I'd like to recognize him again, however briefly, and at least once more I want him to recognize me. Even if it's just to say goodbye. As usual, however, my plans travel only to the end of my mental cul de sac, and I'm left without a clue as to how to rescue a man who's likely lost for good.

****

"Pick a color," she instructed me during one of our sessions.

"Excuse me?"

"Pick a color. One you find calming."

This request came a few counseling sessions after the most recent medication for my melancholy had failed. It's odd that my complaint to her, and my reason for flushing the pills, was that I "didn't feel like myself" while taking them, especially when the non-medicated me felt even less like the person I used to be.

"I want you to close your eyes, focus on a color, then try to relax."

"Isn't that my problem? Learning to relax? You said so yourself."

"And I was right. So let's give this little exercise an honest effort, fair enough?"

Perhaps inferring assent from my return silence, she gave me an approving nod. "Now then, close your eyes. Slow the pace of your breathing. Take deep, slow breaths. There's no place to rush to, nothing else to think about. Listen to the sound of your breath coming in and going out. Let your brain follow the path of the air. Now tell me, what color did you choose?"

"What color?"

"Yes, your calming color."

I gave it some thought, then answered, "Green. Green. Like in the forest." Truth be told, I was only telling her what she wanted to hear. I felt bad for her. She was pulling harder for me than I was for myself.

"That's good. Now tell me, where are you seeing that green? Where are you?"

A long pause, then, "There's a river in Franconia Notch that winds down the mountain in a series of waterfalls. I'd sit on the boulders there to fish. Sometimes nap there if the night before was rough."

"Perfect. Keep focusing on your breathing. Is the rushing of the water too loud for you to concentrate?'

"No. The falls are gradual and shallow. They bubble like white noise."

"All right then. Keep your eyes closed. Take a deep breath and hold it in. Picture yourself sitting beside the falls. Feel the warm, brilliant sunshine. See how blue and vast the sky is. The color green is all around you, wrapping you up. Take a deep breath and inhale it. It's there in the trees and the grass and the vegetation along the banks. It's being blown toward you by the breezes. Accept it. Breathe it in. Fill your lungs with it. Feel the green washing through you. Feel how calming it is."

Her voice, more soothing than I'd ever heard it before, unexpectedly disarmed me. It swept me up and carried me away, and I traveled from her worn couch to the tranquil banks of that familiar river, where the worrisome static spilled out of my brain and drifted away downstream. Imagining those meandering waters moving steadily past a lush green backdrop, I was soon unable to distinguish the gentle noise of their rapids from the sound of my own breathing. My head, suddenly too heavy to hold erect, toppled forward, stopping only when my chin hit my chest. Whatever had been keeping me upright and stoic abandoned me, and I fought the urge to weep like a lost and frightened child. Lasting five minutes at most, this brief escape from myself was restorative, like sleep absent the nightmares. With varying success, we performed our little ritual nearly every session which followed until, along with everything else in my life, the therapy collapsed.

There are still occasions when I resort to this technique, such as right now. Instead of listening to music while running, I'm giving forest green another go, hoping it will distract me from the obsessive thoughts which drone on in my head like monks at vespers, even while I know that, eventually, when my concentration flags in inverse proportion to my fatigue, tranquility will desert me like a good intention, and my mind will return to its customary preoccupations, such as looking out for dogs and berating myself for forgetting to bring the correct change for the newspaper and, oh yes, questioning what I might do to make my existence more satisfying and less frightening. When my run concludes I'll skip the newspapers. I'm in no mood for Edward and there's no time for reading anyway. John will be waiting for me when I return to High Street.

CHAPTER THIRTEEN

Never trust a sunny day.

Jackson Meadows was enjoying an unusual stretch of warm April weather and I'd popped home from Philly without Annie for a weekend of fishing after a particularly difficult trial. Brookies caught earlier in the day had been cleaned and stored in the refrigerator. Archie and I were hanging around the house, as usual saying little to each other, more or less killing time until my mother returned home to start dinner: trout rolled in corn meal and cooked in a greasy skillet with onions and bacon. So far, the day had been a pleasant one.

Later than expected, we heard a car pulling up the driveway. Like me, I'm sure Archie was waiting for the little sing-song hello she always delivered whenever she entered the house. Instead we heard three heavy raps on the side door next to the driveway, leading me to assume she was weighted down with packages and couldn't manage the door. When I opened it, I found a New Hampshire state trooper, hat in hand, wearing a stone solemn look.

Before I could speak he asked, “Is this the home of Mary Taylor?”

“Yes, yes it is,” replied Archie in a shrill voice I almost didn’t recognize. I hadn’t noticed him standing behind me. Shouldering me out of the way, Archie looked the young trooper straight in the eye and said, “Go on, say what you came here to say. Waiting’s not gonna make it easier on any of us.”

“Sir, are you Mary Taylor’s husband?” inquired the trooper.

Drawing a deep breath, which seemed to supply him with just enough air to speak, Archie responded to the trooper’s inquiry in a dead voice. “No. I’m guessing I’m her widower now.”

Sticking to what I am certain was a prescribed script, the trooper quietly began offering details, as if the tone of his voice might soften the devastation about to be inflicted by his words. “Earlier this afternoon your wife was involved in a traffic accident. Apparently she was following a pickup truck when . . .”

“Where is she?” interrupted Archie, his voice elevated to a pitch I’d never heard from him before.

“You see, sir, the truck was carrying . . .”

“Listen to me, son. You’ve done your job and it’s a damn hard one, I’m sure. But I’ve got the rest of my goddamn life to learn how it happened. Right now though, at this moment, I want only one answer from you. Where is my wife?”

After a pause during which he seemed to be weighing the wisdom of deviating from his script, the trooper answered Archie. “She’s at the hospital. In the morgue, Mr. Taylor. I’m very sorry for your loss. If you feel that you need to go there right away it might be best if someone drove you. Very often when someone is distraught it's better to . . ."

"Do I need to sign anything? Do you need written proof that I've been duly informed?"

"No sir, not at all. I just want to make sure that you . . ."

"Then thank you for your time and sympathy. I've got a goodbye to say."

With that, Archie elbowed the trooper aside and rushed toward his car which was parked next to the trooper's, leaving the trooper still on the porch and me in the doorway. Yanking open the driver's side door, Archie glared back at me. "Are you coming or staying, boy?" What else could I do? I closed the door to the house, to a happier chapter of my life, and climbed into the car with him. For better or worse, and from hereon, it would be just the two of us.

We did not utter one word during the five minute ride to the hospital. Bad news can buckle you at the knees or drop you in your tracks like a kill shot on a battlefield. Sadness can sicken your soul to the point where all you ask is that the world agree to carry on its business without your participation. During our death trip to the morgue, all I felt was nothing. It was too soon for the pain, too early to comprehend the loss. For me, and for more reasons than my dear mother's untimely passing, all of that came later.

As for Archie, over the next few days he shed no tears around me. Whenever I'd look at him, his world having collapsed into rubble like a building rocked by an earthquake, I'd think of a poem

I'd been forced to memorize in high school about a country home which had burned to the ground, leaving only its chimney to stand alone. In the few moments it took for the trooper to tell his awful story, Archie had become that lonely chimney, my mother the lost beauty of the architecture which once surrounded it.

Always adept at letting anger supplant sadness, Archie was incensed at everyone involved with the funeral and the burial. The flowers in the funeral home were wilting because the room was too hot. The priest's uninspired eulogy was obviously canned. Traffic on the way to the cemetery should have been stopped for the procession, and goddamnit was it too much to expect that her name be engraved on the pre-purchased headstone in time for the burial? We all understood that Archie needed this anger in order to survive the immediate aftermath of her death. What he might require to get by in the months and years to come was anyone's guess.

As we gathered in the springtime green and deceptive serenity of the cemetery to bid farewell, I thought how much she'd have disliked the burnished wood of the casket and the many extravagant flower arrangements. Unimpressed by all its trappings, my mother reduced life to its simplest terms and lived for its unadorned essence. She possessed a rare gift for being happy that her son did not inherit. An avid churchgoer whereas I was not, she'd prod me to join her at Mass and thank God for giving us everything we needed. I didn't see things the same way. I still don't. Like survivors of mass shootings who manage to ignore the less fortunate souls who perished, are we to be thankful for His giving while ignoring all the cruel taking away?

Just before they lowered her into the ground, Archie stepped forward to the casket and lightly rested his left cheek and the palm of his right hand upon it, as if listening for a heartbeat or feeling for a pulse. Finding neither, he turned away, relinquishing her to eternity. His eyes, to paraphrase another New England poet, had a distance in them like the look of death.

As we later learned, my mother had been following a pickup truck transporting a child's desk in its rear. The desk was cherry red, small enough for a young child to sit at, and light enough to bounce out of the truck's shallow bed when it smashed in and out of a cavernous pothole. I'm sure that when she swerved to avoid the airborne desk my mother, whom we always teased for her excessive caution behind the wheel, was gripping it at the prescribed ten and two. I expect she was still holding fast when she hit the tree head on. Weeks later, when I could bear to visit the spot where her life had been stolen, I parked my car on the soft shoulder and got out to have a look around. The oak, large enough to have withstood the impact, bore a splintered wound from the hit, an ugly memorial to the end of a beautiful life. Tiny shards of glass and bits of plastic and metal from the car still littered the area. Tire tracks in the soil and scraggly grass led straight to the unyielding trunk. I scrutinized the area for any sign of my mother. A shoe perhaps, or a piece of jewelry, or something in her pocketbook that might have fallen as she was pried by emergency workers from her vehicle. I found nothing there to make this tragedy personal. It looked like any other faceless accident scene one might slow down for and gaze upon with detached curiosity. Had she steered five feet to the left or right, my mother would have encountered nothing but pliable saplings and underbrush. It was her fate to have driven squarely into the only object in the immediate vicinity capable of killing her.

CHAPTER FOURTEEN

No sign of John at the conclusion of my run. Nevertheless, as I walk up the driveway, already sprouting early summer weeds, I have the feeling I'm under close surveillance. No matter. John will just have to sit tight wherever he's lurking until I'm good and ready to play. Our rematch, when it comes, will have nothing to do with nostalgia or renewal. On the contrary, it looms as a sobering confrontation with mortality and all things diminished, and by the latter I mean both our friendship and our athletic skills. There's no denying we were inseparable until our late teens, or that in the years which followed we'd randomly catch up with each other's busy lives over a few beers. More recently, after everything turned sour and pointless, I couldn't consider resuscitating a friendship when I was incapable of reviving myself.

After a bowl of cereal that goes down like soggy cardboard, and then a quick shower to rinse off the sweat from my run, I procrastinate like a kid reluctant to commence his homework. Parking myself on the window seat with its expansive view of the neighborhood, I struggle to recapture some of the enthusiasm I once felt when preparing to do something with John. But my mind, which these days has a mind of its own, carries me somewhere else entirely, and instead of John I'm thinking about a present-day Meg standing behind the antique glass candy counter in her emporium. Framed with strips of hardwood, the counter's thick glass covers shallow bins of brightly colored penny candy. Like the several owners who preceded her, Meg still employs a rope and pulley apparatus attached to rings in the wood to raise the glass cover like a drawbridge, until hinges catch and hold it in place, thereby providing access to the candy. Children waiting in line for their treats bounce impatiently from one foot to the other, as if in dire need of the bathroom. At last, when their turn arrives, they step nose high to the counter and solemnly select the candies to be scooped into their small paper bags. I know exactly how they feel. Decades ago I stood at the same counter, squeezing a sweaty handful of change. In those days, happiness was more easily purchased.

****

Still neither hide nor hair of John as I enter the barn. I'd like to think he's reconsidered an impulsive suggestion to reenact our boyhood, except there's never been anything impulsive about him, other than the time in fifth grade when he was curious to see how far he could shove a dandelion up his nose and ended up the emergency room to have it extracted. No doubt he'll show eventually. Rather than wait for his appearance I decide to begin without him.

Although my basketball ballet is now performed in slow motion and I really can't jump to save my life, my shot remains true. It's not long before I am caught up in the beauty of a spinning ball dropping through the net without so much as brushing the rim. Dribble shoot. Dribble shoot. When the shot is pure the ball's tight backspin returns it to your feet. Start with the legs, end with the fingertips. The anatomy of a jump shot: each attempt offering an opportunity for perfection.

"I see you haven't forgotten what I taught you." It's John announcing his arrival. It's also his way of backhanding a compliment in my direction while simultaneously reminding me who helped hone my skills. I was worried he'd be wearing a headband and some tube socks straight out of the 1970's. Thankfully, he's attired in a faded gray tee shirt and some nondescript athletic shorts. The footwear, as he indicated yesterday, is virginal white. He's brought a towel and a water bottle, indicating he's prepared for a rigorous workout, which causes my stomach to execute a quick, nervous flip. To my surprise, he's also brought along his own ball.

"I remember how bad you hogged the ball, JT. Figured I'd best bring one of my own."

No one but John has ever called me JT. I can't tell if he's done so deliberately, or whether our being back in the barn has instinctively drawn it out of him. Hearing my old nickname again softens me up a little. “Are you sure we’re ready for this?” I ask. “We’re not kids anymore, you know.”

“Sure we are,” he replies. “We’re just hangin’ out in middle age bodies.”

“That’s a catchy saying,” I respond tactfully, “but I’m at the age where I congratulate myself for getting up off the floor without pulling a muscle or farting.”

“We didn’t come here to complain about how old we are,” he snaps impatiently. “Grab your ball and let’s warm up. I’m thinking about renewing this rivalry with a game of “Feast or Famine.” Remember that one?”

“Could I ever forget?” He does not pick up on my eye roll.

And so the warm-up begins. Compared to John’s my skills are effortless. There is a ferocity in the way he pounds the ball into the floor while dribbling and in the flat trajectory of his shots, which clang off the rim at severe and unpredictable angles. He warms up as if he still believes, even at his age, that by trying hard enough he can improve.

“Ready to go?” he asks, flipping the ball to me. “You make it, you take it.”

I easily toss a jumper through the hoop, meaning I’ll have the ball first to start the game. John retrieves my shot, hands me the ball, and assumes a defensive stance best described as a Sumo wrestler preparing to battle for life and honor. His chin and nose are practically touching my belly. Looking downward, I notice for the first time that John's brown hair, already soaked with perspiration, is a little sparse on top.

"You're sure you wouldn't rather start with a game of horse or something?" I'm concerned things are escalating too quickly.

"No, I'm good," he replies without looking up at me. His voice sounds a little muffled. This is because he's guarding me so closely he's essentially talking into my shirt.

"Ok then. Here we go."

My first dribble bounces directly off John's right foot, which is sitting more or less on top of my left one. This sends the ball careening off to the side of the court, and John bounds after it like a hyperactive retriever. The ball now belongs to him, and he immediately commences backing me toward the hoop by bumping me with his not inconsiderable backside. I'm reluctant to start pushing back, not because I can't handle the contact, only because it would just feel weird to be pressing my sweaty body against his at this stage of our lives. As a result, I quickly find myself ineffectually guarding him directly beneath the net, at which point he easily flips a baby hook shot through the hoop.

His next shot goes awry and I snag the rebound. Rather than use my quickness to blow past him to the hoop, I take one dribble to my left and fire up a jumper which catches the front of the iron and caroms directly into John's hands. These opening seconds establish the pattern for the rest of our game. On the one hand there's John, totally engaged in the competition and furiously working to prevail. On the other there's me, emotionally detached from the proceedings, offering minimal effort and standing outside myself, as though watching events unfold from the sidelines. The final score reflects our respective efforts. John wins handily yet says nothing when he tallies the winning point.

The second game plays out much like the first. After pounding the final nail into my coffin John is silent. We head for our water bottles, plop onto the barn floor and drink thirstily. From experience I know something's brewing. John slowly mops his face and head with his towel, gives me a sidelong look, and finally asks, "Where, exactly, did you lose it?" There's no hint of disapproval or anger in his voice.

"What?"

"I said, where'd you lose it, JT?"

"Lose it? Lose what? I have no clue what you're talking about."

"Come on, man. You know what I'm saying." John's voice is so soft he's almost whispering, as if trying to coax the answer out of me.

I'm growing exasperated. "Where did I lose it? You mean the game? Well, it's pretty obvious. You made more baskets than me. That's how I lost it."

"Nope. Not even close. But don't worry, buddy, we'll get it figured out."

And with that he rises stiffly to his feet, retrieves the ball, and tosses it to me even as I remain seated.

"Let's finish with a game of horse," he suggests. "Good way to cool down. Need to stay loose for tomorrow."

CHAPTER FIFTEEN

Like the Lone Ranger, John has abruptly vanished. It doesn't take a genius to decipher the meaning behind his cryptic question. He's right, I've indeed misplaced something. There was a time when I guarded an opponent like a terrier latched onto a pant leg, and I practiced law with the same ferocity. I was tenacious, and my bite was worse than my bark. Outhustling my competition, I lived to do battle. That being said, there are times when I wonder if my problems have more to do with what I've yet to find in this life rather than what I acknowledge has been lost.

John still hasn't raised the subject of Annie, inquired about my job status, or even asked what I'm doing back here other than visiting Archie. In other people, such omissions would be deemed irreparably callous. Not so with John. I know that if he were dealing with someone other than his boyhood friend he would've voiced all the socially appropriate inquiries, just as I'm certain that from the moment I pulled up my father's driveway he's been mulling over how best to broach these delicate topics with me, unconcerned that

I'll construe his silence as indifference. We both know that in due course the conversation we've been sidestepping will happen, especially now that we've resumed our basketball together. Years ago, we'd tumble naturally into our most intimate conversations while engaged in something else. It didn't matter if we were walking the golf course, shooting baskets, or sitting in a boat waiting for the trout to feed. Confiding in one another came easily when our communication entailed minimal eye contact, when the physical aspect of whatever we happened to be doing lent our conversations an easy rhythm and a natural ebb and flow.

I don't know where the rest of John's day will take him. With a wife who doubles as a business partner, seven kids, a house in perpetual need of repair, a full-time job and, of course, his prized woodpile, he has much that is worthwhile to occupy his time. In doleful contrast, my days are filled only by the empty hours I aimlessly inhabit. Here it is, barely afternoon, and I can't think of one productive or enjoyable thing to do. Too distracted to read, too pensive to nap, too stubborn to call anyone who's written me off, I opt instead for a walk to nowhere in particular.

Randomly tracing streets and sidewalks which meander like cattle paths toward the outskirts of town, I linger here and there like Leland Caldwell to contemplate the lives of those who might occupy the dwellings I'm passing. One, perhaps, holds a family grateful for the simple blessing of an evening meal around a large wooden table. Another place, more modest in scale, could be a starter home for newlyweds, giddy with love and optimism at the outset of their journey and dreaming of children playing like puppies on a rug in front of the hearth. I really hope tableaus such as these remain possible. I hope other people, luckier people, can lead such lives. There was a time in my own life when I knew who lived in practically every one of these houses. Now I find I'm a stranger in my home town, no longer belonging here, or anywhere else for that matter.

Another twenty minutes of walking takes me to the entrance to the Jackson Meadows recreation center, a sprawling expanse of athletic fields, tennis and basketball courts, and a swimming pool that has yet to open for the summer. It all looks familiar, as well it should. Starting at age nine, from the chilly days of early spring to the last shriveled leaf of autumn, this place was my second home. Today, in particular, it's the steep hill across the street from the center which attracts my eye and carries me four decades into the past.

No older than seven or eight, I'm sitting at the bottom of a snowy incline which looks more like a mountain to me. Kids on sleds and tubes and flying saucers screech with excitement as they rocket down the hillside. As for me, well I'm feeling morose and alone. First, because I'm younger than nearly everyone else, but mostly because my ancient metal flying saucer is bent and dented, and patches of flaking rust on the bottom cause it to stick on the snow. It's an antique, a hand me down from John's much older sister, and essentially useless. Although it might be able to gather speed on the steeper portion of the hill, I'm too afraid to slide from way up there. So instead I sit in a lump at the bottom, fighting tears and eating tiny, crusted balls of snow that dangle like frosty crumbs from the yarn of my mittens.

As I squint into a blinding winter sun reflecting off the snow cover, my gaze strays to a distant figure in the parking lot beckoning in my direction. To my wonderment, I recognize my mother. I have no idea why she wants me. Obediently, I commence my trek toward her, but it's a long walk when the snow is so deep it reaches your waistband and spills tiny avalanches of icy crystals into your snow pants. The day is frigid, yet by the time I reach her, sweat has puddled between my shoulder blades and is running down my face from beneath the itchy woolen hat sitting askew on my head.

Out of frustration I begin to cry. I can't slide with the other kids and now, to make matters worse, I'm sweaty and tired and think I might have to pee from all the snow I've consumed. My mom takes some tissues from her coat pocket to wipe my face, adjusts my hat, and then, without saying a word, she smiles, lifts the trunk of her car, and extracts a brand new plastic saucer. My mind can barely process this unexpected good fortune. There's no reason for this gift. It isn't Christmas. My birthday's not for months. How did she know I couldn't last another afternoon without a new flying saucer? How could she . . . .

"Can I help you, sir?"

These days I'm easily spooked by any voice other than the one inside my head, and I spastically jerk my body to the left to see who's snuck up on me.

"Are you looking for information on our programs? If so, I think there's some flyers on the bulletin board next to the tennis courts."

Embarrassed by how I must have appeared to this kid while staring blankly into an empty field, I decide to chat him up. Just to prove I'm normal.

"Shouldn't you be in school?" I ask, borrowing John's technique of answering one question with another.

"Oh no, not at all. I'm home for the summer. I'm working at the rec center till August."

"Ah ha, a college student." He looks about fifteen to me. "Used to work here myself when I was around your age. Jake Taylor," I say, offering my hand.

"Dan Russell." We shake robustly, and I lose the strength of grip contest. Among my other maladies, it seems I've come down with a case of old man's handshake.

The last ember of vanity still smoldering inside me had been hoping to spot a flicker of recognition when I offered young Dan my name. Clearly he isn't well-versed in his town's ancient athletic history.

"I went to high school with a Sarah Russell."

"That could be my aunt," he responds with all the politeness due his elders. "Her name's still Russell. Took it back when she got divorced." By now he's begun glancing at something over my left shoulder. I can see we're both losing interest in this conversation.

"Nice girl. We had a lot of fun. When you see her, please tell her I said hello."

"Oh, I will, for sure. She still lives in town so I see her a lot. Owns the book store on Middle Street."

"Well, maybe I'll stop by there sometime. Pleasure to meet you."

"Same here. You sure you can't use some information about our summer programs?"

"Thanks just the same. I don't plan on being here very long." With this last statement I'm probably lying to both of us. He walks off toward the tennis courts and I turn back to where I came from. I refuse to call it home.

I'm shocked to learn that Sarah never left town; she was ambitious and devilishly untamable when I knew her. As high school seniors, she and I spent a good many nights parked in my parents' car on the dirt shoulders of deserted back roads topped by washboards that would rattle your teeth if you drove over them at more than thirty miles an hour. With the world outside our vehicle black as coal except for whatever meager illumination the moon and stars could provide, we'd fog the windows with heavy breathing and body heat, and afterwards lie in the back seat, door handles, seat belts and arm rests digging uncomfortably into us. With arms and legs entwined, we'd listen to the radio and talk confidently of the exciting lives we knew we were destined to lead.

I hope young Dan forgets to convey my regards. I'd hate it if Sarah were to learn I'm living here now. Just me, alone with my dead end dreams.

CHAPTER SIXTEEN

By means of a small down payment we'd scraped together and a mortgage we could scarcely afford, Annie and I purchased a modest house a few months after I'd passed the bar exam and landed an associate's position with a boutique personal injury firm in the heart of Philadelphia. She'd already found work as a graphic designer in nearby Merion, which lay conveniently along the busy Main Line extending in and out of the city. Ours wasn't much of a house, really. It sat on a postage stamp lot. Barely a sliver of lawn separated it from the street, and we shared a driveway with our neighbors. Every so often we'd pluck a solicitation for home repair from our mailbox or find one wedged into the storm door, periodic confirmation that our place could sorely use some fixing up.

In the ensuing months, thanks to her clever eye for decorating, Annie transformed our tiny dwelling, with all its quirks and imperfections, into something altogether charming. A unique wall hanging here, some art work there, a few colorful rugs and some antique furniture scattered just so, and before long she'd feathered a snug nest we were delighted to call our own. When winter arrived to cup our home in its icy hands, we'd cozy up on opposite ends of the couch under an old quilt she'd inherited from her grandmother, reclining there to read or chat idly until we both nodded off. On lazy summer evenings, lounging outdoors on a patio bordered on three sides by arborvitae, we'd savor music and wine, the latter mostly red blends. We knew next to nothing about fine wines, but enjoyed sampling new brands with clever names and creative labels. And on those serendipitous occasions when we could synchronize our calendars, we'd fly off to islands lapped by turquoise waters to lounge on sand as fine and white as sugar. Hand in hand, we'd stroll along nighttime shorelines to the sound of invisible waves rolling and crashing near our feet. Love came easily in paradise.

Our life together seemed perfect, and for longer than *I* deserved anyway, it was. We promised ourselves that when it came time for children we'd stage the wedding her parents were not so subtly pressuring her to have and pony up the money for a larger house, maybe a historic old colonial with a spacious yard and at least one tree with limbs thick and sturdy enough to support a swing. In the aftermath of Annie's second miscarriage and her surgery for endometriosis, the topic of children disappeared like something tossed into the back of a messy closet.

I never knew – and am now ashamed to admit I never asked – if Annie's heartache lay in her inability to bear children, or if instead it sprang from some irrational blame she heaped on herself for their absence. Unlike Annie, I'd never given much thought to starting a family, and had more or less been tagging along with the notion for her sake. To me, children were something that showed up automatically in one's adult life like gray hair or weight gain or an enlarged prostate. It wasn't that I didn't want a son or daughter for whom I might be what Archie rarely was. I just never felt an urgency to procreate.

I now confess that I was often too self-absorbed to view the issue from any perspective other than my own. Like the morning mail, clients kept materializing in my waiting room. There were motions to be argued before imperious judges and cases to try in which my client's financial future – not to mention my reputation – rested on the fickle attention spans of six strangers in a jury box, jurors I had to charm, entertain and educate. Over time, my trials evolved into a new type of basketball arena where hustle and talent could once again be rewarded. The more at ease and in control I felt in the courtroom, the more the entire process felt deliciously like the old days when the ball would be entrusted to me at a critical juncture of a game and I knew I had the skills to break down my defender.

As for Annie's job, she was often unhappy about the rudimentary projects handed down to her. In spite of her talent, there was only so much she could do with basic ads for school plays and church fairs. For her, graphic artistry meant just that: artistry, not the rote juxtaposition of words, colors and shapes. Given the chance, she knew how to tease the imagination and lead the eye exactly where she wanted it to go, so when the rare opportunity for more inventive projects arose, she'd pour her talents into them with a fervor matched only by her considerable skills.

One of her favorites, and mine, was an oversized, illustrated map for kids commissioned by the Philadelphia Zoo. Annie's whimsical creatures projected their own unique personalities. On safari, her tigers roamed grassy plains in pith helmets. Majestic lions – kings of the jungle bearing their regal scepters – wore brilliant crowns of gold atop their mighty heads. Meanwhile, an icy world away, cherubic penguins, spiffily attired in candy-colored scarves and knitted hats, slid merrily down smooth mounds of ice and pristine snow. Granted, the anthropomorphic caricatures may have been obvious, even predictable, yet who wouldn't smile to see a desert lizard sporting a fancy parasol to fend off the scorching sun blazing overhead? How I loved watching Annie work beneath the eaves of her cramped, messy office on the second floor of our home. With the patience of a cat eyeing its prey, she'd sit motionless and stare at a blank poster board, then suddenly attack it with fierce precision. With her dark hair pulled carelessly back and loose strands falling forward to brush dollops of paint or marker which had found their way onto her face, she looked little girl cute and big girl sexy. I never burned for her more than in those moments.

The years have a devious way of melting into one another, until you look up one day, startled to realize you've been together for more than a decade. And so it went for Annie and me as we inched closer to our forties. By then her parents had given up on a big wedding for their only daughter, and I'd assumed, conveniently perhaps, that Annie no longer cared about it either. Every so often, seemingly out of nowhere, she'd toss out a lighthearted remark about making this final commitment. I now cringe to recall how I'd either change the subject or lob a joke back at her, often analogizing final commitment to final interment. She never laughed at the comparison. Over time, the topic of marriage sank beneath the surface of our conversations and settled to its murky bottom with the rest of our detritus, as we moved uneventfully into our second decade together. The way I saw it, we may have lacked for children and a legal recognition of our relationship, but not for happiness, and in the days before our love and her patience were stolen, I'd sometimes pause to reflect on our good fortune. Never again will I dare be that happy. There's simply too much to lose.

CHAPTER SEVENTEEN

"Ready for another crack at me?" This time John has beaten me to the barn, which I interpret as a warning that his enthusiasm has not waned. For some reason he has not brought his ball this time, so we take turns shooting while the other rebounds. It's obvious that, like me, John's sore after yesterday's workout. He's wearing a compression wrap on his left knee and I notice he's shooting flat footed. Warming up, we engage in mundane banter about John's job at Burton's and how business at Meg's emporium is perking up now that the tourist season is in full swing. When I follow up with a few questions about his kids I can tell John's struggling to reciprocate with some specific questions about my life. The best he can offer is an open-ended inquiry. "So what else is happening with you, Jake?"

Other than what I glean from my new buddy Edward at the Gas Mart I have no current news to offer. "Not much," I tell him. "Just enjoying the time off till I go back to work in another month or two. It's been a nice break but I can't live off my savings forever."

"So you haven't left Philly for good?"

"No, not at all. I just needed a break. Let me tell you, litigation's a brutal way to make a living. There's no coasting, no taking your foot off the gas or your eyes off the road. The courtroom's a messy and dangerous place, more like a battlefield really, and believe me, it inflicts casualties. Unfortunately, I'm too poor to retire."

John hoists up another shot then remarks, "Funny, I would've said that type of environment suited you perfectly."

"Nope. Too draining," I reply.

He tosses me the ball. "Well, I suppose people change."

We continue our banalities until, once again, it's time to commence play. "My legs feel like concrete blocks," I advise him. "Don't expect too much out of me this time around."

"Now, JT," he immediately scolds me. "Remember what you always used to preach to me about excuses?" He stops dribbling the ball, turns toward me, and waits for my response like a teacher who's called on an unprepared student in class.

"You mean the one about. . ."

"Remember?"

I do recall my annoying old adage about excuses and losers. In fact I remember lifting it verbatim from a sports book I read as a kid. It was incredibly lame then and I refuse to recite it now on John's command. My hamstrings burn, I have zero interest in playing today, and I've had enough of being coerced. Unable to contain my irritation, I deploy John's favorite tactic against him, answering his question with a more explosive one of my own, a question intended to neutralize him.

"Why is it that you haven't once asked me about Annie?"

To my surprise, John's expression doesn't change one bit. In fact, he barely blinks. He takes a few stationary dribbles, then thoughtfully spins the ball for a few moments in his meaty hands, as if weighing it. "Well, sir, that would've been like asking a cancer survivor if he's worried it'll come back. Or an amputee if he misses his limb. Answer's pretty obvious. Same with you. There was no sign of Annie when you came up here to move your dad out of the house, even though they loved each other mightily. And when you pulled in here this last time I could read it in your eyes, plain as day. Dead and lost, that's what they were. Still are. I'm figuring it's over and I'm real sorry for that."

I don't know whether John has just apologized for not asking, or if instead he's told me he's sorry about Annie and me breaking up. I also don't know how to respond to him. Whatever possessed me to bring up this topic? I wandered back into this barn with the vague hope of escaping my problems, not confronting them.

"Every breakup's a timeworn tale," I tell him. "Sometime when we have nothing better to do I'll bore you with it."

Unwilling to let go of the subject matter just yet, John presses on. "Not that I wasn't concerned about you. Meg too, of course. I figured you'd tell me when you were ready. That's always been your way, JT, and you damn well know it. There's never been any use in trying to pry something out of you. You know me about as well as anyone can, so you also know I'm ready to listen anytime you're ready to talk." He holds the ball out in front of him until I'm forced to make eye contact, waits several additional seconds for emphasis, then hands it to me so we can begin again.

Round two proves a struggle for both of us. Maybe our middle age bodies are too fatigued from the day before, or possibly we've been knocked off balance by our foray into the intimate and personal. Whatever the reason, I receive no criticism from John about my effort, nor does he propose an additional game. Afterwards we grab seats on the dirty floor to catch our breath between gulps of water.

"So then, what exactly are you doing with yourself up here, Jake? Been seeing much of your dad?" Evidently John has decided it's time to slice open another vein.

"Some," I reply. "I like to think he enjoys the company even if he doesn't know who I am. But that place is worse than death."

"Your dad lived with a lot of pride, and that's an understatement. But pride's something that gets checked at the door when you're living up there, no two ways about it."

"True enough. Which is why, mostly, I don't visit all that often." I'm hoping he doesn't ask what I might be doing instead. It's also disconcerting to hear John refer to Archie in the past tense.

"Is that because of who he is now, or are you staying away because of where he is?"

"It's the sounds, the stench. It's the people. It's Archie. It's everything. Right now Meadows Retreat is the worst place for me to be." I don't know if John fully grasps what I meant by that last sentence. I'm hoping he won't ask.

"Anything stopping you from taking him out of there?" he inquires, turning his head to look directly at me.

"Anything stopping me? What, are you kidding? Other than the fact that he usually can't tell his ass from his elbow and two weeks ago thought I was *his* father? Or that he needs round the clock supervision? If I were to take him out of there where the fuck else would he go?" I don't know if this is coming from guilt or frustration. Whatever the source, I've quickly lathered myself into a pretty impressive pique.

"You think *I* can take care of him? Listen, man, my little sojourn here will be over soon. I've got a life waiting for me five hundred miles south." Winded by my outburst and egregious lie, I take a deep breath and form a "T" with my hands to signal a time out to the conversation.

John shakes his head in response. "Same old Jake," he says. "Attack first, ask questions later. When I suggested taking him out of the home I meant only for an hour or two. Maybe pushing him down the sidewalk in a wheelchair or just driving him around in the car."

"And what would be the point of that?" I demand. "And by the way, right back at you, buddy. Same old John too. Won't say shit even if he's got a mouthful of it." My one-sided argument has escalated quickly. I suppose it's been simmering for quite a while.

For the first time John appears pissed. “Cut the bullshit excuses, Jake. The benefits are pretty damn obvious. You spend time with your old man – offer him a little recreation – and you avoid that hell hole up the street. So what if he doesn’t know where he is? You used to drag that stupid dog Otis up and down the street when he was so old he could barely walk. Or hold his urine. Or even see. You think *he* knew what the heck was going on?”

He may have a point there, but now I’m sulking and not ready to admit it. Instead I say, “You think I can simply saunter out the front door with him whenever I want?”

“Yup. As a matter of fact, I do. He’s not a prisoner, you know.”

“And how do *you* know Archie will enjoy our two-man parade through the streets?”

“I don’t. But neither do you. And that’s exactly my point.” Whereupon John leans toward me and lightly smacks my forehead with the palm of his hand. When we were kids this was his way of advising me to smarten up. It may be too late for that.

CHAPTER EIGHTEEN

Rain lightly descends in a soupy mist as I limp back toward the house after my little dust-up with John. Too much of today remains with too little to color in its margins. Stronger storms are now darkening the immediate horizon, meaning it would be a perfect opportunity to visit Archie, if I were so inclined. Although I can't see much benefit in John's suggestion I can't entirely dismiss it from my head either. What if I do haul Archie out of there for a spell? What if he actually enjoys it? *What if?* How much of what we might otherwise attempt in life is stunted by the paralysis that often accompanies these two simple words? What if, for example, Archie's waiting for me right now in that foul and depressing facility, silently judging me for my selfish and cowardly neglect? What if I stopped avoiding whatever might upset my precarious equilibrium, as if I truly had any to begin with? What if, for a change, I endeavored to make someone other than myself happy? In so many words, Annie often asked me the same question.

As I stand shivering in the upstairs shower waiting for the water temperature to inch past lukewarm, I try to quiet my restless brain by concentrating on the sound and feel of the spray beating down on me. It does not work. Such distractions rarely do. Toward the end of things with Annie, having embraced the blackness of my depression like a hungry lover, I'd retreat to our basement, kill all the lights, and lie there for hours on a ratty old couch, a comforter pulled over my head. I longed for darkness thick and swollen, darkness dense enough to smother my obsessive thoughts and my fears. For longer than she should have, Annie would dutifully venture down to my gloomy hideout and try to coax me back upstairs. Eventually, once her patience and interest had been exhausted, she left me there like junk to be tossed when the time arrived for spring cleaning.

It seems there's no escaping the sadness and regret of my recollections. Everything I do, even this ordinary act of taking a shower, conjures up old memories. Right now, for instance, my thoughts have snuck back to Archie. This house didn't even have a shower until I reached my teens. Before then, all we had was an old cast iron tub with feet shaped like claws. When I couldn't take it anymore and finally went off on Archie one morning, ranting that I could no longer tolerate sitting in my own tepid filth, he rigged some piping upwards from the tub's faucets and erected a metal ring around its perimeter to accommodate a curtain. He never did get around to installing a ceiling fan. It was a half-ass job, and predictably, the unvented steam buckled the wallpaper and produced mold on the bathroom's painted surfaces.

Standing here beneath the water's spray also makes me think of my mother. When I was a little boy sent upstairs to take a bath on sub-zero winter nights, the hallways and bedrooms seemed as frigid as the frozen outdoors. Ice would form on the poorly insulated windows, ice so thick I could scrape it off into thin shavings with my fingernail. In contrast, the inside of the steamy bathroom was more like a sauna. After allowing me time to deplete most of the hot water in the tank my mother would knock on the bathroom door, inquire if I'd finished, and warn me to wrap a warm towel around my scrawny shoulders because, as she put it, "There's going to be a big change in the air when you come out." Back then I knew the type of change she was referring to and knew how to prepare for it. I've since learned that changes of much graver import often arrive without warning, like the unerring bullet of a sniper.

****

It's presently six-thirty in the morning at The Maple Leaf Golf Club. The ascending sun shoots streaks of golden light through lingering remnants of fog which snake around the taller trees like swirls of cotton candy. Today I stand alone with my rented golf clubs, and my recollections, in the day's first light. I am nearly fifty. I am thirteen. I am every year – and practically every summer – in between. That's how long I've been playing this hilly old course, beautiful only in a craggy sort of way, much like New Hampshire itself or the ungainly moose who populate it. Today I've decided to give golf an opportunity to lift my spirits. I have my doubts.

At this young hour, especially on a weekday, it often seems the course is deserted. Appearances to the contrary, I am never truly alone out here. Accompanied by the chattering ghosts of my former friends and playing partners, I stand poised on the first tee box, briefly survey the opening fairway, then hit my opening drive. As I commence my walk down the fairway my ghosts match me stride for stride, reminiscing with me, swapping recollections of past rounds marked by shots wondrous to behold, or sometimes just wondrously bad.

This first hole, a par five, is one of the easiest on the course. Just play up the left side of the wide fairway and avoid the sparse tree line along the right. Yet even before I putt out on its spacious green, I'm already directing curses at hole number two. "It's just not a fair hole," I grouse to my companions, who uniformly nod in agreement. For years I've detested the second hole, a long and narrow uphill climb bordered on each side by fir trees which devour golf balls with an insatiable hunger, their branches growing magically longer and taller to snatch even accurate drives out of the air. It's a fact; ask any of my ghosts. Predictably, the second hole does not go well. I send two balls deep into the woods, never to be seen again, before ball number three finds the tiny green. Already I've decided not to keep score. The second hole can do that to a golfer.

The third hole is a par four played from an elevated tee pushed back into the woods. As I stand motionless over my ball on the tee box, I can hear John, my oldest and most familiar ghost, chuckling quietly to himself as he stands closely behind me. Far too often for my liking he's seen me play this hole without my drive ever clearing the claustrophobic tunnel of woods leading to the sunny fairway a mere hundred yards away. He has a good idea of what's coming next – and the thought tickles him. Will it be a slice that curves like a banana into the woods, or will my latest catastrophe be a low, bounding ball that hops like a panicked rabbit into the underbrush? Surprise, it's neither. This time a colossal hook sends me – and this is the ultimate horror – back into the adjoining fairway of that miserable second hole. Yes, I have returned to hell, and the trip out is predictably ugly.

When I pause briefly to catch my breath and assess the fourth hole, John seizes the honors and tees off. This has always been John's motto: "It is better to be lucky than good; it is even better to be incredibly lucky." As is often the case, his drive slices high and deep into the dense forest on the right. And, as is our practice, we patiently give it time to re-emerge. Soon enough, there comes the thwack of his ball against a tree, and then another crack, and then, amidst the scattering of leaves and the fluttering of startled birds, it makes a triumphant reappearance, nestling onto the welcoming grass of the fairway. Knowing the level of my annoyance at his unfailing luck, John makes no eye contact with me as I tee up my own ball which, after a swing that more closely resembles the hack of an axe murderer, goes skimming along the ground at a severe left angle. I set out for the left-hand rough while he ambles contentedly forward. I swear I can hear him whistling a jaunty little tune.

It has taken fewer than four holes for the game that's playing out in my mind to poison the round I'm actually trying to enjoy. I simply cannot withstand the assault of memory and what I have lost. The sunny beauty of the green and blue tableau, the competition and the companionship, I once loved it all. Returning here today, I'd hoped to find some comfort in the familiarity of this old course, where I still remember every break in every green. To my dismay, I've instead discovered one more place I no longer belong. I push through two more holes then walk off the course without once looking back.

CHAPTER NINETEEN

Trying to sleep can be exhausting, and last night was another long one. After thrashing about for a few hours I grabbed a blanket, a couple of pillows, and curled up on the window seat downstairs, where I stared out at a moonlit landscape as white and still as bones. Whenever the occasional car passed by, I'd wonder where anyone could be heading at such an hour. Fiery young lovers, exhausted and spent, returning home from wherever new love travels? A farm hand on his way to the early milking? Parents with a wailing, febrile child, racing to the emergency room for medicine and reassurance? Seemingly, even in the lonely quiet of night other people had places to go, purposes to fulfill. Yet there I lay, exactly one month into my retreat, having moved nowhere other than deeper into my solitude.

This morning, therefore, I've concluded enough is enough. The moment for action has arrived, even if I see no clear reason for it. If only for the sake of moving, it's now time to move. Consequently, I've resolved to go for a drive rather than take my usual run, and this time I'm planning on a front seat passenger. It is not lost on me that I'm about to embark upon the exact course of action John suggested. Unquestionably, he'll be pleased to hear it. Although from my vantage point it looks like a long shot, maybe I'll be pleased as well.

****

Step one in the chauffeuring process involves cleaning all the crap out of my car. It's been a long time since it's transported anything other than old newspapers, gym clothes and trash. Step two, which is springing Archie from the clink, proves unexpectedly simple. Per instructions from someone staffing the front desk when I called in advance, all I have to do is track down Joy Foster, still the Foghorn Leghorn of this particular barnyard, and sign the old guy out.

"Will your father be returning by midnight?" Joy inquires after I finally locate her. Even in the harsh illumination of the lobby she somehow casts an imposing shadow.

"Yes, of course. We'll be gone an hour or so at the most." I reply, puzzled by the question.

Looking to the left and right as though someone might care enough about our conversation to eavesdrop, she sidles up to me, her expansive shelf of a bosom nearly knocking me backwards. "Because you know – and I'm really not supposed to tell you this – we provide skilled care here at Meadows Retreat. If one of our residents leaves too often, or for too long, Medicare may cut off their benefits. As a courtesy to the families we do try to look the other way, so to speak, but we really shouldn't bill Medicare for a day in which a bed is not filled. I trust you can appreciate that, Mr. Taylor."

I find her officiousness grating, and I'm tempted to take a look around for my old nemesis Harriet for relief. "Well, trust is a pretty powerful word. However, I'd say you can count on Archie being back in his bed on time tonight. For all I know, this could be the first and last occasion I take him out of here. We'll see how things go."

"Very good then. Have a pleasant day together." And with that, Joy pivots sharply on her heel to attack her next chore, leaving me standing uneasily next to Archie, who's presently sitting hunched over and expressionless in a wheelchair he doesn't really need. I've seen him walk around his room and down the corridors, and usually he manages just fine. Despite that, from a lifetime of experience, I surmised he might be mulish about walking out the door with me. I was also worried I'd have to hold his hand, and regardless of the extent of his dementia, I'm certain neither of us would be comfortable with that arrangement. So he gets the chair.

Evidently some staff member has given it his or her all helping Archie prepare for his big excursion. Notwithstanding the fact that it's 82 degrees and blindingly sunny outside, he's sporting his favorite white nylon windbreaker, zipped to the sagging wattle of his neck, and khaki pants, much too large for him now, which balloon around his lower torso like clown attire. His worn leather belt no longer comes close to cinching around his bony waist and hips. Since he won't be doing any walking, I'm not particularly worried about keeping his trousers up. I'm guessing there's a pair of adult diapers underneath them, though no one's mentioned that to me and I'm definitely not inquiring. Archie's still wearing his slippers. No problem with that, as they're the hard soled, dress shoe type and actually look pretty sharp. His snow white hair, longer than he used to wear it, protrudes in a shaggy bowl below the band of his Red Sox hat.

A sudden breeze picks up as I push Archie through the parking lot, causing his windbreaker to billow like a parachute. Even though he's sometimes chattered at me like an over-caffeinated mynah bird, thus far he hasn't uttered word one to me, nor I to him. Now that he's outdoors he seems to want to look around, yet even with the brim of his Red Sox hat pulled sharply downward he's squinting into the brilliant afternoon sun like someone rousted from bed in the middle of the night by a flashlight beam to the face. I make a mental note to pick up a pair of sunglasses if I'm crazy enough to try this again.

When we reach the car I realize I have no idea how to transfer a stiff jointed, uncooperative old man into a compact vehicle without possibly breaking a bone or dislocating a shoulder. Maybe I can talk him through it. "Archie, this is our car. If I pull you up do you think you can stand and take a couple of steps?"

No answer. Not even a glance my way.

"Archie, I need to get you into this car so we can go for a ride, ok?"

He's now toying with a piece of loose string hanging from the hem of his jacket. He's also sinking lower into his chair, as if gradually melting in the hot sun.

"Archie, can you please help me out here? I have to get you into the car."

His chin is now resting on his sternum.

"Hey, I know you can talk. Less than a week ago you babbled half the afternoon about Ted Williams and how he could fish even better than he hit, and how this country went to straight to hell when LBJ decided not to run again. And oh yeah, you delivered this riveting information while motoring pretty damn well on two good legs down the hallway."

Not a muscle moves. Not a word is spoken.

A fourth try. "Archie, you have to . . . oh fuck it. Fuck you. And fuck me for even trying this." With that I yank open the car door, scoop him out of his wheelchair and plop his bony ass onto the front seat. Before he has time to tilt, fall or slide I surround his torso with the lap and shoulder belts and click them into place. "There, goddamnit. You can stare at your feet or you can look out the window. I don't give a shit. But we're going for a ride 'cause you've got nothing better to do and, damnit, old man, neither do I." I slam his door for emphasis and furiously collapse the wheelchair for storage in the trunk.

Circling around the back of the car I steal an agitated glance through the rear window to see how he's reacted to my outburst. What I observe defuses my anger like a bomb. He looked much heartier within the tiny confines and artificial light of his room. Now that's he's outdoors and exposed, the real Archie looks shriveled and frail, his skin brittle like parchment. And what tears at my heart, yet at the same time offers faint hope for our little journey, is that he has turned his head toward the empty driver's seat as though waiting to be taken somewhere.

CHAPTER TWENTY

"At first we thought your father's problems might be attributable to depression, which is something that often develops in elderly people who unexpectedly find themselves widowed and alone, or possibly from one or more mild strokes that went unnoticed. Both can cause confusion and memory problems." That's the gist of what Archie's gerontologist, Dr. Mumford, told me when we conferred privately following one of Archie's appointments. This, of course, was before he entered Meadows Retreat, eight months prior to be precise. Dr. Mumford went on to explain that after administering a battery of tests, and based on his clinical judgment, he had "regretfully" concluded that Archie had a "touch of dementia."

Like Archie, I've never been fond of euphemisms. "Isn't a 'touch of dementia' like a 'touch of pregnancy,' Dr. Mumford?" I asked bluntly. "It progresses or regresses, or something like that. Bottom line, it only gets worse, right?"

"Over time, yes. Yes, I'm afraid it does."

"And where is Archie on this timeline, doc? How long before it all deserts him?"

"Well, depending on which study one reads, dementia can be divided into several stages based on the severity of a patient's cognitive decline. Generally, however, it's easier to identify only three main stages: early, middle and late."

"And Archie is in what stage?"

"That's a close call, Jake." I learned long ago that the bearer of bad news often uses a person's name before unloading on him, as if to say, *We're in this together because I care enough about you to use your first name.* So I knew what was coming next.

"I'd say Archie did a remarkable job of concealing his problems from you, and from most everyone I'd assume, over the past year or two. Believe me, he had to be acutely aware of them. Now he's slipping from a mild cognitive decline to a moderate one in which his short term memory will continue to deteriorate and, increasingly, he'll have difficulty recognizing his surroundings, as well as his friends and family. At present it's not as if he's lost all these faculties. In fact, at this stage of the process he may enjoy periods of lucidity lasting from hours up to several days or more. What you need to know is that the brain controls the entire body, and when the brain breaks down, so to speak, the body soon follows. As a result, dementia patients frequently develop heart, lung and gastrointestinal problems. As the disease progresses, they also tend to refuse food, which further compromises their health. Should your father live long enough, the time will most certainly arrive when all his psychomotor and communicative skills will abandon him."

"How long would you estimate before we reach that point?"

"Maybe one to three years, on the average. I realize your father's a fighter but force of will has little effect on such an insidious disease."

"One last question: how much longer can he live by himself at home?"

To that, Dr. Mumford simply shook his head.

****

Today's junket, the first and possibly only one Archie and I might ever take, finds us nearly a year into the death sentence pronounced by his doctor. With any luck Archie has forgotten everything about that day. As for me, I'll never forget exiting Dr. Mumford's office to discover Archie sitting alone in the waiting room, staring blankly at a squawking television mounted to the wall. Its channel was tuned to Fox News, a network he'd often railed against for its "pig-headed hypocrisy and phony patriotism." Sitting as placidly in that waiting room as a parishioner in his pew waiting for Mass to commence, he must have at least sensed what was going to happen to him. I hoped by then, with my mother gone and his future shrinking, he'd quit caring.

Keeping one eye on the road and the other on Archie, I putter down Main Street toward the center of Jackson Meadows. Unlike the newer homes on the outskirts, the houses in this older part of town are squeezed tightly together like elderly people leaning on one another for support. As we poke along, I swivel my head back and forth in exaggerated sweeping motions to peer at the mundane sights, hoping Archie will mimic my actions. Instead he remains locked in his dead man's stare which, given his diminished stature, means he's looking directly into the dashboard. Not much of a view. I assume he's enjoying none of this.

When we began our little trip I'd turned on the air conditioning to cool off the car, which had sat baking in the sun while I collected my passenger. Now, with Archie looking so fragile and pale, I shut it down and fully open both front windows for a little warm air. As if on cue, Archie immediately lifts his right elbow and plunks it on the bottom frame of the passenger window. Although his elbow is now awkwardly positioned about two inches higher than his right ear, Archie leaves it there while the wind briskly snaps the sleeve of his nylon jacket like a flag.

I'm stunned. Entirely unresponsive to anything I've said or done today, he's now gone and shoved his bony arm out the window which, due to fundamental body mechanics and an old man's lack of flexibility, has forced him to raise his head to such a degree that he's physically compelled to look out the front windshield. Suddenly wide-eyed, he appears startled by what he sees. I'm tempted to offer him the flat of my palm for an enthusiastic high five, until I recall that Archie always drove, and later rode, with his bent elbow hanging out the window like a coat hanger. Most likely this is nothing more than an incidence of muscle memory, like a chicken running to and fro after its head's been lopped off. Still, insignificant as it might be, it *is* at least something. Unwittingly, I have coaxed Archie into having a look around, even if he no longer recognizes what he sees.

It takes no time to traverse the main thoroughfares of the village proper, and it takes even less time for me to realize I'll need to drive more slowly if we're going to stretch this experiment into anything longer than a half-hour trip. Despite the minimal number of streets in Jackson Meadows, I've avoided driving past our house on High Street, worried that if Archie spies it he'll think I'm taking him home. As we tool around town at our turtle pace, Archie maintains his awkward posture, elbow protruding from the window at an acute angle. I'm assuming he's lost all feeling in it by now. Still no conversation though, so I give it a go. Summoning all the false enthusiasm I can muster I ask, "See anyone you know, Archie?"

One might expect that after years of questioning witnesses I could come up with something better than asking a demented old man what he recognizes. Problem is, I'm motoring through uncharted territory right now, uncertain if any part of this little adventure of ours is even registering with him. Of course, nothing has ever been easy when it comes to Archie, and the suspicious part of me suspects he's doling out some measure of delayed punishment with his silence.

Having run out of local streets, we set off for a rural area of town commonly referred to as "Out East," where the narrow roads snake around foothills and undulating fields. It's a bumpy ride, especially this time of year, since the municipal paving crews never make it this far from town until mid-summer. Consequently, last winter's frost heaves have had time to collapse into themselves in the heat of the June sun. No matter. Nobody much cares about holes or bumps in these roads because nobody can travel very fast on them anyway, not with moose and deer to drive around, or into, and not when one is routinely forced to creep along behind farmers pulling loads of hay from field to barn by means of rusted old tractors billowing smoke from their exhaust pipes. Out here, it's also common to happen upon any number of empty vehicles parked next to the crisscrossing trout streams generously fed by waters from the nearby mountains. Archie truly loved this region. It was almost sacred to him. It's where he taught me to fish. "Keep only what you can eat, boy," he'd say. "Let the little ones get bigger and smarter. Give 'em a fighting chance." When I was little and the tall grass in the fields leading to the brooks rose nearly over my head, Archie would tuck me under his arm like a football and carry me to the easier fishing holes. Once there, he'd cast my line into a pool of calm water and tell me to wait for a bite. Years later he confessed that he'd never hand the pole over to me until he'd already hooked a fish. "You needed the confidence to believe you were a real fisherman," he told me. And he was right.

Life was simpler Out East, where we had but one objective: land a big one. We'd root about for just the right hole, such as a shady pool split by a fallen log or some rushing water interrupted by large rocks, then let our fly drift in the lazy current until a speckled trout breached the surface to snatch it. Like upscale food service, successful fishing was all about the presentation. Though he was not exactly the most patient of instructors, Archie did teach me his angling tricks and reminded me each time we came here to take an appreciative look around at the sky and the mountains and the majestic beauty of the forest. He'd offer the same advice to John, who usually tagged along on our trips. Later on, after we'd acquired our drivers' licenses, John and I began striking off more and more by ourselves to fish; at that age it was much more fun being on our own. Turning our backs on Archie like that must have sorely wounded him. Always the stoic, he never uttered a word of disappointment.

Our route this afternoon leads us past the McLain farm, slavishly worked by generations of the large McLain family, including its present owner, Bunghole McLain. I've never known Bunghole's true first name, nor do I know the provenance of his peculiar nickname. I'm quite sure I don't want to. The McLain farm boasts the standard array of cows and sheep, as well as a smaller, fenced-in enclosure populated entirely by goats of various sizes and colors. Noticing that Old Bung has deposited a massive hollow tree trunk inside the goat enclosure, I pull over to the side of the road to look through Archie's window and watch the goats climb in, up and over their wooden playscape.

"The whistle. Where's my whistle." Startled, I quickly look around to see who might have snuck up on us from outside the car. There's no one in sight.

"Where's the damn whistle?"

Astoundingly, it's Archie. Outdoors his voice sounds more high and nasally than back at the home, kind of like an agitated duck. The good news is he's finally talking. The bad news is I have no clue what he's talking about. I have no recollection of his ever owning or using a whistle, and even if he did, what would he need with one right now?

"Archie, what did you say? What is it you want?"

No answer. Nor is he looking at me, as he's now turned his head to peer directly out his window.

"Little buggers will fall right over. Scare the bejeezus out of 'em."

Eureka! We have a connection. Years ago when Archie would taxi John and me to the brooks, he was forever telling us how some goats, when startled, would stiffen up and topple over, their limbs temporarily paralyzed by fear. To demonstrate, he'd often sound the horn whenever we'd drive by a field of goats, who'd perversely refuse to drop and would instead glare back at us with the malevolent look most goats have. I now recall him guaranteeing we could get them to fall if we snuck up from behind and blew a whistle. John and I were in agreement that even if Archie happened to be correct, watching goats tip over was not especially uproarious fun. Today, however, hoping to further engage Archie, I enthusiastically lay on the horn with all I've got to see if I can knock one over. Unfazed, the goats don't even look up. Instead, I succeed in scaring the everlasting crap out of Archie, who instantly throws both arms straight up in the air like the victim of a stick-up, then drops them to pull his Red Sox hat over his eyes.

Although his mind may be nearly kaput, there's no denying his heart remains strong.

CHAPTER TWENTY-ONE

I'm not sure what to think about yesterday's experience with Archie. I wouldn't characterize it as a success, nor was it a disaster. After depositing him in his prisoner's quarters I sped directly home for two aspirin and a nap. My muscles ached from the tension of the afternoon, as though I'd spent it lugging heavy rocks. Notwithstanding the rigors of the experience, before dropping off into a dead sleep I chuckled perversely at the recollection of Archie practically jumping through the roof of the car when the horn blared. It was comically ironic to watch his old trick backfire. And besides, it wasn't as if I frightened him on purpose, so I didn't feel especially guilty about it. I promised myself I'd somehow make it up to him the next time. Yes, the next time. I can't say the experience was fun, exactly, but I didn't hate it nearly as much as I'd expected.

This morning I've commenced my run later than usual. To my surprise, I'm rather enjoying the solitude, which is saying a lot considering I'm always alone. The songs on my shuffle do not render me quite so melancholy and contemplative, and the cool air which trailed in on the heels of last night's heavy rains feels refreshing on my skin. Strange, really, since nothing has changed. I can't put my finger on a reason for feeling this upbeat. Whatever the cause, my pace today seems faster and my steps lighter, and instead of setting out as usual for the outskirts of Jackson Meadows, I decide to change things up and head toward its business center, which the old timers still refer to as "down street." On this new route I pass Meg's Shop in the Barn, where larger items for sale have been arranged on the sidewalk outside her store, almost certainly in violation of local zoning ordinances. I smile as I run by the large granite horse trough erected by the town's early settlers on the occasion of its centennial birthday. Fed by four elevated spigots of highly pressurized water, this is the same trough that John and I filled late one night with several boxes of laundry detergent, producing mountains of soapy bubbles which spilled out and covered a considerable portion of Main Street. Good clean fun.

Turning left up the mostly empty sidewalk onto Middle Street, I push onward for about fifty yards before clicking off my music to drink from a stone pedestal fountain that's been hydrating Jackson Meadows pedestrians since before I was born. In refreshing contrast to the mid-morning heat, the fountain's water is icy cold. After satisfying my thirst, I splash several handfuls of water onto my face and lift the front of my ratty old shirt to wipe it off. Exposing my sweaty, hairy belly in public is a little crude but I'm certain no one's around to notice.

"Jake? Jake Taylor?" I don't recognize the voice, nor can I see the speaker with my shirt still covering my face. Immediately uncomfortable at having been recognized, and doubly so because of my unflattering pose, I warily drop the front of my wet shirt to see who's addressing me.

"Jake, I thought that was you. How are you? Remember me?"

If I were inclined to panic, and lately I have been, now would be the perfect time. This woman appears to be about my age and even though she's let her long, thick hair go gray she is remarkably attractive in an Emmy Lou Harris sort of way. Still nervously drawing a blank, I know I need to say something. "Yes, of course I do," I lie, as I initiate a frantic scan of my memory bank. "We went to school together and . . ." And then I notice the backdrop behind her. A book store. On Middle Street. I'm pretty certain this is the store young Dan Russell told me his aunt owned. And that would make this woman Sarah Russell, clearly winning her battle with middle age. Kicking its ass, really.

"On second thought, I guess there's no need for me to remind you what we did together in school. Hi, Sarah. It's good to see you." Surprisingly, I think I actually mean what I've just said.

"What's it been, Jake. Something like twenty five years?"

"All of that," I reply. "Are you the owner of this fine establishment?"

"I am indeed. One book store for a one horse town. No competition, and unfortunately not a whole lot of customers either.

I can push *Fifty Shades* or *Harry Potter* out the door but forget about selling real literature. Would you believe I actually had one customer ask if *To Kill A Mockingbird* was about ornithology? But listen to me prattle on like an old snoot. What brings you back to town?"

"Just taking a little break after some difficult trials, spending a little time with my father."

"Oh, that's right. I did hear Archie's living in Meadows Retreat. That's a shame. He was . . ."

I can tell she's fumbling for the appropriate words. "A real fighter?" I offer.

"I was going to say, 'Someone who truly relished life, and every bit of it.' I remember how faithful he was about going to all your games, and how you told me every Saturday night was date night for him and your mom. He was a wonderful dancer, am I recalling that correctly?"

She's right. Archie was immensely proud of his dancing ability. There was no tempo or rhythm tricky enough to stymie him. He could dance to anything. He knew all the steps and all the styles, and he'd badger my poor mother into learning them as well. Occasionally, with a still sleepy smile over a cup of coffee on a Sunday morning, she'd tell me how, the night before, Archie had been calling for one more number while the poor, exhausted band was ready to pack up and head home for bed. But enough about Archie and enough about me. Safer to steer this conversation back to Sarah.

"Tell me, Sarah, do you have any children?"

"I do indeed. One. A boy. He's fifteen and a great kid. What a shock to hear a parent say that, right? He's getting ready to spend two months with his father up in Maine, near Brunswick. I'm going to miss him like crazy. That's the consequence of being divorced with children. You never entirely jettison the ex-husband."

"And how about you, Jake? A wife? Any children?"

"I was . . . no. . . I was with someone for about twenty years. We're not together anymore. We never married. No children, although we did have a dog we spoiled rotten, if that qualifies. Splitting up was a mutual thing, best for both of us. I know she's happier now, both her and the dog." That last quip cuts too close to the bone. Time for the escape artist to perform his act.

"Listen, Sarah, I can't stand here cooling off for too long. These days my aging muscles tighten up fast. It's really great to see you, and I do mean that. I jog around town most every day so I'm sure we'll be bumping into one another again. Let's agree to talk longer next time. It'd be fun to catch up." Edging away, I find the thought of seeing her again a little exciting, by no means a familiar feeling for me over, let's say, the past five years.

"I'd like that. Take care, Jake. Enjoy the rest of your run. You certainly have a beautiful day for it."

Sarah gives me a goodbye smile that says she's genuinely happy to see me, then turns back toward her store. Before striking off I pause surreptitiously to watch her leave, reminding me of an old saying which goes something like, "I hate seeing you leave but love watching you walk away."

CHAPTER TWENTY-TWO

No John sightings in the past few days. I presume he's back at work after his vacation, and as a result I haven't expected him to be nosing around for more basketball. In those haughtier days before life dealt me a well-deserved comeuppance, I considered his job to be little more than a glorified shelf stocker. I knew I could net more from one trial than John could bank in five years, and back then I was far too impressed by the size of my own portfolio, as if that had anything to do with my worth as a person. Life, I've since discovered, has a harsh way of reshaping one's point of view, and nowadays I'm more impressed by how John offers a hard day's labor in exchange for an honest wage, with the emphasis on "honest." In direct contrast, my role at trial is to play the magician with a deft sleight of hand, misdirecting the jury's attention toward what I want it to see and burying damaging evidence by obfuscation and outright trickery. Over the years I've manipulated and flustered hostile witnesses until they could barely recite their phone numbers, and I've called experts to the stand who – for enough dough – testified exactly as I wanted with all the sincerity of a minister delivering a Sunday homily. It's profitable work as long as one doesn't allow a little thing like a conscience to stand in the way.

Two days of soaking rains followed by abundant sunshine have produced a lawn lusher than usual for early July, and consequently I'm out here this late afternoon pushing the lawnmower up and down its front portion. Archie's mower is a tired old plow horse which burns through nearly as much oil as it does gasoline, and coughs out the clippings in thick clumps. Regardless of the cloud of smoke it emits and the multiple piles of grass I'll have to rake up later, I welcome any activity after being cooped up indoors. Yesterday, with the dark sky dumping buckets of rain, I drove up to Meadows Retreat to see Archie, where I found him asleep in his recliner, mouth agape, snoring loudly. I didn't have the heart to rouse him from the escape that I hoped his sleep was providing. Having little to do afterwards, I took a drive Out East to inspect the turgid brooks. Their rapids of silver and green were rushing off into distant fields and deeper forests. In the old days, even with all the rain, I might've been tempted to grab a pole, wade downstream, and try my luck. After all, wet is wet. Sitting there yesterday in my car, I tried to resurrect my old fisherman's enthusiasm. Not a chance. It was like attempting to cry after running out of tears.

To my surprise, I glance up from my mowing to see John spraying weed killer on his lawn, which I predict will finally extirpate any remaining green and leave it entirely dirt. At least then it will match his house. Maybe he has plans to seed the areas he's spraying, although he has to know that July is just about the worst month for growing grass. John pops his head up and offers a hearty wave, which I return. I haven't finished mowing the front lawn but conclude that's it for the time being because John is now heading my way. I cut the mower's engine and wait for him, a little warily as usual.

"Jake, glad I spotted you. Meg's been up one side of me and down the other about inviting you over for dinner. She's convinced you've been existing on nothing but canned beans and frozen dinners."

"Actually if you subtract the beans and add a steady diet of ice cream you wouldn't be too far off," I say, trying my best to keep the conversation light. It irks me that I remain so tense around John.

"So whatta you say? Dinner at our place then? We'll kick the kids out of the way so we can eat in peace."

Knowing John will never take no for an answer, I feel compelled to accept his offer, preferably for some indefinite date. "Sounds great. We'll have to do that for sure."

"No time like the present," he persists. "How about tonight? Unless you've been hiding someone in that house with you I expect you're planning to dine alone again."

John's invitation has morphed into something of an insult. Invite the loner holed up in his house over for dinner. Pointing this out to him would be a waste of time, as would be resisting.

"I'm sure I can clear my calendar. What time?"

"Six sharp. And bring your appetite. You're looking a little gaunt with all this running of yours. We'll see you later then." He gives me a hearty slap on the shoulder and strides off without another word.

As I stow the mower in the barn it occurs to me that the sociable thing to do would be to bring a bottle of wine with me. Because I'm smelling a little ripe after my yard work, and grass clippings are clinging like magnetic filings to the legs of my jeans, I opt for the informality of the Gas Mart rather than the supermarket. Although the selection there is limited I'm pretty sure I can find something to suffice.

When I arrive at the Gas Mart, I discover that the large cooler for wine and beer also holds small Styrofoam tubs of worms and night crawlers, a juxtaposition of items I never encountered at the package stores in Philadelphia. Selecting the priciest bottle of red wine, which is to say it costs slightly north of eleven dollars, I step up to the register.

"Good afternoon, Jake. Are we entertaining this evening?" It's Edward. Who else.

"Hi, Edward. Not really," I reply in a clipped monotone meant to discourage conversation. Pointless, really, since Edward is deaf and blind to social cues.

"Oh, I thought you might have rekindled one of those old high school romances," he says in a conspiratorial voice, as if he's just one of the guys and we're schmoozing about babes.

"No such luck," I tell him, forking over the money.

“Well, no harm either in partaking of a glass or two alone at night,” he offers with exaggerated empathy. “It relaxes a person. Good for the ticker too, or so they claim.”

I can think of nothing intelligent or friendly to offer in response while awaiting the hand-ironing of my bills, and so I silently count along with Edward as he painstakingly doles out my change.

“You take care of yourself, Jake. Enjoy your refreshment.”

“So long, Edward.”

The little bell that tinkles when the door opens reminds me that in no time Edward will be disseminating his latest news bulletin: Jake Taylor, former star athlete and big time Philadelphia litigator, is now drinking alone in his father’s old house on High Street.

CHAPTER TWENTY-THREE

The interior of John's house is a his and hers combination of John's spare, New England practicality and Meg's creativity, and as I stoop to permit Meg to deposit a hello peck on my cheek I realize the place looks and feels so familiar it's as if I've taken a magical step backwards into my boyhood. From the front door, the narrow hallway entrance leads to an old fashioned octagonal-shaped parlor heated in winter by –what else – a wood stove. The parlor's walls, together with the ones I can see in adjoining rooms, are a soft cream color stenciled with borders of varying pastels running from corner to corner, and garnished with wreaths of sticks and dried flowers. Smooth, gray pieces of driftwood from the Israel River, which courses through the downtown center of Jackson Meadows, are arranged on antique wooden shelves and several nearby table tops. Colorful braided rugs lie scattered atop wide hardwood planking, and an ornately framed full length mirror, before which generations of Caldwells have paused to adjust a tie or a hat, hangs sturdily next to an old-fashioned coat rack in an alcove between the parlor and the spacious living room. The high ceilings and oversized windows make me feel as small as when this place was my second home.

Steering me by the elbow, Meg says, "Come right on in, Jake. Let's get you something to drink."

"Well, you might consider opening this bottle of wine," I say, handing it to her. "I can't vouch for the quality. And don't mind the bottle; it might smell like worms."

"No problem there," says John, more or less directly into my right ear. He's been hovering over my right shoulder. "Last year I bought part of the wine collection from the old Wentworth Resort when it finally closed. Remember that place? They asked you to lifeguard for them even though you could barely swim."

"Hey, that's not entirely true," I protest. "I could stay afloat well enough to save myself from drowning. I was dating Sally Something or Other, the owner's daughter. Can't believe I've forgotten her last name. Anyway, their only requirement for lifeguard was someone athletic looking, since most of their guests were on the wrong side of seventy and more interested in wading than swimming. In any event, they would've been perfectly safe with me on duty. The pool was only five feet deep."

"My guess is that pretty little Sally wanted to know where you were at all times," counters John, "more than Mommy and Daddy needed a lifeguard. Oh well, that's ancient history now. Long story shorter, I've acquired part of their wine collection. Let's you and I pick out a bottle or two from the cellar before settling in."

While Meg bustles back to the kitchen, John and I open a narrow door in his dining room and descend a set of wooden steps into the basement. Glancing to my left, I notice that the portion of the cellar running beneath a shed attached to the house still has a dirt floor. To the right, it's a different story. The walls, rough and irregular owing to their composition, namely boulders and large stones cemented into a foundation, are ringed by free-standing shelves holding tools, neatly stacked boxes, and jars of vegetables, presumably canned from last summer's garden.

Gesturing in the direction of the shelving, I remark to John, "We raided a considerable number of dill pickle jars over there back when your parents used to can and preserve stuff. Not to mention the brownies and cookies in the freezer. I can't recollect, did you ever get into trouble for pilfering any of that stuff?"

"Those were serious crimes, my friend," he intones with mock solemnity. "Thankfully, I never served any time."

"So where's your wine cellar?" I ask.

"Where else?" he replies, pointing with his right thumb directly behind us.

I turn to look in the direction he has indicated and there, looming in the far corner of the basement, sits a familiar hulking cube of cinder block construction. "You're kidding me," I exclaim. "You still have that fallout shelter down here?"

"Once built, they're pretty difficult to dispose of, wouldn't you say?"

"Leland had that thing built in the early sixties, right?" I ask incredulously.

"Possibly even the late fifties. Always had it stocked and ready for full occupancy in case the Ruskies ever dropped the Big One."

"Ah yes, the Big One. We had a much more peaceful use for that shelter, like sneaking beer in there and drinking half the night when we were teenagers."

"And then passing out," John adds.

"Oh yes, I woke up sick and hung over in there more times than I like to remember. And before morning came we'd sometimes stagger over to the dirt part of your cellar to pee or puke. It was kind of like our own private latrine."

John corrects me, "That latrine was for emergency evacuations only, when we couldn't make it out the hatchway to the back yard."

"Nothing says back to nature like peeing under the moonlight."

"Speaking of drinking too much," John says, "I'm sure you also remember the night we spent at that hole in the wall bar near the border crossing for Canada. The one next to the railroad tracks?

"Of course I do. Or part of it anyway. We were pretty wasted."

"Remember the band that was playing?"

"Are you kidding? How could I ever forget? Cheesy little mustaches. Powder blue blazers. Hair slicked back. And as impossible as it seemed, their music sounded worse than they looked. They were imported directly from Canada, right?"

Warming to the story, John chuckles and says, "Indeed they were. And the drunker we got the more we yelled at 'em, 'Hey, you Canucks! We're shelling out good American dollars here. For Chrissake, sing something in English!'"

"We were heckling, not yelling. Definitely heckling."

"And the one and only song they could sing in English was . . . ?" asks John, barreling ahead with the narrative.

"Oh, that's easy. A little number from the sixties, written before most everyone in the bar was even born: *Wild Thing.* Three chords, simple lyrics. I swear they must've played it a half dozen times. All at our request, of course."

"More like a threat than a request," John chortles. "And each time we sang along at the top of our lungs, till the manager had heard enough and finally gave us the boot. At least *he* knew English."

"Particularly the four letter words."

John flashes the first genuine, unrestrained smile I've seen from him since returning to town. It reminds me he wasn't always so serious. It also reminds me how harmless and fun our youthful escapades really were, way back when we were brothers.

CHAPTER TWENTY-FOUR

Back upstairs, saying hello to John's kids is akin to meeting the Von Trapp Family. There's no mistaking that they've been admonished to be on their best behavior, extend a polite greeting to their guest, then disappear for the evening into the nooks and crannies of their capacious old home.

While awaiting our meal, John and I opt for the cool evening air of the front porch rather than the living room. We sip our wine as Meg scurries back and forth from porch to kitchen, briefly pausing each time to chat before returning to check on the progress of the meal. Viewing the neighborhood from this perspective, looking *at* my house rather than out from it, is oddly relaxing. It's as though I've stepped outside my existence and temporarily escaped from wherever it is I've been holed up these past months.

"You certainly have a model family," I remark. "Meg is still Meg, which means she's great. And the kids all seem like they have it together."

John reflects on my compliment for a while before replying. "Life's not without its issues," he says, with reservation detectable in his voice. "But yes, I'd say we're about as happy as anyone has a right to expect."

"Hey man, I'd say that even being in a position to *expect* happiness is a great place to be." I'm not entirely sure what I mean by this. I do know that I'm irked by John's lukewarm assessment of his family situation.

True to form, John offers no direct response and instead reaches for his glass of wine, which sits on a small wicker table between us. Gesturing across his yard with his free hand he asks, "Tell me, JT, what are your plans for your dad's house? It's lookin' pretty decent now. That being said, it's no secret empty houses go downhill fast, 'specially when winter hits. Pipes burst, roofs collapse, mice move in, all sorts of bad stuff goes on."

He's not fooling me this time. I recognize his gambit. Refusing to inquire directly about my long range plans, he's hoping instead that I'll I cough up the information on my own. As he well knows, divulging my intentions for the house will necessarily involve telling him how much longer I plan to stay there. It could be that Meg's also pressing him to extract more details out of me about my situation, particularly the subject of Annie, and this is his scheme for acquiring them. Who knows? One thing I do know is I'm uncomfortable with the topic.

"I don't exactly know what's going on. Just riding out the summer for now."

“Given any thought to winterizing it?”

“No, I can’t say that I have. Not yet anyhow.”

Before John can follow up, Meg reappears on the porch, wiping her hands on a checked dish towel. I’m struck by how thin, almost gaunt, she appears standing alone in shorts and an oversized tee shirt without John standing nearby to add bulk. “Dinner’s on the table, fellas. Come and get it.”

As we adjourn to the dining room I remark to John, “I remember a time when your mom would’ve stepped out onto this porch and rung that big old cowbell of hers to summon you guys to come indoors for dinner. Seemed like the whole neighborhood knew when the Caldwells were fixing to eat.”

“My stomach still growls every time I hear a bell,” John replies, assuming his seat at the head of a long wooden table, gouged and scratched from decades of use. I’m wondering if the initials “JT” and “JC” are still carved into its rough underbelly.

Toting a long platter, Meg arrives at the table and airmails a smile and a little smooch my way. “I’m hoping you still have a taste for rainbow trout, Jake.” She is obviously pleased with her choice of entrée.

“It looks delicious, Meg. I can’t recall when I last had trout. I do know it’s been years since I’ve caught one.”

“Thanks, Jake. Tonight you’re the guest. No catching or cleaning required.”

I heap my plate with one of the larger trout, some sautéed green beans and rice, then turn to John. “How many times did we fish with your dad on Mirror Lake? There's no way we ever caught this many with him in the boat."

"Him and that damn pipe of his," replies John with a rueful smile. "Every time we dropped anchor he'd figure it was time to clean and refill it."

Meg chimes in excitedly as if she's come up with the answer on a quiz show, exclaiming, "Oh, I've heard this one! He'd empty the pipe by whacking it against the outside of the boat, right?"

"Not just any old boat," I reply. "A metal one. That old Lone Star with the stubborn motor. And he didn't bang it just once or twice. Oh no, he had to remove every last speck of old tobacco in the bowl. He'd rap that thing like an angry blacksmith."

John chimes in, "Thereby delivering an advisory to every trout in the vicinity that skedaddling was a more prudent choice than sniffing at our worms."

"Can fish even smell?" I ask.

"Who the heck knows. But you get the idea."

"It was always clear to me that he was more interested in our company than the fishing anyway. How many years since he's been gone?"

"Just hit ten," says John. "Hard to believe when he's still so alive in my mind. Every once in a while, out of habit, or maybe instinct, I catch myself picking up the phone to call him. Or sometimes, when I look at pictures of him taken when he was about the same age as I am now, I wonder if life looked the same to him then as it does to me."

"And do you hope it did?" I ask him.

"Most times I do. Yeah . . . most times."

Amidst the clatter of plates and silverware, dinner ensues as one would expect. From sports and music to academics and club memberships, Meg enthusiastically describes the many activities their kids are immersed in, and she eagerly fills me in on how the emporium is faring. She's still as peppy as ever, no question about that, yet her voice sounds thinner than I recollect. As for John, per usual he is content to assume a back seat in the conversation and let his wife steer it wherever she chooses, interrupting every so often to add color commentary to her stories. Despite the lighthearted conversation I sense John's eyes boring in on me intensely, as if he's waiting for my tell. As it turns out, the wait isn't long.

"And the cancer, Jake? Meg inquires earnestly. "How are you doing with that? You look good. A little undernourished maybe. But good just the same."

And just like that, as my fork stalls halfway on its trip to my mouth, the air gets sucked out of the room and for several uncomfortable seconds we're on radio silence. Already I'm mentally kicking myself for creating such childish drama. It's not like I haven't answered this well-meaning question a thousand times before. Tonight, the mature and polite response would have been to assure Meg I'm doing just fine, thank her for asking, and ease gracefully into the next topic. Instead I've grossly overreacted, mostly because my reservoir of patience ran dry long ago. I no longer have the tolerance to smile nicely and recite the sunny lie everyone expects, and indeed, demands. I've learned that nobody wants the truth. It's too messy, too unpleasant and difficult to respond to. It's obvious from her deer in the headlights expression that Meg realizes she's struck a nerve.

"Oh, Jake, if I ..." she says. Worried that she's going to cry, I interrupt what sounds like the beginning of an apology.

"It's ok, Meg. Really. I hesitated only because it's a very difficult question to answer."

"I didn't mean to put you on the spot," she adds with a couple of sniffs.

"And you didn't. Not at all. It's just not that easy to explain in a short answer. I don't want to get all preachy here, but cancer's like a tornado. It sweeps you up, then drops you somewhere else, someplace miles away where nothing's comfortable or familiar. Maybe you find your way back home. Maybe you don't. But even if you do, you quickly realize that home doesn't feel the same anymore. Or as safe."

By now Meg has sidled down the table to sit next to me. "I understand perfectly," she says, giving me a tight hug around the shoulders. "Believe me, Jake, I really do. It's a huge upheaval. We heard what you were going through with the cancer, plus all the other complications. We haven't seen much of you since then, so I just thought . . . ." Trailing off into the uneasy air, her voice is laden with the solicitude I've grown to detest. Far too often I've listened while it turned to pity.

My overblown reaction to Meg's question has been hurtful, and I feel an obligation to explain myself further. "It's more than that," I add, trying to soften the tone of my voice. "I'm four years out from the surgeries, so everyone pats me on the back and calls me a survivor which, I'll concede, is true to an extent. But 'survivor' is a burdensome label to pin on someone. It comes with obligations, one of which is that I should be happy and grateful simply to be alive."

"But you *are* alive; you *are* a survivor," interrupts Meg. "And that's all anyone can ask for, right?"

"No, not really. Not the way I see it. There's more to survival, and certainly to happiness, than steady breathing and a beating heart. Cancer's a skilled assassin. In one fashion or another, it *always* hits its mark. Let's face it, the other elephant in this room tonight is Annie. Did *she* survive my cancer, or did it destroy something inside her the way it did in me?"

"Well said." This remark comes from John, who has been leaning forward with both elbows on the table, his brow furrowed. I'm not sure if his concern is for me or for Meg.

"Perhaps," I reply with a dismissive wave, "or possibly I'm making way too big a deal out of it." I wait for John to agree with me. At first he says nothing.

"And what's stopping you from being happy, JT?" John finally asks. "What's the problem there?"

"That's a good question, one I still can't answer very coherently. In part, it's because death changed from an abstraction to a reality I couldn't escape. I nearly died from the peritonitis when my colon unexpectedly burst while I was waiting for the cancer surgery, and could've easily died a second time from the cancer itself. I know it's a tired cliché, but it took those critical illnesses to make me understand how brief and fragile life really is. After I physically healed, I became consumed by an urgency to make my days count, to make every single moment of every single day meaningful and important. Take it from me, that's an impossible way to live. Life will never be good enough. It can never live up to such lofty expectations. Instead, yesterday's frustrations get heaped onto today's dissatisfactions, until eventually your world becomes a big, steaming pile of unhappy tomorrows."

Having said more than enough, I simply shut up. John and Meg are now studying the pattern of the tablecloth, while somewhere behind me a large clock noisily counts off the seconds. At last Meg breaks the silence. "At least you're physically doing ok," she says, looking into my eyes, almost pleading with me to consider the bright side. "At least you're moving on."

"Oh no, it was Annie who moved on," I correct her. "All I did was move back."

CHAPTER TWENTY-FIVE

Dessert was served, hugs and handshakes were exchanged, as were promises to do this again soon, and dinner with John and Meg was salvaged by our deliberate re-routing of the conversation back to happier topics. Rather than pick our way across the mine field of current events and my medical history, we doubled back to the safe, easy path of reminiscence. They laughed when I told them how, during my first sweaty palm year of law school, I'd utilized John's foolproof technique for avoiding being called on in class, which was to take out a tissue and begin blowing my nose whenever an especially difficult question was posed. In the "Rules According to John," no instructor with any sense of etiquette could ever call on a student thus engaged.

We spoke of the time in high school when a thoroughly inebriated John spent the night in the guest room of my parents' house. As I lay passed out in my bed, John realized he had to throw up, and fast. Stumbling and bumping his way to the bathroom, he frantically raised the first lid he could locate and promptly unloaded the contents of his rebellious stomach. Unfortunately, what he'd found was the clothes hamper, which he identified as such only after it refused to flush. Drunk as he was, he had sufficient wits about him to apprise me of his mistake. When my mother inquired the next morning why I was doing a load of wash at three in the morning, I told her I needed the clothes for tomorrow. I had no answer for her when she asked why it included my father's clothes, and hers.

And John and I reminisced about one teenage summer when our favorite late night recreation was tossing back beers and driving desolate country roads. With flashlights guiding our way, several of us would break into abandoned farmhouses hoping to conjure up the restless spirits of their former inhabitants, now deceased. Emboldened by youth and plenteous amounts of alcohol, we felt no fear, until the night we found ourselves congregated on the second floor of a particularly creepy place and suddenly heard an eerie, out of tune piano being played one story below. Like spooked mice we scrambled wildly from room to room seeking escape, crashing heavily into walls and one another in the process. We soon discovered that our sole egress was by means of the first floor, and we sure as hell weren't going down there. That was, until we heard John, who'd happened upon a piano no one else had noticed, calling up to ask if the fraidy-cat little boys upstairs would prefer a different musical selection. The myth of our bravado having been debunked, we soon decided that ghost hunting wasn't that much fun after all.

"Those were some great times," John observed.

"They were, for sure."

"And just think, Jake. They all took place right here in Jackson Meadows."

****

Early August, and the weather was too perfect to last. Sunshine kissed the still-green lawns, producing tiny rainbows in the rhythmic droplets from sprinklers. Bikers and runners swooshed through the warm summer air while kids frolicked on playgrounds and splashed in pools. I'd made plans to golf later in the afternoon and was eager to tee it up. I was never more optimistic than when standing on the opening tee box, where the best round of my life was still a possibility. First on my itinerary, however, was the inconvenience of what I'd assumed would be a routine abdominal CAT scan, ordered in response to some nausea and cramping I'd been experiencing. My doctor, whom I teased for being excessively cautious when it came to treating litigators, had assured me my gastric distress was a product of too many hours at work and deplorable eating habits. Driving to the course following the scan, to which I'd not given a second thought after its completion, I was concerned with one affliction only: a looping slice off the tee that had recently materialized to infect my game. Then came the call.

"Hi, Jake. Where are you?"

"Hey there, Doc. About twenty minutes away from Raven's Nest. I have a 2:15 tee time. What's going on?"

"I hate to spoil your afternoon, but would you consider turning around and meeting me in my office? We weren't entirely pleased with the look of your CAT scan."

And that's how, in less than a minute, my life detoured from its charted course and drove dead south. Soon – three weeks to the day to be exact – I lay on an operating table having a cancerous section of my colon excised and another portion of my ruptured colon repaired. In the terrifying days and nights leading up to the surgery, I recited a mantra of optimistic predictions my doctors and friends had offered to assuage my fears. They were of no avail, as it quickly became clear to me that any power ascribed to positive thinking was easily trumped by an even stronger truth, a truth I'd been able to ignore until now: one day this world will roll on perfectly well without me. When I'm gone the moon won't be swallowed into a black hole. The sun will continue making its scheduled appearance on the eastern horizon, and those who loved me will find ways to be happy in my absence. No doubt they'll miss me, and from time to time they'll reminisce through a few tears about the days we shared. Ultimately though, their lives will go on. Life, I was forced to acknowledge, merely pauses for the dead. It does not stop.

Imprisoned within my own traitorous body and suddenly isolated from all those healthy people around me, I felt frightened and helpless. All the good wishes and prayers sent in my direction were little more than a tepid washcloth to a brow on fire with fever. Everyone glibly assured me I'd be just fine. It was, of course, the socially appropriate thing to say, and what it meant to me was less than nothing. It was Annie alone who refused to sugar coat anything or dismiss my fears. She held my hand. She hugged me. She listened to me for hours on end while my mood shifted direction like wind in the desert. Assuming the roles of nurse, wife and mother, Annie remained faithfully glued to my side in the days prior to surgery and during the painful and complicated period of recovery which followed. For that reason alone, I will always love her. Later on, as we'd painfully learn, even love's strongest glue fails if those whom it binds pull hard and long enough in opposite directions.

CHAPTER TWENTY-SIX

"Ready for another tour around town?" I am leaning against the doorway to Archie's room at Meadows Retreat, not quite as nonchalant as I'm striving to appear. This will be our fifth time in the car together, and I like to think he's warming up to me. His interest in his surroundings seems to have broadened, as has the range of our conversations, if one can call them that. Keeping up a conversational pace with him remains a challenge whenever he breaks his silence and leap frogs from one decade to another. I have quickly learned that in order to enjoy our time together I need to follow and react to his words the best I can, and therefore I let him ramble on rather than try to steer him in a coherent direction. There's no point attempting to impose my reality on him, and so I do my best to share the one he's experiencing. Besides, his versions, as I have come to appreciate, are often more enjoyable.

No windbreaker this time. Even in the White Mountains the hot, mid-summer air is thick and syrupy. Today Archie's scrawny white arms extend like pipe stems from the short sleeves of his checked dress shirt. For some incomprehensible reason, he's wearing his leather wristwatch this time, someone having adjusted it to the tightest fit. Despite the adjustment, it's in danger of sliding off his hand. I make a mental note to look for it on the floor of the car before dropping him off. No more wheelchair though. We have wordlessly negotiated an arrangement: I hold his elbow and steer, he walks. Today he's wearing the sneakers I bought him, which resemble large white canoes attached to the bottom of his spindly legs. Together we toddle our way toward the front door and the world beyond.

"Take a spin past my beauty queen's house, see what's cooking," he orders as I buckle his seatbelt. This is a reference I get. The first time he mentioned his beauty queen I panicked a little, presuming he was talking about my mother. Turned out he was referring to Sally Evans, someone he dated back in high school, a comely lass (his words) who, in her junior year, was crowned Poultry Princess at the Jackson Meadows Fair. I am tempted to make a crack about Archie's chickens coming home to roost but of course it would sail right over his head. Not that funny anyhow.

"Sally can fill out a dress, that's for sure," remarks Archie, his bony elbow assuming its position outside the passenger window. "Good luck getting underneath it. Money's not all she's saving."

"Well you old rascal, Archie. Making the moves on Sally Evans are you."

"Who?" he asks. And so ends that topic.

As we cruise up and down the streets of the village like teenagers looking for trouble on a Saturday night, I consider stopping for a bite to eat. Nothing fancy, just somewhere we can grab a quick meal or, if need be, make a quicker getaway if Archie becomes uncooperative and our patronage doesn't pan out. It's mid-afternoon and my rumbling stomach is informing me that it's been a long, empty stretch since breakfast.

"Are you hungry, Archie? Did you eat lunch today?"

No answer.

"I said, did you eat lunch?"

"What day is it?" he finally asks.

"It doesn't matter what day it is. I'm simply asking if you had lunch today."

"What day is it?"

"Archie, I just want to know if you ate lunch. It doesn't matter what day it is."

"What day is it?"

"Listen, I understand you like to know what day it is, but that has nothing to do with eating lunch."

"You sure about that?" he sneers. "You eat there too?"

"Of course not. What difference does that make?"

"Makes a big difference. All we ever get is Shepherd's pie. Hate Shepherd's pie. Looks like cat puke. Friday's pizza day. I'm pretty darn fond of pizza."

Today is Wednesday, and I'm not going there. It's easier just to go hungry.

As we near the far end of North Main Street Archie makes his first observation of the day. "Wynn Dailey's place is looking ok. Good choice, that funeral home. Lots of customers. Don't care much for the sign."

Indeed, there is a sign out front, and it happens to be advertising Italian food. Archie has recognized the two-story Victorian structure that once housed Wynn Dailey's funeral home. I believe Wynn himself was waked there. After Wynn took his eternal leave the place closed for at least a decade, until it reopened as a video rental store, which was kind of creepy. Each category of movie – comedy, adventure, adult or what have you – was displayed in separate rooms, all formerly viewing rooms for the recent and dearly departed, which was something I could never get out of my head, especially when renting a movie from the horror section. The newest iteration of this old building is a restaurant, the owner having been savvy enough to retain the historic exterior design while knocking down several walls inside. Archie, as expected, sees only what he remembers from years before.

Not that I know for sure, but I assume the dinner bell rings early at Meadows Retreat. In any case, Archie and I have prowled around town long enough for today, and I slowly taxi him back to the home. When we arrive at the doorway to his room he turns to face me directly, as though we're two kids on a date about to exchange a good night kiss. Scrutinizing my face, he squints his cobalt blue eyes with steely concentration, then offers his hand for me to shake. Surprised, I give it a firm squeeze. Archie does likewise, and holds our grip for several seconds before he releases me back to my world and turns away to face his.

CHAPTER TWENTY-SEVEN

The cancer surgery came sooner than planned. Earlier that day, with my abdomen burning to the point of distraction, I'd driven home from work at lunch time, thinking I'd have some ginger ale and crackers, perhaps rest on the couch for the remainder of the afternoon if need be. Annie wouldn't be home till five. My recuperation on the couch didn't last long, as no more than an hour later I was curled in a fetal ball on the floor of our bathroom, gasping for life like a fish out of water and debilitated by a searing pain in my belly coupled with an engulfing nausea. I thought about calling an ambulance, but after some woeful attempts to crawl to my phone in the bedroom, found I was already too weak to move even a short distance. So that's where Annie found me later that day. Dying on the bathroom floor.

In the emergency room the enormity of the pain exceeded anything I'd ever experienced, or indeed could've imagined. Like a grievously wounded animal, I moaned and thrashed about on my gurney for what seemed longer than I could withstand, until silence

– serene, comforting and mysterious – suddenly dropped like a warm blanket around me. Blind to whatever might've been happening in that hospital, I fell deep into myself, landing in a place where, I somehow understood, nothing could harm me anymore. Like a tiny boat dropping off the edge of a far off horizon, I vanished into the welcoming glow of a setting sun within me. Although my outer shell may have been dying, the me inside it was compressing into a pulsing core of energy seemingly centered in my chest. I intuited that the process of my death had commenced, and I was all right with that. Floating tranquilly beneath the sound of my breathing, I trusted the mysterious force drawing me inward, and I surrendered to its power.

A day or so later I awoke in intensive care, sensing more than seeing the people hovering around me. As if the cancer weren't enough, I eventually learned that my colon had also come down with a staggering case of diverticulitis. One of the large, inflamed pockets had popped open like a cheap tire rolling at eighty miles an hour, spilling bacteria-laden fecal matter into my abdomen and causing a massive infection. The medical diagnosis was acute peritonitis. For a while afterwards I would've preferred a diagnosis of death.

Early on during my descent into hospital hell a male nurse, looking properly Satanic with a full, black beard and eyes dark as coal, roused me from a recurring morphine dream I'd been having, one in which fierce gargoyles leapt out at me as I ran through a labyrinth of burning brick. "I've been asked to inform you that you have a colostomy," Satan announced flatly, as if delivering a stock market report. "Do you understand what that is?"

I don't recollect saying anything in response. I'm sure my expression looked puzzled.

"Your doctor had to pull a piece of your large intestine through the stomach wall in order to give you a chance to heal inside. It's called a stoma and it's attached to a bag for depositing your fecal matter."

There may have been more to this conversation. I'll never know. What I do know is this: before I passed out again that asshole never made it clear to me that the colostomy was only temporary. Drifting in and out of consciousness over the next few days, I lay like a sweaty lump in intensive care, rarely speaking, often wishing I'd never made it through surgery. Occasionally I'd wake to find Annie holding my hand, or would open my eyes to see Archie's face, foggy and indistinct, hovering above me. At times I was certain my mother, love and concern etched on her kind face, was standing over me as well, which would've been quite miraculous, given her death one year before. From the snippets of conversation I could absorb, I understood we were waiting for biopsy results. I was dozing and alone when my doctor materialized at my bedside a few days later.

"Jake. You there? Are you with me? The lab results were good." He had my attention at "Jake."

"We excised the diseased portion of your large intestine and there was no sign of any cancer cells in the edges. It's all great news."

"Which means?"

"Which means there's no indication your cancer had spread."

"Chemo?" The tube running down my throat made it hard to speak, and my mouth was so dry it felt as if my lips had been glued together.

"None. No need for it. We'll just do some regular follow up and scans for a while. You're a lucky guy, Jake."

"Not so lucky, living with a bag full of crap attached to me."

"How's that again?" he asked.

"The bag. The stinking bag."

"You've had a lot of pain medication and so you're probably forgetting. The colostomy is only temporary, remember? In fact, for medical reasons we have to reverse it no later than a year from now. You won't have to put up with that nasty thing for too long."

"Can you do it now?" I rasped.

All cheer and optimism, he replied, "Oh no, not a chance. Your poor colon has taken quite a beating; it needs time to heal. Let's give it six or seven months. Then we'll get rid of it for you." When I opened my eyes again he was gone, and I worried that, like my mother, his appearance had been part of another morphine dream. Then came the rehab and the fever, and just like that I was too sick to care.

****

"Time to get you into the chair." The words I dreaded most during my ordeal in intensive care. As each new morning broke I would listen with growing apprehension while the floor came to life. Doctors hurriedly made their rounds, call buttons sounded, and for the fortunate ones who could eat, breakfast arrived. As for me, like a turtle trapped on its back, I'd lie in my bed, alone and helpless, wondering how I might summon the energy to brush my teeth or sit up while the aide washed and shaved me. But by far the most grueling endeavor was traversing the chasm of pain which stretched between my bed and the chair next to it, a distance less than four feet. The searing pain in my abdomen precipitated by that journey from chair to bed blinded me until I'd wretch with nausea. I felt like a bit player in the westerns I used to watch with my grandfather, the ones in which some cowboy gets shot, usually in the shoulder, and needs to have the bullet cut out before it kills him. A large knife is sterilized over a campfire. Whiskey, frontier anesthesia, is poured down the victim's gullet, and he's given something to bite on, usually a rolled up bandana or a stick. Then it's up to the scalding hot knife to begin its awful task of cutting through flesh and muscle while the patient, wild-eyed with pain, endures his torture for the sake of survival. Praying to live. Begging to be put out of his misery. That would be him. That was me. That's what it felt like to struggle from bed to chair, and then all the way back again.

Not surprisingly, a fever ensued, drenching me in sweat and making even the simple act of opening my eyes a near impossibility. For several days I lay sweating in misery, a wet washcloth draped over my eyes and looking, I would imagine, like a condemned prisoner facing a firing squad. That's when some knucklehead on the hospital staff decided I should view a short video about how easy and fun life could be with an internal organ emptying its contents into a bag attached to one's waist. I did not watch. Actually, that's not entirely true. I did see the first scene, in which a smiling and vivacious young redhead sat on the edge of her bathtub, attending to her stoma as if applying makeup for a big night out. That was it for me, and I left it for Annie to view the rest. The months which followed weren't nearly as enjoyable as suggested by that cheerful redhead.

CHAPTER TWENTY-EIGHT

August has now made its arrival and my routine hasn't changed all that much, except of course for Archie. Each morning I faithfully take to the road, renewing my efforts to outrun regret and the awareness that I'm squandering precious time. John and I continue to hook up sporadically for basketball, and these days I'm beating him regularly at whatever game we decide to play. I find I'm enjoying our contests more, mostly for the companionship, not for the winning. John has the feel of an old sweatshirt. Nothing flashy, just a warm and comfortable fit, now fraying a little at the edges. I did return for a second dinner at his house, its exterior having been slathered with a fresh coat of paint the color of milk chocolate, and we've exchanged nonspecific promises to go fishing before summer draws to a close and the October chill renders the brooks too cold for wading. Hard to believe I've been here this long.

To a degree, Archie has helped me move beyond some of my old resentments toward Jackson Meadows – and toward Archie himself – mostly because I enjoy listening to his colorful ramblings while I squire him through town and we weave in and out of time. Knowing I cannot pull Archie into my world, I've found my way into his. We even have a running joke of sorts. When he recognizes one of the many deer crossing signs on the outskirts of town, he'll sometimes perk up and ask how they trained the deer to cross next to these signs, which used to be my question to him when I was a kid. Those were the years when he'd proudly chauffeur us around in a big shiny Pontiac, jet black with polished chrome. On Sundays the three of us would drive thirty miles east to Berlin where both sets of grandparents lived. The return trip usually came after dark, when I'd curl up in the back seat with a blanket and pillow and doze to the sound of my parents' voices blending in harmony with the steady hum of tires against blacktop. I consider our little drives my opportunity to return the favor.

These days the old Jackson Meadows railroad station, now a run-down laundromat, looks too filthy to accomplish its advertised purpose. As we motor past it, Archie wonders aloud if the trains are running on time, and then, like the straight man to his comic, I wait for him to tell me how the "B" and the "M" in the Boston and Maine company name should really stand for "Bust'em and Mangle'em," given the careless way it handles freight.

Every so often we turn around in a weed filled parking lot abutting a boarded up building where Harvey Stevens predicted he could turn a handsome profit selling nothing but potato chips made from fresh potatoes imported from Maine, as if local families would actually elect to climb into their cars and trundle down the road for three or four miles in order to sit and eat potato chips. It took Harvey about six months to spot the error in his math, and his marketing, at which point he took to selling ice cream instead and built an arcade in the field next to his store. Archie recalls only the potato chips. I've been made to understand that they were never greasy and always reasonably priced.

"You really loved this town, didn't you," I remark to Archie. It's an observation, not a question, and I do not expect a response. Right now he's staring blankly out the passenger window and paying no attention to me, something that's been happening more frequently over the past few weeks. Assuming he's neither listening nor understanding, I've felt liberated to jabber at him the way one confides in a faithful dog. I do all the talking and supply the responses I want.

"You've got a lifetime of memories wrapped up in this place," I tell him, with a melancholy I'm hoping no longer touches him. "Sometimes I picture you as an old cowboy riding west on his horse, stopping to turn in his saddle and taking a final look back at what he's leaving behind."

"Not that damn horse Virgil Tucker bought!" exclaims Archie from out of nowhere. I had no idea he was processing anything I'd been saying.

"So you've been eavesdropping on me," I respond with a smile. "No, Archie, it wouldn't be Virgil's horse. You're right about that."

The story of Virgil Tucker and the defective horse he purchased is the stuff of legend around here, a bitter courtroom drama about common sense and reasonable foreseeability. The case, which engendered a feud between two generations of prominent farming families that simmers to this day, has been retold so many times it feels as if I attended the trial myself, though it played out decades before I was born. In fact, I once referred to this case during closing arguments while defending a breach of contract claim for a friend of mine.

Shortly after victory was declared in World War II, when money was scarce and veterans were trying to make their way in civilian life, Virgil Tucker returned home from the Pacific and offered to buy a working horse for his farm from Luddy Newell, himself a struggling farmer. After dickering for a spell, the parties agreed upon a fair price and the horse, a three year old filly, was duly handed over to Virgil.

Things went well between Virgil and his new horse until, about two weeks later, she kicked him upside the head and knocked him out stone cold. As one might imagine, this did not endear the horse to Virgil, nor was he too pleased about purchasing an animal with such violent propensities from Luddy Newell who, in a rather unsettling analogy, had assured Virgil that the young filly had the type of makeup one might seek in a new bride: she was gentle, patient, and eager to please.

Even before the egg-sized knot had disappeared from his forehead, Virgil dragged his new horse back to Luddy's farm and demanded the immediate return of his purchase money, together with an extra hundred bucks tossed in for pain and suffering. Luddy was having no part of this new negotiation and, in so many words, told Virgil the kick to the head must've made him crazy if he thought Luddy was going to fork over even one red cent.

To no one's surprise, their dispute ended up in the county courthouse several months later. With neither party able to afford an attorney, they butted heads like two angry rams for the better part of an afternoon before a packed house. When it was Luddy's turn to respond to Virgil's allegations that he'd knowingly sold a dangerous horse which, with reasonable foreseeability, was sooner or later bound to plant a hoof somewhere on its owner's head, Luddy claimed total innocence. His closing argument, a model of brevity, raised only one point: "She weren't no kicker," he declared. "Besides, everyone in these parts, including this here court, knows all about Virgil Tucker. You name me one person who hasn't had damn good reason to plant a foot somewhere on that son of a bitch. It's justifiable, that's how I see it. Justifiable even for a horse." Luddy won the trial and gained an enemy for life in Virgil.

"You still with me, Archie?" I ask. Not a word in response. Like spotty reception on a cell phone, he's cut out again.

"We never did have many heart to hearts, even after Mom died. Oh, I know you loved me, but you more or less left that up to me to figure out, didn't you. I haven't heard you speak her name in a long while. You can't possibly have forgotten her, right? Am I right? Then again, sometimes I think forgetting might be the best thing for both of us. It's not easy living back here, watching you forget everything while I remember too much. It's pointless telling you this stuff, I know, but I guess there's no harm in rambling on like this."

"No harm," parrots Archie. "No harm."

CHAPTER TWENTY-NINE

Late last night found me ravenous and scavenging about the barren kitchen for food. I ended up stuffing my face with handfuls of stale onion and garlic croutons and washing them down with flat diet root beer. Clearly I'm overdue with my grocery shopping. Unable to stomach more croutons this morning, I skipped breakfast after my run, grabbed a quick shower and now stand at Burton's deli counter with a belly that's complaining loudly. Right now everything in the store looks delicious. A few elderly women, dressed impeccably for the social occasion of food shopping, hold numbers ahead of mine, and I'm impatient to get back home to eat. I wait in frustration behind them while they painstakingly decide upon their choices, until my eye catches a display of cheese samples, nearly hidden and situated way off to the side of the counter. Without hesitation I make a beeline for the display, greedily grab a couple of the larger, pre-cut chunks of cheese and pop them into my mouth. Almost instantly my gag reflex overwhelms me. I've always had an embarrassingly weak stomach, and at the moment it's not putting up much of a fight. The cheese, which I now realize must have been part of an old display not yet taken down by the staff, tastes like warm, rotten eggs. My mouth is now filled with this odious product and there's no place to spit it out, nor do I see any napkins on the display table for spitting into. I think I'm about to be sick.

"Well look at you, Jake. I never realized you were so domestic." It's Sarah Russell, appearing out of nowhere. Matters have now reached a crisis stage. I can't respond to her without emptying my mouth, and I can think of only two ways to accomplish this task: swallow or spit. Raising my index finger in a "just give me a second" gesture, I gamely chew the contents in my mouth, which causes my eyes to water up in response to the rank smell and equally repulsive taste. One final, sickening gulp and it's down. The aftertaste is a killer. It's clear to me that this cheese is not going to stay put for very long.

"Sarah, great to see you," I gasp, stifling the onset of a dry heave. "Would you give me just one minute? Be right back." I have no clue where the restrooms are located but I do know the fastest route to the front door. Bolting outside, I run between two cars parked outside side the store and forcefully vomit. Goodbye, cheese. Farewell, last night's croutons. As I wipe my mouth and dripping nose with the back of my hand, it occurs to me that whoever owns one of these cars is going to have one miserable time accessing the driver's side door.

Vanity, to say nothing of the chunks of vomit showered onto my right sneaker, would ordinarily compel me to go home, brush my teeth and wash up, if not for two problems: First, the deli was my last stop in the store, and I therefore have a week's worth of groceries piled in the shopping cart. Second, and even more important, I assume Sarah's still standing there waiting for me. There's nothing I can do about my smelly sneaker except give my right foot a few vigorous shakes like a wet dog drying off. To counteract the horrid aftertaste burning in my mouth, I pause on my way back into Burton's to buy a Gatorade from the vending machine, then saunter back to the deli with as much dignity as I can muster.

Sarah spies me coming, and I offer a little half wave of hello and an apologetic grin. When I reach her she takes note of the Gatorade and jokes, "Boy, you must've really been thirsty. You took off like you were being chased."

"Sorry, I had a little something in my throat." I spot her trying to look without looking at the right side of my tee shirt. Nonchalantly flicking a chunk of something from its front I add, "It might've migrated to my shirt."

"Well, I notice you've got detergent in your cart, so problem solved. How's life going for you in Jackson Meadows? I've seen you jog past the store a few times since we spoke."

"I have indeed. Seven days a week, I'm out there patrolling the streets, keeping this town under surveillance and safe for everyone. Other than being flashed by a few old ladies with loose bathrobes on windy days I have no problems to report."

"Who knows," she responds laughingly. "Maybe they're doing it on purpose. You know, a young, skinny guy stalking them each morning."

"Not so young anymore, Sarah. Right? And who are you calling 'skinny'?"

"Seriously, Jake. Do you own a bathroom scale?"

"Can't say that I do."

"Have you looked in a full length mirror?"

"That would also be no."

"I'll bet you weighed more at our high school graduation. Who's been feeding you?"

"That's a rather tragic story. You see, I was recently compelled to fire the maid. I gave her one last warning after I caught her stealing the silverware and fine china, but had to let her go when she pilfered the candelabra." Am I flirting here? I really think I am. It's been so long that I barely recognize what's occurring. I also think I'm catching some return signals from Sarah, who's laughing a little too boisterously at what I've been saying and has yet to break eye contact.

Lightly resting her hand on my elbow and affecting her own haughty tone she replies, "Good domestic help is so terribly difficult to find these days." Then, just as quickly dropping the snooty persona, she declares, "More than a maid, you could use a good meal or three. You know, there's a farm to table restaurant about a half hour away. It's on the main route between Littleton and Whitefield. Granted, it's a long way to travel for takeout. It's well worth the trip though. The meals they offer are fully prepared and absolutely delicious. You might consider giving it a try."

Sarah is wearing tight designer jeans which accent her slender legs and the curve of what I've been imagining is still a tight little butt. The loose fitting peasant blouse she's wearing is clearly not intended to hide excess pounds. Her gray hair – somehow she makes that work – is pulled back, and although I'm not a practiced observer I cannot detect much, if any, makeup. Not that she needs it; even the harsh illumination of supermarket lighting attaches to her attractively. My next step is pretty much instinctive.

"Does this place have a dining area too?"

"It most certainly does. It has a cozy little dining room overlooking the river, with white lights sprinkled into the trees outside." I swear she has just licked her lips, and not because we're discussing food.

"If you're interested, maybe we can make a reservation for this Saturday night. It might be fun to catch up on things. That is if you're free. And if not, or it's a problem, or if . . . ."

"Jacob Taylor," she interrupts, "no need for the bashful invitation. I think it would be fun to have dinner with you again."

"Perfect," I exclaim. "I'll make reservations for around eight and pick you up?"

"That sounds wonderful."

I decide against a hug or a peck on the cheek as we part. Too much too soon, and besides my breath surely reeks from the fetid cheese. After taking a few steps in the opposite direction, Sarah pauses to call back to me.

“Hey, Jake. Two questions: First, no cheese at dinner, agreed? And second, whatever happened to the Jake Taylor who’d pull me out of a party like a cave man for a little action?”

“As for the cheese, you’ll get no argument from me about that. And if you want me to pull you out of Burton’s I’m going to have to start drinking very early in the day.”

CHAPTER THIRTY

Here's how to assassinate a romance. Like a baby in need of a diaper change, let the woman whom you once seduced and made love to change your colostomy bag for five degrading months because you're too squeamish and repulsed to look at it. Pretend it's not there. Let her deal with it. Wallow in despondence and fear while you await what you're certain will be the inevitable reappearance of the cancer cells. Paradoxically, now that you've been reminded that much of life is beyond your control, try to grab hold of yours and shape it into something more meaningful and satisfying. Immerse yourself in whatever you hope might offer enlightenment, or at the very least, an escape from the life you're leading. Hike desolate mountain trails. Sit by yourself on rocks next to bubbling forest streams and wait for a voice to tell you everything will be all right in the end. And when, of course, you hear nothing, shake a mental fist at the inscrutable sky above you. Most of all, try to save a relationship by trying to save only yourself. Disregard whatever she might be working through, and when she reaches out to talk about problems which have arisen between you, by all means cross your arms, arch your back, and refuse to discuss them. Do this long enough and you'll reach a point where there are too many words to take back, too many selfish acts to apologize for, too much damage to repair.

At first I was bitter at how things fell apart. In the months of resignation and grudging acceptance which followed, I adapted in order to survive. I found ways to numb myself to the losses and hide from the inevitable pain that accompanies daily disappointment. Eventually, out of self-preservation, I snuffed out the one remaining candle I'd left burning in my window on the off chance that comfort or mercy ever came looking for me.

****

Our third trip to the dating well is a home-cooked meal at Sarah's house. Having spent most of my adult life with Annie, I'm not sure if the unwritten rules of the dating playbook still call for physical intimacy on date number three. If so, we appear to be right on schedule. There's no mistaking the heightening sexual tension between us, even as I worry that like a dog chasing a car, I may not know what to do if I run down what my libido is after. Yes, once upon a time Sarah and I did burn our way through a thrilling back seat romance, but that was long before gravity gained the upper hand.

One of the pleasures of a fresh romance is telling the story of your past to someone who's interested in becoming part of your future. It's an opportunity to reinvent one's self, rework a few details of the script, and present things in a more flattering light. The account I've offered Sarah to date has been sketchy. Thankfully, she's thus far appeared disinclined to snoop about in the drawers and closets of my life where all the bad stuff has been stashed.

Sarah's home, surely among the major spoils of her divorce war, appears aged and rustic. In actuality, it's only five or six years old. Built by her ex-husband, a successful third-generation contractor, it's a post and beam Cape centered about a large hearth of brick and fieldstone. The home's wide-planked floors of distressed wood, comfy country furniture, and hand painted bookcases stuffed with literature and photography collections entice one to curl up with a good book and a cup of hot chocolate.

Tonight she's preparing pot roast in a red ceramic Dutch oven, and she's arranged some cheese and crackers, together with slices of fruit, on the black soapstone countertop of the kitchen's center island. I resist the impulse to remind Sarah of her admonition to me at Burton's a few weeks back about the cheese. Why replay that scene for her? While we talk, an undercurrent of music softly pulses from the living room, with an emphasis on folk rock new and old. Lots of acoustic guitar, piano and Memphis soul horns in the background. Thankfully, I've yet to hear any of the songs from my I-Pod, all potential mood killers. Already I'm finishing my second glass of wine and thinking maybe I should ease up. Simultaneously, a voice in the back of my mind reminds me I may not be driving home tonight anyway, a prospect I find both exciting and mildly terrifying.

As Sarah chops vegetables on the kitchen counter, I'm standing close enough beside her to inhale the seductive aroma of her perfume. The smells and the food, the music and the wine – their mixture has created a swirling, sensual ambiance. However, as much as I'd like to, I can't just stand here sniffing at the air and mentally salivating, so I deliberately dial down my libido and turn up the conversation.

"You certainly have an attractive place here," I remark. "And a solid business too, it seems. Tell me the truth though, do you ever regret not leaving Jackson Meadows? I still recall how, as teenagers, we planned our escapes to big cities and exciting jobs."

"Regret," she repeats contemplatively. "Hmm, that's a strong word. I'd say 'curious' is more apt. We all wonder, don't we, what might have happened if we'd turned left instead of right, or said 'no' instead of 'I do.'"

"That's true enough. And you'd agree, wouldn't you, that many people born in this town end up dying here. They never go anywhere. Who knows what they've missed?"

"But I did leave, remember? College in Boston. A few years of entry level work at that publishing house in New York? I'll grant you that life was radically different there, yet I'll never concede it was any better. And let's face it, almost everything we decide to do in life is a trade-off of sorts, and up here folks are pretty savvy horse traders. I believe many of them have weighed the excitement of bright lights and culture against the cost of an urban lifestyle and judged it to be too high."

"I suppose, for some people anyway, it can be. On the other hand, when I lived close to Philly I enjoyed museums and professional sports. I could attend the theater or dine in the finest restaurants. I could attend lectures at a half dozen prestigious universities. Jackson Meadows doesn't even have a restaurant open after 9:00 p.m. on weekdays."

"And when you lived there, you worked five – sometimes six – long days a week, as I understand it. And then you came straight home, relaxed, possibly did some work around the house or ran errands on weekends, right?"

"That was more or less my routine," I reply. "That's pretty much everybody's routine."

"Exactly. And how many times a month did you find yourself at one of these museums or the best restaurants, or at a Phillies or 76ers game?" she asks.

"Some months, three or four times."

"And in others?"

"Not at all," I concede.

Sarah gives me a satisfied smile. I've seen it before. Not on her, but on the faces of litigators who know they've backed a witness into a corner. "And that, Mr. Taylor, is my point. Most of us, no matter where we put down our roots, lead comparable lives. I may have chosen to reside in Jackson Meadows, but I'm only a three or four hour drive from a weekend in Boston. And precisely because of where I live I've made it a point to travel regularly. I'll bet I know my way around New York City better than you do, and if you're asking for the best places to stay or dine in Venice or London I can point you in the right direction."

"So, in response to my question, I hear you saying you're satisfied with life you've made up here."

"I'm not finished making it, Jake. Life's always under construction."

"Well, I've never been any good at building. Seems I'm more of a demolition man."

"Such a stubborn pessimist," she scolds me playfully. "Then I hope you're more enthusiastic when it comes to eating because dinner is ready."

Sarah has laid out an inviting table. Our plates rest on mats of colorful fabric which, to me, look more like fancy dish towels. An old Mason jar holds a spray of summer wildflowers, and two small candles in tarnished holders throw off their flickering light as the evening settles comfortably around us. Our salad bowls don't match the style or color of the plates, the silverware is old and tarnished, and the navy blue water goblets match nothing else on the table. Nevertheless, the overall palette is pleasing to the eye. I try to ignore the thought that Annie possessed a similar talent for arrangement.

Sarah and I sit across from each other, and even though the meal is truly delicious I barely register its taste. That's because

Sarah is sending me an assortment of half smiles, and the message I'm reading in her brown eyes is that, if I want, dessert will be served in the bedroom. If so, I really hope it will be dark in there, because for the first time in over twenty years I'm feeling self-conscious about what I look like without clothing to camouflage my defects. What if her ex was a real stud? Should I have been doing pushups in addition to all the running? I mean, I'm in reasonably good shape with a generous amount of hair on my head and none to speak of on my back, yet who knows what imperfections a critical eye might seize upon? Plus, in the past few weeks I've been cheating a little bit. Every time I've anticipated her touching my bicep area I've been flexing my arm muscles. Tonight she's bound to notice that my guns look more like derringers.

And what about my lovemaking technique? My repertoire is limited. For years I faithfully stuck with what seemed to work for Annie. Or at least she never complained. What did it for Annie, what carried her across the finish line, so to speak, might be the entirely wrong approach with Sarah. What's the protocol these days? Am I supposed to inquire in advance? And why does that question remind me of the public service announcements issued by utility companies advising the public to "call before you dig"?

****

Sure enough, here I am, nervously perched on the edge of Sarah's bed while she washes up in the bathroom in preparation for tonight's main event. My pounding heart is shooting waves of adrenaline through me to the point where I can barely sit still. It's the same feeling I'd have just before exploding out of the locker room for pregame warmups, although right now I'm feeling a lot more vulnerable sitting here in nothing but my best boxer shorts. I didn't have the foresight to bring a toothbrush or mouthwash. Consequently, I've stuffed a few pieces of chewing gum into my mouth, which I intend to spit into a tissue and toss into the nearby wastebasket as soon as I hear the bathroom door opening. The mood created by the room's lighting is indeed romantic. I hope my performance can match it. Except for some mismatched electric candles burning in the windows, the lights are extinguished, and moonbeams bleach the walls of the darkened bedroom. All is quiet indoors and out, except for the persistent thud of my heart.

Hearing the door open, I swiftly chuck my wad of gum and attempt to look calm. Like a vision, Sarah appears in the bedroom with a fluffy yellow bath towel wrapped around her. Offering me a demure smile she whispers, "It's been a long time since we were teenagers, Jake." After which, revealing only a hint of bare skin, she lifts the covers on her side of the bed, deftly sheds the towel, and slips in next to me. I'm both surprised and relieved to discover she's as apprehensive as I am, and we giggle and joke a bit as I lose the boxers and we commence our clumsy efforts at foreplay. Passion has a way of dispatching inhibition, and we're soon resuming what began and ended nearly thirty years before.

****

I would love to report that last night's lovemaking with Sarah was unfailingly spectacular, my performance nothing short of masterful. Regrettably, that account would be grossly inaccurate. Things were proceeding extremely well until, in the throes of pleasure, Sarah cried out, "Ooh, baby." Seems innocuous enough. Hardly a distraction, right? Not true. Not when it comes to Jake Taylor and his monkey brain swinging non-stop from limb to limb. "Ooh, baby" sounded a lot like "You, baby," which immediately reminded me of a bubblegum pop song by the Turtles that Annie used to sing when we were driving in the car and things were light and playful between us. Suddenly, without warning, Annie had materialized in Sarah's bedroom to transform things into an unworkable threesome. Angry at myself for letting my mind wander in such a pernicious direction, I was even more pissed at the Turtles, particularly their two vocalists, Flo and Eddie. *What kind of a name is 'Flo' for a man anyhow?* I asked myself. *What self-respecting guy calls himself 'Flo'?*

For some reason, this inane query reminded me of "Go-Flo," a product intended to improve urination in aging guys like me. From there, it was a short and easy mental leap to the topic of erectile dysfunction, which of course I promptly began experiencing first hand. When it became apparent to both of us that my ascending passion had taken a serious nosedive, Sarah gave me a chaste peck on the tip of my nose and uttered the words every guy dreads:

"That's ok, Jake. No need to be embarrassed; it happens to every man."

After that we simply lay there for a while, glued together by drying perspiration, Sarah's head resting on my chest, one leg swung over mine. When I clumsily tried to explain the convoluted thought process that had led to this mortifying result, Sarah reassured me that this was an unfamiliar place for both of us, and it would be unrealistic to expect that our pasts would never intrude upon our present. I wanted to believe her.

"Do you remember our very first skin to skin contact?" I eventually asked, breaking a silence so protracted I thought she might have drifted off to sleep, most likely from boredom.

"Was it the bedroom at Becky Jordan's party?"

"Oh no, you'll have to travel back a lot farther than that. Picture lots of ice, like a snow globe with a winter scene inside. You know, the kind you shake to make the flakes fall through the air."

"You've lost me. I need a better clue."

"Ok, how about this? The season is winter and we have blades on our feet."

"Blades?"

"Yes indeed. Blades."

"Like skates?"

"Not 'like' skates. Actual skates."

"Are you talking about the town skating rink?"

"Correct. When school had been dismissed for the day and it was starting to get dark in the late afternoon."

"That much I do remember. The lights would kick on around four."

"Right again. They helped set the mood."

"We were only in grade school then, Jake, and there was no mood to be set. About half the kids in town under the age of twelve were there with us. I'm absolutely certain we did *not* have sex at the skating rink."

"Well, no, not exactly. However we did have sex for twelve year olds. I remember it like it was yesterday. You'd wear the white skates with little red pompoms dangling from the laces. They looked like colored cotton balls. Huge walls of snow would be piled up around the rink from weeks of shoveling the ice, and then you'd appear out of the girls' warming hut and step onto the ice."

"I was never in the boys' hut, but if you're wondering, I can tell you the girls' building smelled like wet sheep and dirty socks."

"Clearly I've been carrying around a more romantic recollection than you for all these years, Sarah, but stick with me on this. Remember how I'd ask you to skate around the rink with me? And how it was an unwritten rule that if a girl said yes she'd have to hold the boy's hand and circle the rink at least once with him? She was allowed to leave her mitten on, even though we boys were too cool to wear anything on our hands."

"I do recall that. Most everybody did it. What I don't recall is what any of this has to do with sex."

"Oh, but it did indeed. If the girl really liked you she'd let you escort her around the rink twice. Do you at least remember that?"

"Most definitely. It was a bold move to allow a boy take me twice around. To mix metaphors it was, what, like getting to first base?"

"I'll stick with your analogy, Sarah, and remind you that you let me reach second base many times back then."

"Mr. Taylor, I never," she exclaimed with mock indignation.

"Oh, you were a scandalous little vixen. Not only did we circle that rink *more* than twice, you'd strip off your mitten and lace your bare fingers into mine. Skin to skin contact, baby. Come on. You remember. Don't deny it."

"Oh yes, I do remember now," she cooed seductively, slowly inching her hand down from my chest to my waist. "You were the little boy with the ice cold hand and the big bulge in his corduroys."

As she spoke, her hand slid lower and lower, lightly tickling my skin with her fingertips. I rose eagerly to meet it. It was hardly conventional dirty talk. Still, it worked like a charm. The rest, one might be tempted to say, came easy.

CHAPTER THIRTY-ONE

When someone reminds you how patient they're being it means only one thing: you're talking with someone who's run out of patience. And that's how it went with Annie and me, as her smoldering anger and frustration flamed into outright warfare. Although I was the lawyer, supposedly with the power of language in his arsenal, it was Annie who proved the more capable verbal marksman. I quickly learned that my greatest strength lay in defending myself, in dodging her bullets and evading the direct hit. From her perspective, ample time had elapsed since my illness, and there was no reason why we couldn't pick up where we'd left off prior to the unkind interruption life had imposed upon us. When I'd try explaining why I couldn't just slip back into those old days like a pair of comfortable shoes, Annie wasn't buying it. Repeating almost verbatim our arguments from the night or day or week before, we'd sit across from one another in the living room like opposing litigants, each with arms crossed, each unwilling to concede the validity of the other's position. I'd futilely struggle to explain how precarious and hollow living felt, and how I was spending too much of each day swallowing a grief for the loss of my security and happiness, a grief so strong it would surface and burn like bile in my throat. It was as if, I would tell her, we'd previously been speeding down the highway at seventy-five, carefree and untroubled, never suspecting that a half mile ahead traffic was jammed tight and we'd be forced to change our route.

"Remember the interview with John Lennon I told you about," I once reminded her, "the one he gave in 1980 shortly before his death? He was incredibly optimistic about the new decade and his own future. He kept saying how he couldn't wait for the next chapter of his life to unfold. A few days and several bullets later it was all over. He never saw the end coming."

"You want life to be perfect," Annie would reply heatedly. "You're looking for someone who can promise you that nothing horrible or frightening or unexpected is ever going to happen to you again. And that's not all. Oh no, not you. You want to do your so-called 'important' and 'meaningful' stuff while skipping all the miserable crap we slog through every day. What you're really searching for, buddy, is something *better* than life. Well, good luck with that."

"No, you're wrong," I'd tell her. "Of course I accept life's uncertainties. I'd be a fool not to. What I can't accept is wasting the time I have left, and right now I'm struggling to figure out the best way to make each day count."

"You might want to begin by being grateful for today."

"That's such a glib response," I'd tell her. "There's nothing wrong with wanting more than simply more time. How about finding fulfillment, or even sleeping peacefully through the night? Is that too much to ask? Most people I know haven't been where I've been. I want to warn them. No, that's not entirely accurate. What I really want to do is scream at them and say, 'You don't know what it feels like to be dying, to almost touch the other side, whatever that may be. Unless you've teetered on the edge of extinction, you cannot comprehend how unimportant much of life is. So don't be so frivolous with your time.'"

"Tell me something, Jake," she'd ask sarcastically, "how is it, exactly, that you alone possess this remarkable power to intuit how others are feeling or thinking, or what they do or don't understand about life?"

"Come on, Annie, that's unfair. I have no idea what's running through their heads, and as a matter of fact that lack of a connection is part of my problem. No matter where I am or who I'm with, I feel isolated from everyone because of what I've gone through. I've become life's great imposter. I'm like the drunk feigning sobriety, pausing to consider his words before speaking, or carefully placing one foot in front of the other to avoid the telltale stumble."

Invariably, Annie would respond in the dead voice she reserved for me alone. "You could always try worrying about someone other than yourself for a change. That might be a good place to start."

But I didn't. I couldn't, or so I believed, and after nearly two years of circling and sparring in this fashion we were spent. Indifference, supplanting all the bitterness, settled like a shroud over the corpse of our love. Annie's been gone more than two years now. For a while after our demise I'd swear I'd spotted her from the corner of my eye crossing hastily against traffic or ducking into the doorway of a shop or restaurant. The second glance always disappointed, so in time I gave up looking.

****

"Taken a gander at the brooks lately?" It's John calling to me while both of us are doing what we seem to do best. I'm walking up the driveway after a Sunday morning run and he's outside working his woodpile.

"No, can't say that I have. What about 'em?" I ask as I cross into his yard. The grass seed he planted earlier in the summer has barely taken hold and looks like a botched hair transplant.

"Starting to see leaves and crabapples floating downstream. Won't be long till fall."

"I suppose you're right. Hard to believe September's almost over."

"Which means," as he plods forward in the conversation, "if we're planning on going fishing we'd best do it soon. You know how it works. Once the water gets too cold the trout get sluggish, especially the big ones."

On several occasions since my first meal at his house John has suggested a fishing trip together, and I've always yessed him without really meaning it. This time it's obvious he's mulish about the idea and prepared to press the issue until I capitulate. Regardless of how I feel about striking off downstream together, I know how this conversation is going to end. Why not feign some enthusiasm.

"My dance card is free," I tell him. "You're the one with the job. Just pick a day and I'll be ready.'

"Sounds like a mighty fine plan," he responds, almost before the words have left my mouth. "You don't, by any chance, happen to own a pole or any fishing gear, do you?"

"Nope. Nothing at all. And in case you're wondering, I'm too old to dig worms in your compost pile."

"No problem there, JT. I'll supply everything we need, including the night crawlers."

"I don't suppose that old geezer up on Causeway Street's still selling them out of his kitchen," I say, adopting a jocularity I don't especially feel. "Remember how we'd knock on his door at five in the evening or five in the morning? The time never mattered to him; he'd be eager to display his product, like a jeweler pushing a watch. 'Got some good fat ones here,' he'd proudly tell us, 'tossin' in a few extry too.'"

John gives me a sigh. "Sadly, he's rooming with those worms now. We'll try the Gas Mart instead."

"I suppose I'll have to break down and buy a license," I remind myself aloud. "The only game warden I've ever run across was at the Clark Fork River when I spent a summer at the University of Montana. The way my luck's been running this would be occasion number two."

"You can buy a one-day license. Let's plan on next Saturday morning, say five sharp. Buy your license the day before if the weather looks ok."

"Five a.m.? You realize, of course, that trout bite all day. There's no need to be shivering next to a brook just waiting for the sun to come up."

"You're forgetting tradition and sound fishing logic, my friend. When have we not had our lines in the water before six? This way we can't miss the morning feed."

"Guess I'll be in bed early on Friday."

John assures me, "You'll be fine. Just don't spend all night with your lady friend."

I had no idea he knew, which is precisely why he's grinning at me, obviously pleased with his sleuthing. I stare back at him with blank innocence and say nothing.

"We'll catch our limit on Saturday then cook 'em up for a big Sunday brunch," he adds, grabbing my left shoulder and shaking it. "It'll be a fun weekend, just like the old days. We can sit around afterwards, watch some football, toss a few cold ones back."

"Sounds like you've got it all planned out."

"I do indeed, assuming you remember how to hook a decent size trout."

"That's it?" I ask. "Anything else?"

He's not smiling anymore. "Yes, one more thing: For one day at least, quit beating yourself up and enjoy the moment."

****

I still can't figure out why my happiness matters so much to John. Everything else that's going on in his hectic life should be more than ample to occupy his attention. Instead, he's spent the spring and summer acting like a rabbit in a cross country race, that runner whose function it is to set the pace for his faster teammate. Problem is, I've no clue why we're racing or where he's leading me. There's no finish line or reward in sight, no one to cheer us on as we pass by them on the home stretch. Nonetheless, I've been blindly running this race all summer, each encounter with John pulling me faster and farther in a direction I'm uninclined to take on my own.

And, paradoxically, there's Archie, who always looked like a wonderful father, unless of course he happened to be yours. At this stage of the game, why should *his* happiness, if that's even possible, mean anything to me? My efforts are almost certainly lost on him. Alone and confused, that's certainly how he'll die, even if I'm there holding his hand when the lights go out. Have I been trying to make him happy for his sake alone, or has my time spent with him been more about satisfying some ambiguous need of my own? Lately, until the rattle of his snoring startles him into consciousness, he's been nodding off more and more on our trips around town, and on the increasingly infrequent occasions when he does speak, his voice is weaker, his thoughts even more disjointed. How much pleasure could he be deriving from being tossed into a car and hauled here and there? Maybe he'd rather burrow under the covers of his bed and stay there. I know the feeling.

And let's not forget Sarah, who's warm, funny and radiant. Since our first clumsy foray into the bedroom we've shed our middle age inhibitions and courted a hunger which, once satiated, leaves us panting and exhausted. What I cannot tell her is that she's not Annie. No one ever will be, including, I suppose, Annie herself. Even as I find myself falling into Sarah's world as if parachuting to safety from a plane descending in a death spiral, I can't help critiquing her. Unwittingly, she's locked in competition with a revenant, a memory, a woman with whom I shared my youth and my dreams, a woman whose harsher edges have no doubt been smoothed over in my memory by the unceasing waves of time.

"Feeling tongue tired?"

"Huh? What'd you say?" While I've been sorting through my thoughts like mismatched socks, Sarah's been resting her head on my chest. It's been a while since either of us has spoken. I'd assumed she was sleeping.

"It's a pun, a joke. 'Tongue tired.' Instead of 'tongue tied.' Get it? I thought you weren't speaking because you needed to rest your mouth. Poor thing just had quite a workout," she purrs while pressing her forefinger to my lips, which in truth are a bit tender.

"No, I suppose I'd taken my mind off its leash. As usual, it ran off."

"Anyplace interesting?"

This is a good spot for a fabrication by omission. "Not really, except to ponder how much longer I should keep chauffeuring Archie around town. Each time I do, a little bit more of him seems to be disappearing."

"Well, the end probably won't be dramatic or heartwarming like in the movies. That seems like a safe prediction. Are you planning to see him all the way through?"

"I really don't know. I'd hate to be that son who skips out on the death watch, then shows up racked with grief at the funeral when it's too late to matter. Or it could be that it already doesn't matter. And what if he holds on for another six months? Or what if it's a year? He's just stubborn enough to do that, you know. What am I supposed to do then?"

"I'd say 'supposed to' is what other people expect you to do. On the other hand, what you *need* to do is an entirely different consideration."

"And if I don't know what I need to do?"

"I'm not sure. It could be you keep feeling your way along until you do."

"Even on a wasted cause like Archie?"

"As I see it, it's only a waste when it means nothing to either of you. Although you've never spelled it out for me, I know how you feel about that old guy."

"You mean the guy who's disappeared?"

"True. Or mostly true anyway. Then again, from the little I've observed, the patient fisherman in you will hang around for hours hoping to see the old Archie surface again. And who knows? Every so often, whoever or whatever remains of him, might recognize you and enjoy your company. Give a little get a little. Could be there's still something in there for you too."

I pull her up to me and kiss her. Because she's smart and sexy. But mostly to stop her from talking.

CHAPTER THIRTY-TWO

Friday night. Tomorrow's weather report promises fair skies with temperatures in the low fifties for the early morning, topping out at a high of sixty-eight. I'm now the proud owner of a one-day New Hampshire fishing license, my first in several years. Knowing from experience how groggy I'll be at five a.m., I've laid out my attire ahead of time. Two tee shirts (long and short sleeves), jeans and sneakers, and a hooded fleece sweatshirt to ward off the morning chill. Given the low humidity and relatively cool temperatures, I doubt we'll be pestered by bugs. With the heat of summer having departed the North Country, the trout should be running closer to the surface rather than hiding in deep, shady holes more difficult to access. Tomorrow will be "Fishing 101," meaning worms only. No fly rods necessary. The place we're headed for is a confounding maze of intersecting brooks and tributaries, mostly narrow, all of them edged by thick forest shrubbery and trees which bend over the water like green arches. It would no doubt prove a frustrating venue for someone like me, rusty with a fly rod and short on patience.

When I was young and John and I would ride out to the brooks with Archie, I'd lie shivering in my bed the night before our trip, giddy in anticipation of the next morning. I couldn't wait to plow through the tall grass in the fields and meadows which led to the rushing waters, when the day's early dew would soak us as thoroughly as the brooks we were about to wade through. Then, at long last, the morning's first cast would be sent out over the water, soon followed by the first thrilling tug on the line. Sometimes the smaller brookies could fool you by snatching the hook and running with it as forcefully as the big ones. Other times, when the weight at the end of the line was so heavy it at first felt like a snag, you knew you'd latched onto something sizable. Once we'd all caught our limits, we'd kneel next to the stream to clean the fish right then and there before storing them in plastic bags for the short trip home.

Just like the old days, I find myself tossing sleeplessly the night before, this time for an entirely different reason. Despite the comradery which has accompanied the basketball and the dinners, and now perhaps the fishing, my extended stroll with John down memory lane has remained largely uncomfortable. I didn't come to Jackson Meadows to relive my past. Far from it. What I've been doing with John strikes me as ironic – or possibly moronic. I took off for these mountains to escape my recent history, sort things out, and devise a plan for starting over. Instead I'm hanging out with my boyhood friend, dating a high school flame, and cruising familiar streets with my demented father. I've abandoned my law practice and left it to my former partners to wrap up my pending cases. No job. No map. No direction. No Annie.

Admittedly, not every aspect of my time up here has been awful. Sarah's been a comfort, even a source of happiness, if such things still exist for me. There have been serendipitous moments when I've slipped back into my friendship with John, and they've briefly warmed me, even while his unexpressed intentions remain an enigma to be solved. Overall, I've been more curious about the reemergence of our relationship than enthused about it.

On several occasions I've visited my mother's grave and traced her name with my finger on the cold stone, as if by doing so I might touch her again. Never imagining I'd be one of those people, I sometimes speak aloud to her, unburdening myself, hoping to garner some motherly advice by concentrating on her mute stone. My words, futile and sad, merely sail away on the summer breezes.

Then there's Archie and my ambivalence toward him. It pains me to be a spectator to his protracted demise. He used to be strong as granite. Now his life has become a slow dimming of light on its way to extinction. Most days, I want it to be over for him, for both of us. Sarah's right. I do savor the fleeting moments when the Archie I loved in spite of the distance he kept from me, the Archie who infuriated and, yes, at times inspired me, emerges unexpectedly from darkness into daylight and recognizes me once more. Each time this happens I think it will be the last time.

****

Morning arrives, as does the ever punctual John. His red pickup rumbles up my driveway, its diesel engine running loud and rough, headlights casting a wide beam on the shadowy frame of the barn in the backyard. At such an early hour, the morning remains black as midnight, and as I step onto the side porch and shiver when hit by the chilly dampness, I dread the inevitable soaking to come. As in the old days, there'll be no way to access these brooks other than through fields of tall, wet grass and shrubbery which will sweep across us as though we're moving through a car wash, and there'll be no way to fish them other than wade down portions of their lazy, meandering length. The place we're heading for is mostly forest, so thickly overgrown that the sun will not provide appreciable warmth until it has risen to its peak in the noontime sky. Until then, we'll be soaked and shivering. Or at least I will. I briefly contemplate feigning an illness and promising to reschedule our excursion very soon, then quickly decide against it. John knows me too well. He'll see right through the ruse and will prod me into following this thing through. I'm reminded of my reluctance while standing outside Archie's door before my first visit with him. Once again, having nowhere else to go, I open a different kind of door and enter.

"Welcome back, JT. Perfect morning for fishing."

"Morning, John." My words come out more like a cough as I try to clear my throat at the same time. "How exactly can you tell it's a perfect morning when it's still dark?"

“Ah, come on, can’t you smell it? The air’s clear, no storms on the way, still Indian summer. The brooks will be rushing again after a dry summer. Perfect. Just perfect.”

“All I can smell is the heat you’ve got blasting into the cab of this truck and that big mug of coffee sitting next to you. Have to take your word for the rest of it.”

“I’ve got everything we need. Plenty of crawlers. Those little gold hooks you always favored, you know, the ones with the red beads that look like fish eggs attached to the leader. Got clippers so we don’t have to cut the line with our teeth like we used to do. Our old choppers aren’t so sharp anymore, you know. And all sizes of sinkers. I’ve got plenty of everything.” It’s clear that nothing’s going to dampen John’s enthusiasm.

Feeling somewhat guilty about my sullen demeanor in the face of John’s obvious need to make this day special, I try to perk up a little for his sake. “I was thinking of buying a couple of prewrapped sandwiches from the Gas Mart, and maybe some granola bars and stuff. By the time I drove up there last night they were closed. Everything shuts down early around here.”

“No problem there. Meg made us a full lunch for when we’re done. Come noon time we’ll be plenty hungry for sure. And I brought a couple of small thermoses filled to the brim with libations, more than enough to take away the chill and toast our success.”

“I’m assuming you also brought along your own brand of bug spray, just in case?”

"Of course. Two cigars each to smoke away those little critters and plenty of matches to light and relight them."

"Now if only the trout will cooperate," I say with a smile.

"The trout are gonna be easy. The hard part was getting you to cooperate."

"Yet, here I am."

"Yes indeed, here we are." With that John shifts his truck into reverse and we commence our trip by moving backwards down my driveway and into a past John seems determined to relive.

****

The ride Out East is a short one, no more than twenty-five minutes. John spends much of it telling me about the fall inventory that's been arriving piecemeal in Meg's store and the exciting plans they've hatched to improve the way it's marketed. Even though the eastern sky is now brightening, the combination of the heat blowing in on me, John's familiar voice, and the rocking of the truck as we bump along familiar roads, not to mention the boring topic of conversation, is making me pleasantly drowsy. Unable to resist, I close my eyes and allow the voice and the truck to carry me where they will.

The soporific effect ends abruptly when John stabs at the brakes and executes a sharp right into a small gravel pull-off next to the road. Killing the noisy engine, he looks my way and declares with gusto, "Well, here we are. Ready to shove off?"

With the grim resolve of a foot soldier doomed to charge enemy fire I reply, “Let’s do this thing.”

After collecting our poles and equipment from the back of the truck, we strike off across an expansive field toward the dense tree line which hugs the ragged fringes of the water. Once we breach that barrier we’ll be entering a more elemental world, a world of water and deep woods and, please, no bears. It has not escaped my attention that fall is the time of year when they’re feeding ravenously in preparation for winter’s hibernation.

John and I commence our trek. Almost instantly I’m soaked nearly to the waist by the tall, wet grass, and like big sponges, my sneakers squish and seep water with the weight of every step. Five minutes into our excursion and already I’m shivering. I’ve no way of keeping my lower torso dry. The best I can hope for is not to soak anything above the belt. Hunching my shoulders and drawing my arms close to my side for warmth, I plow forward and, as always, allow John to take the lead.

Minutes later, with the sound of running water growing louder, we break through the tree line and find ourselves at the steep bank of the brook we intend to follow. In its deeper spots the water looks to be three or four feet deep. Clinging with one hand to the pliable limb of a sapling for balance, John eases his way down the muddy bank and steps into the foamy rapids. There’s no turning back now. I follow his path and make the same awkward descent into the stream. In an instant my feet are numbed by the shocking cold, and when I hurriedly wade to a shallower spot, the rocks beneath my feet feel much slipperier than I recall. Never, in all my years of fishing, have I fallen into the water. I remind myself to be cautious. I'm a lot older and a lot less agile now.

Having already traversed the deepest portion of the stream, John's now waiting for me to join him on some large, flat rocks on the other side. "You look a little out of practice there, JT," he remarks when I at last reach him. "Ever seen the movie *Bambi*, when the fawn can't stand up on the ice? Don't know why that came to mind just now."

"Funny. Very funny. You know, I wouldn't have objected to fishing at Mirror Lake. A nice, dry boat would've suited me just fine."

"What, and miss all this gorgeous scenery!" John exclaims, opening his arms like Moses parting the Red Sea. "Besides, stuck in a boat we'd have been faced with our old fishing dilemma. If we anchored near shore we'd feel compelled to cast our lines out as far toward the middle as possible, and if we were sitting near the middle we'd want to cast toward shore. Never satisfied. Remember? Out here we can cover every inch of water."

"That's a lot of water," I say.

"We've got a lot of day left."

With that we sit on the rocks to divide up worms, hooks and sinkers. John has brought army green, over the shoulder fishing bags for both of us. They'll hold the tackle, and the trout, thereby freeing our hands for the business of fishing. For the second time this morning John asks if I'm ready to go. I'm not. I tell him yes anyway.

Wending our way down the brook, not another fisherman in sight, we soon fall into our familiar patterns and habits. I've always tended to give a hole only a few minutes to yield a fish. My philosophy, born mostly of impatience, holds that if a brook trout is inclined to bite it will do so almost immediately. After all, the worm's dangling right in front of its nose. What's there to consider? The fish is either hungry or it isn't. It's also been my experience – or so I've convinced myself – that the biggest trout in any hole is generally the first one to bite because it bullies the smaller fish away from the worm. As a result, whenever the first catch is disappointing I move on to the next hole. John used to call me the brook sprinter.

In contrast, John's technique is patient and downright plodding. He lingers at even the least promising holes, carefully probing every inch of them with precise casts like a dentist with an explorer, staring intently at the tip of his pole, as if by willpower and concentration alone he might entice a fish to bite. On more occasions than I care to recall, he's caught up with me on the brook toting a string of impressive lunkers. When I'd ask where he'd caught them he'd pause for dramatic effect and then reply, "Oh, I pulled 'em out of that spot you gave up on a while back." He passionately loved the fishing. I'm positive he enjoyed one-upping me even more.

For several hours we continue our progress down the brook, and in the process I manage to land some respectable natives. A sudden, forceful tug on the line followed by the violent bending of the pole into a fiberglass question mark still retains the power to excite me, though I wonder if it's because I'm truly enjoying the moment, or because I'm pleasantly distracted by the memories this activity engenders. For me, it's never enough simply to be happy. I need to understand why.

I used to be adept at estimating time by the position of the sun. Today, with the morning fog stubbornly hugging the cooler waters, I really can't tell how long we've been out here. Plus, the brooks we've been navigating are like watery green tunnels, meaning there's precious little sun and sky to be glimpsed overhead anyway. I'm also becoming a little concerned about finding our way back upstream when the time comes. In our quest for better holes and bigger trout, we've followed a succession of promising detours, one winding tributary after another, each leading us deeper into unfamiliar geography. And as much as I'm warming to my re-acquaintance with this sport, the farther downstream we trek the more I dread slogging through these rocky waters on the long journey back to our entry point. If we can locate it.

Unlike the old days, I'm also apprehensive about bears. The slightest rustling in the thickets along the banks activates my "fight or flight" response, an entirely useless reaction, since I can neither outfight nor outrun a bear with bad intentions. Unarmed and reeking of fresh fish, I'm a tasty offering on a bear buffet. For this reason, among others, I'm keeping John in close sight rather than striking off too far ahead of him as I usually do, figuring there's strength in numbers, even if that number is increased by only one. I've also been reminding myself that black bears are supposed to be harmless. However, it's not like they've signed off on that.

The morning air is much too cool to rouse any annoying gnats from their torpor, which means John's cigar has not made its customary appearance. Every so often I find myself glancing his way, sometimes for reassurance that a bear sighting has not caused him to abandon his pole and flee for safety, and sometimes for a different sort of reassurance altogether. The sight of him poised motionless as a statue, the clear waters swirling around him, right hand lightly grasping the pole, the left one pinching a section of line between thumb and forefinger to detect even the slightest tug, is a familiar and comforting tableau. It's kind of like coming across an old photo pasted into a forgotten album, a photo with the power to remind you how things were, and to distract you, momentarily, from how they now are.

As morning inches toward afternoon we are nearing the completion of our fishing. Mostly it's been a matter of catch and release. Heeding Archie's iron-clad rule from years ago, we've been tossing the little ones back and keeping only the few worth eating. When we were kids, New Hampshire's daily limit was ten. It's since been reduced to five, meaning we've been especially finicky about the ones we've kept. I'd been stuck on four trout for quite a while, but when my line drifts beneath a fallen tree and the tip of my pole is suddenly pulled almost into the water, I know I've hooked my fifth and final one. I signal John to toss into the same spot, which quickly yields his last catch of the day as well. It's even bigger than mine. So much for my theory.

"Good spot to end at," John remarks. "We've got a nice little sandy spit here to clean our fish and grab ourselves a bite to eat."

I agree with him. The curve of some heavier rapids diverted by rocks has created a large sandbar where we can sit and relax. Best of all, the late morning sun has now climbed high enough to bathe our private beach in its radiant warmth. I can't wait to remove my wet sneakers, roll up my pant legs, and let my toes regain their feeling. For the moment, at least, I'll ignore the fact that I'll have to put my soggy footwear back on.

"I don't recollect the forest being this dense when we were kids," I comment while we kneel to clean our fish at the water's edge. "Everything stopped looking familiar a couple of hours ago."

"Not sure we've ever ventured this deep before," offers John. "Kinda fun, though, exploring new territory. Wouldn't you say?"

"You mean you've never fished these parts before?"

"Nope. Not even once. You've been gone a long time, JT. Adventures aren't nearly as fun when you're having them alone." That said, John rises to retrieve the backpack he's been carrying with our sandwiches and drinks, leaving me to finish the task of cleaning the trout.

CHAPTER THIRTY-THREE

Like a kid racing home from school to deliver exciting news to his parents, I stopped in to see Archie shortly after John had decreed we were heading for the brooks, foolishly hoping the news would miraculously coax the old Archie out from his hiding place so we could talk fishing one last time.

"Hi, Arch," I greeted him breezily upon entering his room, where I found him lost in his recliner, still in pajamas and bathrobe, even though it was nearly lunch time. At the sound of my voice he blinked a few times, then groggily opened his eyes. I wasn't sure who he thought he was seeing.

"Decided not to get dressed today?" I asked. His only response was to rub his bony hand along the uneven stubble of his jaw, lift his chin in my direction, and squint at me suspiciously. No sign of recognition. No hint of Archie.

"We must have a bad connection here, Archie. You're not hearing me. I said 'hello.'" He continued eyeing me as if I were someone at a class reunion whose name and face he might possibly recognize but just couldn't place. I could see that pleasantries were taking us nowhere, so I cut directly to my big news.

"John and I are heading Out East on Saturday for some fishing. Remember? That's where you taught me to fish? Remember that?" I could hear an urgency creeping into my voice.

"I'm buying a New Hampshire license, just like we used to do. We'll be wading down the brooks. We're using worms this time." Like machine gun fire, my words shot out in quick, staccato bursts, as if intended to rip holes through the barrier of his dementia. I was barely pausing for breath between them.

"And don't worry, if it's sunny I'll remember to keep my shadow away from the water. We don't want to spook the big ones, no siree. And those little ones, well, we're gonna give 'em time to grow, aren't we. And just like you always told me, I'll be sure to look around and appreciate the trees and the water and the sky. I haven't forgotten anything you ever taught me. I can't forget a thing. . . Damnit, I can't forget a single thing."

In the face of Archie's mute incomprehension, I found myself tearing up, and before I knew it I was flat out crying. "Come on, Archie," I pleaded, nearly choking on my words. "It's me. It's your son. How can you forget me? How can you leave me here all alone? I know you're strong enough. You've always been stronger than me. Come back to me, please. Tell me what to do. Just once more? You can do it. Please?"

As if exhausted from the effort of trying to place me, Archie plopped his head back against the recliner and shut his eyes. His gnarled fingers moved up and down as if striking letters on an invisible keyboard, and though his mouth twitched promisingly once or twice, he said nothing. There were no words at all, just silence interrupted by the sound of me sniffling and blowing my nose. I stood there watching him for a few minutes until, reluctant to leave, I sat on the edge of his unmade bed to compose myself. From the steady rhythm of his raspy breathing, I could tell he'd drifted back to sleep. Short of death itself, it was surely his best escape. As for his only son, now an orphan of sorts, *his* only discernible avenue of escape was a trip back into the woods, and time, with John Caldwell.

****

"Meg rose early this morning and put together a real feast for us," John announces when he returns to where I'm luxuriating in the sun at the edge of the stream. "We've got ham and cheese sandwiches with all the fixings inside, plus chips – always need chips – pickles and macaroni salad. Soda and water too."

"You've been carrying all that food? Didn't it get a little cumbersome?"

John responds with a dismissive wave of his hand. "Nah," he says, "had it all wrapped and sealed in the fishing bag. I did put the trout in a separate compartment though. Along with the worms. Didn't forget about your notoriously weak stomach there, JT. I knew you wouldn't eat sandwiches smelling of fish or bait." As John lays out our spread on the rocks between us, the sight of food makes me ravenous, and I greedily reach for a sandwich wrapped in tinfoil.

"And like I told you, I've also got a small thermos for each of us here. A little something to toast our success."

"What'd you bring?" I ask between bites of the sandwich I've stuffed into my mouth, bits of bread sprinkling from my mouth as I speak.

"Tequila, very smooth, perfectly aged. The thermoses have kept it nice and cold and I've thrown a few lime slices into each one. Just keeping up the tradition, like when we used to take out the boat on a hot, sunny day, cast our lines and bobbers as far as we could, and then sit there with a cooler of beer between us."

"After a few cold ones we'd have solved the world's problems. That much I remember. Never did pay much attention to the fish."

John's eyes are now smiling. "I'm sure all the drunken conversation and peeing off the side of the boat didn't much help. Have some chips," he says, tossing the bag my way. "They'll provide the salt for the tequila."

While the early afternoon sun warms our chilly extremities, we each devour one of Meg's overstuffed sandwiches and split a second one. We've migrated even further inland to a sandy shoal with some smooth rocks to lean against. Bathed in the welcome heat, I've positioned my bulky sweatshirt behind my head and back to form a pillow against a large rock. Propped up on his left elbow, John's reclining on his side. We barely touch the macaroni salad, and it goes back into John's bag with the remaining sandwich. The chips, however, sit between us, as do the thermoses.

Suddenly pushing himself upright to sit cross-legged on the sand, John grabs each thermos and loosens its top. Handing one over to me he raises his to shoulder height and says, with unexpected seriousness, as though speaking at a testimonial dinner, "Here's to what survives after all these years."

Clanging thermoses with him, I feel compelled to reciprocate with a toast of my own: "And here's to forgetting what doesn't."

It's been a long time since I've drunk anything other than wine or beer. As a result, I'm unprepared for the engulfing warmth the tequila sends through me with the first sip. "That's really good stuff," I remark, smacking my lips. "Really good."

John's only response is to hoist his thermos my way and take another hearty gulp. Returning his silent toast I lift the thermos to my lips and savor the inner glow it produces. For a good quarter hour our only interaction consists of wordlessly handing the chips back and forth between drinks. Lulled by the tequila and the white noise of the brook, I stare at the foamy rapids rushing past us and squint from time to time at the sunlight reflecting at angles off the waters. It occurs to me that these currents will continue to run, in the same pattern and direction, long after John and I have disappeared from this existence, and long after those who might remember us have reached the end of their journeys as well. It will be as though we never existed. Plenty of fresh waters, but no sign of the boys and men who once fished and enjoyed them.

“It’s funny how the older we get the more we cohabit our lives with ghosts,” I eventually comment to John. “Out here I can feel twelve years old again and still sense Archie hovering over me, critiquing me while I fish.”

John turns away from the brook to face me. “We’re kind of like bears in that regard,” he replies. “Our forefathers are in our DNA. They tell us what to do and how to react.”

“Like bears? Really? Bears? You might want to cap that thermos, buddy.”

“Ah, JT. Must I always be the one to enlighten you? Why do you think a four hundred pound black bear will run like crazy from a fifteen pound house cat? It’s because when the world was young and bears came into existence, felines were dangerous predators of theirs. Mind you, I’m talking seriously big, mean felines, weighing in at a hundred pounds or more. Out of necessity the bears, especially the younger ones, learned they had to flee from these killer cats if they wanted to survive. It became burned into their genetic code. Survival of the species and all that Charlie Darwin stuff. And to this day, thousands and thousands of years later, their DNA survival instructions still warn them that cats are killers. Check it out on YouTube. It’s filled with videos of cats chasing bears. They’re pretty hilarious.”

“Again, your point is what?”

“What’s that?”

"I believe you were making a point."

"Oh yes, indeed I was. And it's this: you think you're so all-fired different from your old man. And I'll grant you, aspects of you are. Certainly you've evolved differently. But take it from one who knows. You are most definitely your father's son, based on stubbornness and perfectionism alone. And hell, you think I'm any different? You think I don't understand why I cut and burn wood or why I live in the same house my parents owned, and their parents before them? Or why I'm out here today fishing with you? It's who and what I came from. It's what I am."

"And is that also why you have seven kids, which tops your parents' head count by exactly one? It would appear you definitely took that lesson to heart."

Taking advantage of the escape route my quip has offered him from the unexpectedly serious path of the conversation, John protests, "Oh no, that one I learned all on my own. Jake, my brother, I have two rules for happiness in this life: first, take in more fiber than you think you need; and second, have yourself some serious sex every Saturday night. The kids are the upshot of rule number two and, of course, my unmatched bedroom prowess."

In our history together, John has always planned our next activity even before we've finished the present one. It's an old habit, and there's little John loves more than old habits. Consequently, I'm not at all surprised when he switches topics and begins planning our Sunday. "It'll be a good day of football tomorrow," he proclaims. Patriots are playing the late game. We'll have ourselves some beer and chips before that. Gonna be fun. You still like fun, don't you, Jake?" His question comes out a little slurred. I think he's zinging me again, and I really don't care. Right now I'm floating on a pleasant tequila cloud.

Having reached its zenith a couple of hours ago, the sun has commenced its downward arc on the western horizon. My belly is full, my clothing is mostly dry, and whenever I look around at the trees and sky they seem to be swirling in dizzying unison with the water. My strong inclination is to grab a quick nap, and my assessment of John, who's now lying belly up in the sand with his head resting on his backpack, is that he's not exactly busting at the seams to vacate our comfy little resting spot. Funny how, at odd moments, John and I can still connect, as if all our years apart and life's many obligations and distractions haven't been enough to separate us. Not bothering to cap my thermos, which is nearly empty anyway, I toss it aside and close my eyes to ponder matters further.

CHAPTER THIRTY-FOUR

When our day of reckoning arrived it did so with little drama. No vitriol, no tears, not even a hug or a mumbled apology. The moment was simply about resignation and acceptance, much like the final stage of dying, I'd imagine. A scant two years earlier we'd have never contemplated such an ending, but once it arrived we were almost relieved to be done with it. Already, it seemed, our best times had faded into memories only dimly recalled, like a dream from the night before.

It ended on a Friday evening in early May. Annie was planning to go away for the weekend with some friends while I stayed behind to clean out my agreed-upon portion of our belongings and cart them over to the apartment I'd rented. Still harboring the meager hope that an extended absence would magically clarify my needs and lead me back to Annie, I'd negotiated a short, nine month lease with my new landlord.

That night, Annie and I sat directly across from one another at the kitchen table, each with a yellow legal pad, and like two store clerks we ran down the inventory of everything I'd be taking with me the next morning. Our bank accounts had already been divided, and we'd agreed that by year's end Annie would either keep the house and buy out my portion, or sell it and share half the proceeds. She would retain all the photo albums and cull from them the photos she thought I'd want, not that I really cared what she did with them. They were painful reminders of everything I'd lost.

"That about does it then," she said, pushing her chair back from the table as though finished with a meal. "I think we've covered everything." She had wrapped her arms around herself, and was staring at me with her beautiful blue eyes, as if trying to read my thoughts. It was zero hour and I understood she was calling my bluff for the absolute last time.

"I guess so."

More silence. Annie combed her fingers through her long, thick hair, her habit whenever she was nervous or upset. She knew, as did I, that once we rose from the table and killed the kitchen light we'd be over forever. There'd be no turning back. Annie wasn't quite ready for that, and so she gave us one final try.

"You know, I still believe the Jake I've loved is hiding inside you somewhere. All I've been asking for is reassurance that he'll come back to me, or that he's at least trying to anyway. All I've ever needed is a reason to hope, a reason to keep trying." Her voice, more tender than I'd heard it in a long, long while, was pleading for a commutation of our death sentence.

Breaking eye contact, I traced the grain in the table's wooden surface with my finger, as if it might lead me to some destination other than the inevitable. Part of me ached to promise whatever she needed to hear, to take her beautiful face in my hands and assure her that someday – not now but someday – everything would be all right. Instead, my only response was to reach across the table and take her hand, which she promptly withdrew.

The next afternoon, after everything had been loaded into the rental truck, I removed the front door key from my ring and stuck it under the mat. I had no realistic plans to return. Annie had no intention of asking me back.

****

"Whatta you say, Jake? Ready to head back?" I raise my heavy eyelids to discover John casting a shadow over me. My first impression is that his words sound a little throaty and difficult to understand.

"Did I nod off?" I ask stupidly. My tongue feels like it's been pasted to the roof of my mouth.

"Five or ten minutes. Fifteen, tops, till I began tossing pebbles at you. I was worried you were going to swallow some gnats lying there with your mouth wide open like that."

Unbuttoning the breast pocket of his shirt to extract his phone, John takes a quick look at it and declares, "It's about three o'clock. We'd best be starting back up the brook."

"Which one?" I ask. "We took a shitload of left and right turns after the first one split off."

"I don't rightly know," John concedes. "I'd say we head upstream and hope for the best. It's the only way back. The woods are way too thick. Come on, get up sleepyhead. Time to rise and shine."

Which I do. And it's not easy. Struggling to stand while my spinning head begs me to sit, I watch John preparing to forge his way upstream against the modest rapids. In no time the rapids have prevailed, leaving him sitting chest deep in the water where he has fallen. He looks so confused and undignified that, despite some rising nausea, I have to laugh.

"Decided to crawl up the brook, have we?"

"These rocks have turned a might slipperier," he declares in response, badly mispronouncing the final word. He continues sitting there, slapping at the water around him like a baby in a bathtub.

"You might want to consider getting up," I suggest.

After a couple of false starts John manages to rise by turning on his side in the water and pushing himself up to a kneeling position, apparently unconcerned that he's now drenched nearly to his chin, or that his empty thermos has escaped from the backpack and is floating downstream. As I watch it bob past me I am not the least bit inclined to chase after it. My eyelids still aren't cooperating, and what I'd really like to do is return to my nap.

Now sopping wet, John has made it upright. Giving me a hearty thumbs up and a loopy grin, which I instinctively return like a father watching his kid perform acrobatics in the pool, John resumes his clumsy struggle against the currents and signals me to follow, which of course I do. However, my first few steps over the stones leading to the water are intensely painful, as if I'm stepping on broken glass. I'm totally befuddled by the unexpected pain, until I look around and spot my sneakers still lying where I left them next to my napping spot. Footwear. Never a good thing to forget.

After what seems like an hour of sloshing and slipping our way upstream, we've traveled a few hundred yards at best. It's safe to say things are not going well at all, and I'm now sober enough to know that afternoon will soon become evening. I'm about to call ahead to John when, suddenly, he stops dead in the water and scours the terrain, as if trying to locate a set of missing keys. Peering toward the suffocating wall of green and black surrounding us, he wades with much difficulty to the muddy shoreline. I tag after him like an obedient mutt.

When I reach John I see that his eyes are bloodshot and glassy. I imagine mine look the same. Clearly struggling to organize his words, he enunciates slowly and deliberately. "We need another plan. We need a Plan B."

I'm dull and weary enough to believe he can come up with one, preferably something that doesn't involve walking.

"Yes, a good solid Plan B," he continues.

"So what is it?"

A lengthy silence follows while John squints his eyes in a far off way and nods his head several times, as though he's Leland

Caldwell arguing and then agreeing with himself. Snapping to, he practically shouts, "Here it is. Here's our plan. We're Out East, correct? Isn't that what we've always called this place?"

"Um, yes. But I don't see what . . ."

"Stay focused here, Jake," he says, which is pretty ironic under the circumstances. "We drove east to fish out here, right?"

"Yes, yes we did." I hope I'm simply missing his logic, because I don't know where he's going with this.

By now he's inched closer to me, which throws his face out of focus. I can smell the tequila and chips on his breath. A little of the ham, too. "We came east!" he exclaims. His enthusiasm for Plan B is mounting, along with my confusion.

"It's simple. All we have to do is walk west. We can skip the water. We'll just cut through the woods and follow the sun, which we of course know is setting in the west. We're bound to come upon the road or some houses sooner or later if we just maintain a straight line."

I sense something fundamentally flawed in John's logic, but can't seem to articulate my misgivings. My brain just won't shift out of neutral. In the meantime, John enthusiastically plows ahead. "There's no chance of us wading all the way back up this brook before dark," he argues in support of his plan. "Unless we want to spend the night here, our only option is to hit the woods."

"And head due west?" I ask weakly.

John is now brimming with confidence. "Right towards the sun."

"Remember though, these brooks run in all directions."

"Forget about the brooks," John snaps. "We're shooting straight as an arrow for the sun."

"Don't you think you should call Meg to tell her you're gonna be late?"

"Already thought of that," he replies.

"And?"

"And unless you've got a phone it's not gonna happen."

"Which I don't. Why can't you call?"

"My phone took a little dip in the water with me. It's as dead as these trout we're carrying."

CHAPTER THIRTY-FIVE

Archie loved preaching that desperation drives a person to foolhardy choices. "Don't panic," he'd advise. "Think things through and take 'em slow." His words are a nagging echo in my brain as John and I plunge into the tangled underbrush to chase the falling sun. Raking aside nearly impenetrable bushes and low hanging branches which persistently thwart our efforts, we're soon compelled to take our poles apart and store the reels in our fishing bags in order to free up our hands for bushwhacking. In no time my arms and face are scratched and bleeding from contact with the sharp spines of thorny plants and tree limbs snapping back at me like whips. There's no question our progress through the woods is slower than up the brook, and I'm worried we've made a bonehead decision.

Stubborn as an old mule, John holds steadfast to his plan. "Keep your eye on the sun, JT," he tells me, having just spat out a mouthful of spruce needles from a branch which caught him flush in the face. I don't know what he's seeing up above. Whenever I look skyward I spy only brief glimpses of the sun. What I mostly see is a smothering green foliage of trees interlaced above us like fingers. The hour can't be later than five o'clock, yet already it's becoming spooky dark in these woods. When we were trailing the brooks I felt much more at home. Now, in frightening contrast, we're trespassing where we obviously don't belong. Each arduous step carries us farther into the unknown and the inhospitable, and I briefly consider suggesting a retreat to the brook. However, we've been at this for more than an hour, and turning around would undoubtedly mean spending the night out here. A speech from *Macbeth* has supplanted Archie's words in my head, the one about wading so deep into a river of blood that going back would be as difficult as going forward. Meanwhile, we've been regularly tripping and stumbling over tree roots and partially hidden rocks, and I can think of few worse places to snap an ankle.

Surely I'm approaching the desperation Archie was referring to, and from John's body language I can tell he's traveling in the same emotional direction. Pausing every so often to peer up at the sun, he's been wordlessly adjusting our course, signaling adjustments to it by means of improvised hand signals. The problem is, we can't strictly head west. Too many trees, rocks and thickets impede our progress, forcing us left, right and sometimes even backwards in a succession of vexing detours, while the sun we're struggling to follow continues dipping lower and lower in the early evening sky. As much as it pains and frightens me to admit it, escaping by nightfall has gone from improbable to impossible. John has now stopped exhorting me onward, and whenever we pause to catch our breath it's evident from the look on his face that he too is exhausted and worried. Years ago we loved camping in the woods. That's when we had a spacious, waterproof tent and comfy sleeping bags, plenty of food, and the latest in camping gear. There'll be no such comforts tonight.

"Hold up a second," I call ahead to John, just as he's preparing to crawl on all fours beneath the boughs of a huge spruce tree, the latest obstacle in our path. Sitting there, hunched over and breathing hard, he turns his head to stare glumly back at me, a look of defeat in his eyes. He looks old and tired. This is a John I've rarely, if ever, glimpsed.

"Listen, man, there can't be more than an hour of daylight left, if that. Let's face facts. We're here for the night. Instead of wasting what's left of the light searching for a way out, we're better off looking for a place to hunker down till sunrise."

John's breathing has returned to normal, and I can practically hear the desperate pep talk he's undoubtedly delivering to himself. For the better part of a minute he sits there in silence, rubbing his dirty right hand over his chin. Then, removing his hat to scratch his head, he looks left and right, casts one more glance toward the darkening sky, and says with what I'm certain is trumped-up enthusiasm, "Jake, my boy, now the real adventure begins. Like true woodsmen, let's assess the situation and review our options."

Even if I can't buy his phony optimism, at least he's given me the response I've been conditioned to expect. I'm ready with suggestion number one. "Remember those large rocks we passed five or ten minutes ago?"

"I think so, yes."

"Well, they were arranged in kind of a semi-circle with lots of small trees, including some blow-downs, on all sides. I don't think there's any rain in the forecast tonight but at least we'll have a little bit of shelter there. We won't be much warmer there though." I want to add that we won't have any protection from bears, but don't want to cop to my fear in front of John.

John's face lights up. "We can build a fire for warmth. It'll keep the critters away too."

"A fire? Are you adept at rubbing two sticks together?"

"No, but I *have* learned how to strike a match. I brought the cigars, remember? And a whole book of matches. They were sealed in the plastic bag with our sandwiches so they didn't get wet."

"Well done," I congratulate him. "And unless you jettisoned them along the way we still have a sandwich and the macaroni salad."

"And ten trout," John reminds me, "ten marginally fresh trout."

****

"It's a short life." Such were my words to Archie the one and only time we visited my mother's grave together. Her headstone had now been added, and the brevity of her beautiful existence was starkly memorialized in her dates of birth and death engraved onto it. This came a month or so after her funeral, when I'd stopped back to see how Archie was faring by himself. We'd been running some errands around town. Archie needed topsoil and seed to patch several bare spots in the lawn, and the refrigerator, which was dismally empty, needed re-stocking. Still the alpha male, he'd insisted on driving. As we neared the gated cemetery entrance he braked hard at the last second and turned in. He must've been weighing the pros and cons of visiting all afternoon. I was surprised we were stopping yet didn't say a word. We exited the car and stood with heads partially bowed before the rich, dark soil blanketing her gravesite. Before long, new grass would be taking root, making her resting place look like all the others.

"It can be a long one if you live it wrong," was what he said to me in return.

"And how do you know if you're living it right?" I asked.

"When you can rest your head on the pillow at night and think about your day without regret, maybe even with a little bit of satisfaction. And if you can rustle up some enthusiasm for the next one, well then, you're doing about as well as a man can hope to do."

"Isn't that setting the bar pretty low? Surely we can ask for more than that from life."

"You can ask, boy. And you might just get it. Not for long though. And not forever."

Although I mostly disagreed with him, it was hardly the time or place for a debate on the meaning of existence. Had this conversation occurred a few years later, I surely would've concurred with Archie. I might've even told him he was too optimistic, that the best we can do is suspend our disbelief, ignore what we know, and pretend that anything of what we do really matters in the end.

****

Too weary and disheartened for conversation, John and I double back in the approximate direction of the spot I'd suggested. Along our tenuous route, the forest's inky shadows make it impossible to distinguish green branches from the darkness enfolding them, until they announce their presence by thwacking us soundly across the face. Prickly barbs on unseen bushes hook my clothing as I pass, compelling me to wrestle myself free. Inwardly, the struggle is equally fierce, as I battle conflicting urges. Do we abandon this nearly sightless march and huddle beneath a tree right where we are; or do we scramble and claw through the darkness to search for the location where we hope to wait out the long night to come?

All too soon, blackness envelops us, leaving only the pale illumination of a three-quarter moon to light our way. Accompanied by the chirping of peeper frogs and the tremulous calls of male whip-poor-wills searching for mates, we carefully place one foot in front of the other like tight rope walkers. Every so often the spooky caterwauling of an owl reaches us from some invisible tree, heightening the eerie atmosphere of the forest. Even more unsettling are the sounds I cannot identify. Memory warns me that bears are mostly nocturnal feeders, and this is as nocturnal as it gets. Tripping and nearly pitching headfirst over the root of a tree, I vow to stifle my fears, if I can, and fixate instead on reaching our destination without injury. It's been several minutes since John has uttered a word. I wonder if, like me, he's worried that in this darkness, we won't even recognize the rocky area we're searching for.

With falling spirits and failing energy, we push onward until, rising like an apparition in the mist formed by the clash of cold and warm air, the rock formation we've been seeking materializes. It looked a lot cozier in the daylight. Regardless, it will be home for tonight. The giant rocks and trees which form the perimeter of our crude shelter might at least offer minimal protection from the elements. They will be of no assistance warding off bears or other creatures feeding in the night. We need a fire. Fast.

"Time to break out those matches," I say to John, the urgency in my voice surely unmistakable.

"Agreed." John's voice comes out thin and fatigued. "First we need to scrounge up some kindling. Might be easier to do if we could see more than our hands in front of our faces."

"Roger that. There's no sense breaking off any boughs; the wood's too green to burn. What about if we crawl underneath some of these trees? There's got to be dead branches or twigs near the bottom of the bigger ones."

"Agreed again," rasps John. "Let's give it a shot."

We quickly begin rooting about on hands and knees, and in no time my pants and forearms are covered with pine and spruce needles, and probably ticks. Although we do manage to gather armfuls of dry sticks and small branches, the unforeseen consequence of our foraging is that we're soaked all over again, rendering the fire a necessity rather than a luxury. I can almost hear Archie squawking in my ear: "Wise up, boy. You'd have been a damn sight smarter to have crouched and squatted rather than crawled." Despite my two shirts and the hooded sweatshirt I'm wearing, I'm beginning to shiver more steadily.

Dumping our pile of sticks on a patch of hard dirt next to a couple of the smaller rocks, I begin stacking some of them tepee style while John digs out his matches. In a stroke of good fortune, we've managed to pull some bark from a couple of spindly birch trees in our quest for firewood, giving us something to use as kindling. I construct a small mound of bark strips beneath the scrawniest of the twigs, only to feel my stomach do a quick flip when match number one applied by John flames out on smoky contact. John is more patient with the second one, and soon we have a modest fire going, a fire whose light far exceeds the intensity of the heat it's sending out. Nevertheless, it makes me feel safer and warmer than before. In fact, I'm feeling upbeat enough to toss a compliment John's way.

"Good job with the fire, buddy. You haven't lost your touch."

"It won't last long unless we keep feeding it. I propose we take turns scrounging for more wood. Maybe sleep in shifts so one of us can keep it going."

"Sleep? You really think we're going to sleep?"

"Not much, probably. But now that we can see better we can break off some spruce and pine boughs to use as bedding. Plus, I've got the knife if we need to cut some of 'em. We only have to last till daybreak. Let's make camp then divvy up that sandwich I've been carrying around all day." Once again assuming command, John appears to have been energized by the fire and the prospect of food.

Half a sandwich each takes no time to devour, then it's back to work. John's knife, while impressively sharp, proves a poor excuse for a hatchet when it comes to separating spruce branches from their trunks. Every cut produces a wet, gooey effluence which gums up the blade, not to mention our hands. An hour or so of cutting produces about a dozen boughs for each of us, which we arrange in long piles on either side of the fire.

"Make sure to lay all the branches in the same direction," John instructs. "Otherwise you'll get jabbed by the needles when you lie down. Be less comfy that way."

I tell him, "Comfy's hardly what I'm shooting for. Making it to daylight without freezing or getting too intimate with whatever's lurking out there in the darkness, that's all I'm asking."

"I figure it's close to ten o'clock," says John, looking up at the moon as if he might tell time by its position in the black sky.

"That gives us about eight hours to wait this out. A little sleeping, a little wood gathering, and before we know it it'll be dawn."

All the while he's been speaking John's also been furiously whittling with his knife on some slender branches about three feet in length, until they've been stripped to bare sticks. The end of each one is shaped like the letter "y." When he begins collecting nearby stones the approximate size of softballs I'm compelled to speak. "Ok, I give up. What're you doing?"

"For a smart guy, JT, you sure have forgotten a lot. Don't you remember how we used to make a fire and then smoke the trout over the open flame? The process is simple: hold the sticks upright with rocks, spear all the trout with the long sharp one, then rest it on the side supports just high enough so the fish cook without everything burning up. Come on, we've been doing that since we were kids. Don't tell me you've forgotten how."

"Not *since* we were kids. *When* we were kids, which was like, thirty-five years ago."

John gives me a dismissive wave. "Whatever," he says. "In any event, a man's gotta eat so let's cook up these trout before they turn on us."

Holding up the flat of my hand like a cop stopping traffic, I register my protest. "I understand it'd be nice to have some more food in our bellies. However, and I cannot say this emphatically enough, so do bears. What do you think's going to happen if, out here in this wilderness, we introduce the mouth-watering smell of trout cooking over an open fire? Don't you think that maybe, just maybe, something with teeth and claws might show up at our little barbecue looking for an easy meal? And do you think ten shriveled fish will be enough to satisfy that creature's appetite? Might he, or they, be looking for something more in the way of food? And by food, in case you're not getting any of this, I mean us."

Even in the feeble light of our fire there's no missing the look of concern which crosses over John's face. Doffing his hat to scratch his head, he already knows that *I* know he needs a new plan, another of his Plan B's, and I'm certain he won't speak until he's come up with one. Repositioning his hat, he rubs his chin with a grimy right hand while staring into the fire. Soon enough he looks up and asks, "Well then, JT, how do you feel about sushi?"

"Sushi?"

"Sushi."

"You're suggesting we consume raw fish?"

"Right."

"Fish that have been left unrefrigerated for several hours."

"Fish that have been covered and not exposed to the sun."

"Fish without the bacteria and parasites cooked out."

"One and the same," he says. "The risk is slight."

"And what if," I ask, "having assumed this slight risk, one or both of us come down with nausea and diarrhea? The way our luck's been going it's practically inevitable."

"What are you talking about?" John asks with obvious disgust. "What's wrong with our luck? We had a nice day of fishing, shared some tasty food and, ok, I'll grant you, too much to drink.

And now here we are in the woods with a fire, some more food – don't forget the macaroni salad – and no one's been harmed. Things could be a darn sight worse, my friend. I know it's dark out here but for once anyway could you try to see the bright side of things?"

I'm not entirely convinced that John means what he just said, and even as he's been scolding me I've been keeping one eye on the spooky perimeter of our campsite. With luck, our loud voices have been keeping any predators at bay, although it's best that we do something about this food quickly. So I propose a compromise. "Ok. How about if we cook the fish really fast? We can move them closer to the fire and more or less char-broil their outsides and at least get the insides warm. Then we eat 'em fast, and whatever's left over we bury good and deep somewhere on the other side of these big rocks. Agreed?"

"They'll be cooked, enjoyed and disposed of in fifteen minutes. Twenty, tops."

Which is precisely what we do. Given our ravenous hunger, the fish taste delicious, and since they're not that big and there's no time to be fussy, we peel out only their long spinal bones and chew the remaining fibrous ones along with the warmed meat. Just to be cautious, we leave the macaroni salad in its tin foil. Who knows if there will be a second meal tomorrow? In the meantime our bellies are full enough to stop their growling and my bed of spruce boughs next to the crackling fire looks more inviting than I'd earlier believed possible. Regrettably, I've already volunteered for the first wood-gathering detail, and consequently my rest will have to wait until I've confronted my fear and foraged in the darkness for more dry wood. We've agreed to alternate shifts every hour, which we'll have to approximate since neither of us has a watch.

For John anyway, exhaustion trumps discomfort and anxiety. After some initial twists and adjustments on his woodsy bed he drops fast asleep, his body nearly hugging the fire. Lying there, he looks serene and trusting, as if while drifting off he'd been peacefully confident I'd keep the fire alive to protect him from the nighttime chill and, if need be, from whatever might be stalking our unprotected campsite. *Imagine that,* I think to myself. *There's actually someone who still relies on me, someone who trusts me to look out for him.* It again occurs to me, that for the past several months and in his own understated style, John's been trying to help me through problems he may not even understand. Still the elder brother shouldering responsibility for my well-being, he's tried reconnecting with the old Jake Taylor through basketball and dinners and excursions down memory lane, with only marginal success. Now, with summer waning and winter on the horizon, our time together is running out. Which is why, I'm sure, he's brought us back to these woods, knowing we were often happiest here. It's clear he's been doing whatever he can to remind me how to be happy, even when John himself is actually much more somber than his younger version. Could it be, during these several months, he's been struggling to recapture something inside himself as well?

The least I can do is make sure the fire doesn't go out.

****

Dawn arrives dressed in a somber gray, and the temperature is much colder than expected. My rest was fitful. Curled into a tight ball beside the fire, I'd lapse into a deep, dreamless sleep, then wake with the side of me not exposed to the flames numbed by the chill, the branches from my bed stabbing me like dull pins. Despite all that, I must admit I've endured worse nights. In other beds, at other times, I've not been able to escape my sad dreams of Annie and the loneliness of my life beyond our time together. Last night was merely about physical discomfort and a more elemental need for sleep.

Apparently John slept through his final shift tending to the fire, which has cooled into red and grey ashes. A silvery dew coats the surrounding vegetation like giant spider webs, and my joints crack and pop in protest as I push myself up from my prickly nest. When I glance over at John, who is lying with his back to me, he stirs but seems disinclined to get up. I'd be tempted to toss some kindling on the fire and lie back down myself, were it not for my already escalating dread of our looming ordeal. Just because we lasted through the night and made it to daylight, that doesn't mean we're guaranteed safe passage out of this place. It wasn't as if we lost our bearings yesterday because of darkness. So we can't afford to waste time and daylight dawdling. Still, with last night's sentimental ruminations about John still fresh in my memory, I make an effort to keep my tone light when I call over to him. "Hey, man, there's no snooze button to hit. Rise and shine, give God your glory, and all that kinda stuff."

Emitting a low groan and a couple of grunts, John groggily turns to face me. Despite our predicament I have to chuckle. He has a tiny spruce twig glued to his cheek like a postage stamp.

"Something funny?" he asks.

"A little. You're not exactly looking like Daniel Boone." John gives me a puzzled look. I decide not to tell him about the face decoration and instead ask, "Ready to clear out of here?"

"Breakfast," he croaks. "I always need something to eat first thing. Toast. A muffin. Coffee."

"Oh, no problem. I'll just scoot over to the deli and get you something. How many sugars in the coffee?"

John is not amused. "I meant in the morning I always require food right away. And, smart ass, I was referring to the macaroni salad. It's in my backpack – which also happened to be my pillow. I spent all night inhaling that stuff."

"You can stomach macaroni salad at, what, six in the morning?"

"No, not really. But that mayonnaise isn't going to hold out much longer, so we'd best be eating it while we can."

He makes a valid point. And thus John and I perch side by side on the trunk of a fallen tree and force down Meg's salad. Attempting to chew without actually tasting, I'm reminded of my misfortune with the cheese in Burton's. I'm hoping this stuff, which has turned warm and gooey, stays down. I'm chasing it with large gulps of water, unconcerned about draining the thermos; there will be plenty of water where we're going. Possibly too much.

Having finished our mushy meal, we stand and brush ourselves off. Then, like two inept workers who realize they've painted themselves into a corner, we exchange panicked "What are we gonna do now?" looks. After a night of reasonably beneficial rest, we have the energy and the inclination to strike off for civilization. What we don't have is an informed idea of which way to proceed. Before John can suggest blindly heading west again, I break with our usual protocol and make the decision for both of us.

"We have about twelve hours of daylight," I tell him. "That's plenty of time to retrace our path back to where we were fishing. Once we're there, we can simply follow the brook upstream to your truck. It may not be the fastest route, but there's no question it's the surest one."

John offers no objection. "You're the one who's been doing all the exercising. Set the pace. I'll keep up."

For a while it's a relief just to be moving again, or more precisely, escaping. In fact, for me it feels downright natural. Figuratively speaking, what else have I been doing lately other than navigating through unfamiliar terrain in search of refuge? I feel pleased with myself, even a little buoyant, at having played a tamer version of Jeremiah Johnson. I found us a place to sleep, where we cooked nourishing food and drank pure mountain water from our remaining thermos. From the heavy sound of his breathing behind me, it's evident that John is not feeling equally upbeat, and he has already begun stumbling and tripping while laboring to keep up with me in the early morning fog, which offers no hint of lifting.

The temperature at the moment cannot be any higher than the upper forties. At first, the physical exertion of pushing onward toward the brook we're desperate to find was keeping me just warm enough. Now, however, I'm too warm, dangerously so, and the sweat which initially formed between my shoulder blades has begun trickling like a melting ice cube down my back until I'm simultaneously shivering and perspiring. If I keep sweating I'll just get colder. There's no alternative; I have to ditch the sweatshirt.

"Hold up for a second, ok?" I call back to John. "I need to make a wardrobe adjustment."

Manifestly grateful to be stopping, John assumes a seat on a nearby rock and says, "Take all the time you need."

"We can't be too far away from that brook," I tell him as I wrestle my sweatshirt over my head and cinch it around my waist. "We're moving a lot faster this morning than we could last night, and even then I don't think it took us more than an hour to travel from the water to our camping spot."

"Provided we're headed in the right direction. Have you considered the possibility that we're not?" he asks, while removing his sweatshirt as well.

I'm uncomfortable with this latest role reversal in which John, entirely out of character, plays the pessimist. "Yes, the thought has crossed my mind. Still, there's a hundred streams out here, and all we need to do is find one of them."

"And you think they all lead directly back to my truck?"

"Maybe not the truck, but I'll bet most of them flow from Mt. Bartlett which, as you'll recall, is on the *other* side of the road from where we parked."

"Then lead on," says John with an acquiescent wave. "I've had enough of this place."

Off we go, ducking beneath tree limbs that would otherwise skull us and tearing a path through the wet, thorny clutches of dense thickets and fallen trees. Each time the wind rustles through the treetops it mimics the sound of rushing water, and whenever we hear it we never fail to look ahead expectantly. Meanwhile, the soupy fog still attached to the ground floats around us, limiting our vision to whatever stands immediately in our path. John's probably correct to question the accuracy of our direction, as I don't recall the wilderness being this difficult to negotiate last night. Regardless, we have no place to go other than forward.

A wise man doesn't ignore his doubts, but an indecisive man gets nowhere. Weigh your options, choose your course, and then be bold about it. That's not John addressing me. It's Archie. It's how he bulled his way through life. Chin up, chest forward, eyes straight ahead. He had no tolerance for the weak-spirited or the cowardly. Life posed risks he was prepared and equipped to confront. *Nobody needs to show me where the bear shit in the buckwheat*, he'd declare to anyone who'd listen. I never grasped what he meant by that, but intuited it had something to do with acknowledging life's minefields without succumbing to a fear of forward movement.

"Straight ahead. Hear it?" This time it's John speaking. "Listen. Hear the bubbling?"

We pause, alert and still as prairie dogs sensing a danger. Sure enough, the sound of rushing water is reaching us. After all our despondent slogging, it plays like a heavenly melody. Revitalized, we rush forward to the muddy bank of a wide, bubbling stream. After a congratulatory high five, we kneel at the water's edge, form dirty cups with our hands to drink gratefully, and then replenish our thermos to its brim.

"Now all we have to do is forge our way upstream," John declares, already taking a few steps in that direction.

"Agreed. This time you can lead. I like it better that way."

****

By my estimate, we've been at it now for close to two hours. With the vegetation on the banks dauntingly thick, our escape route upstream has necessarily been a watery one. Every so often we've been forced to suspend our trek and take refuge on a large rock or a piece of dry land to allow our freezing feet, which feel heavy and about as limber as concrete blocks, to partially regain their feeling. Unlike yesterday's brilliant blue, today's sky is the dull color of lead, and I'm not certain if the droplets occasionally splashing onto my face emanate from the brook or from above. Rain, if it arrived, would make matters infinitely worse, even dangerous. *Be bold,*

Archie reminds me. It strikes me that Archie would never have gotten himself into this predicament in the first place.

More troubling than the possibility of rain is the status of the brook we're following. Almost every turn has taken us to the left and decidedly uphill. I don't recollect any hills where we were fishing yesterday. Even more disturbing, the brook we've been counting on to deliver us to safety is clearly shrinking. Its banks have narrowed, and its waters, which at times reached our waists, now run ankle deep at most. I've fished this region enough to know that even the fastest running tributaries can begin upstream, and uphill, as trickling brooks too small to be worthy of the name. I'm convinced that's the type of brook we're now following, and the realization that we remain lost sets my heart racing. I splash ahead to catch up with John.

"Hey, hold up. You see what I'm seeing, right?" I ask, wondering if he can detect the panic in my voice.

"Are you referring to the fact that this brook is drying up?"

"Exactly. Were you going to say anything, or were you just going to keep following it?"

"Well, eventually, yes. In the meantime I was hoping it'd hook up with something bigger."

"I don't see that happening. There's nothing feeding this thing from above. At least nothing worth following."

"Right now I can't feel one blessed thing below my knees," John remarks while looking downward. "Let's pull up a rock and think this situation through."

Wading over to a large boulder several yards away, we perch atop it in gloomy silence. I'm sure John feels as discouraged and cold – not to mention hungry – as I do. Though it can't be later than noontime, I'm fearful we've already wasted too much of the day and too much of our energy. It was a surreal moment when the doctor informed me that I had cancer. It's only slightly less unimaginable to contemplate enduring another brutal night in these woods.

Eventually John pipes up. "The floor is open to suggestions."

Our communications have never been dependent upon the spoken word, and when we turn to look directly at one other I see my worry reflected on his face. Our adventure has turned from a comic mishap we might someday recount for the amusement of our friends over drinks or dinner, to a truly dangerous situation. We're not properly clothed for the chill of this cloudy fall day, or for a night that could very well produce a frost. And we're out of food.

"I can't believe I'm about to suggest this," I tell him. "We don't have time to search for another brook. No way that will work. We have only one option."

"Bear on the right," mutters John in a low voice, looking over my shoulder as he speaks.

"Exactly," I say. "This miserable excuse for a brook keeps taking us left, so we have to bear right on dry land."

"Nope, not what I meant at all," John responds in an urgent whisper. "I meant there's a bear on your right. A big black one."

If this bear can smell fear then I'll be the first one attacked. I don't dare turn around to look. "What's he doing?" I hiss.

"What'd you say?" asks John, leaning in closer to me. "Can't hear you."

"I said, what's he doing?"

"Eating."

"Eating? Eating what?"

"They appear to be berries."

"He's hungry then?"

"Apparently so."

"Aren't we supposed to stand and wave our arms? Shouldn't we try to make ourselves look big and scary?" I ask. "I'm sure I read that somewhere."

"Possibly. But it might work a darn sight better if he didn't have his back to us."

"You mean he's not looking at us?"

"Would you prefer that he was?"

"No, of course not, but what do we do? We can't just sit here waiting to be noticed."

"I believe we just agreed to head right," John replies, keeping one eye on me and another wary eye on the foraging bear. "Now might be a good time to do it."

Tip toeing across the brook – if that's even possible – we crawl quietly up the bank and disappear into the same woods from which we've been attempting to escape.

CHAPTER THIRTY-SIX

Back when the three of us – Archie, John and I – fished this region together, Archie and John would often compete with one another while we hiked to see who was better at identifying the forest's many different trees and plants. Is it a red maple or a sugar maple? Apparently one can tell by scrutinizing the leaves. Beech or white ash? Frasier or Douglas fir? What type of fern did the impatient Jake just trample down? I had no patience for their game; the only plant I needed to identify was poison ivy.

Curiously, even under these dire circumstances, it seems that for John not that much has changed. As we detour around blowdowns and fight our way through invasive stands of barberry and other bushes, which I've always identified simply as pricker bushes, I swear I've spotted him lingering every so often to study a leaf or a shrub, which strangely calls to mind my autumn grade school projects, when our teachers would assign us the task of collecting different types of leaves. Clutching my textbook of leaf descriptions and photos, I'd scavenge through my neighbors' backyards in search of every kind of leaf. Then, taking care not to crush my discoveries, I'd carry them home, where my mother would iron each leaf between sheets of wax paper. Right now, in contrast, I've had it up to here with all the foliage, much like a drowning man who's been offered a drink of water.

While I walk, I wonder if, in addition to our current physical predicament, John's also struggling inwardly with disappointment. His ambitious scheme to transport us back in time, seemingly his last, best effort to reclaim what both of us have lost, has imploded into dismal ruin. I can't help thinking that after we've found our way out of here that will be it for our friendship. Winter is fast coming to the North Country, and soon everyone will be huddling indoors for its duration, isolating even the closest of friends. It will be too cold and dark for running the streets, and I wouldn't last two weeks cooped up in my old house. The time to move on is drawing near. If only I knew where.

"Hey, does it look brighter to you over there on the left?" John calls out to me.

There's still no sunlight to speak of, as the fog has now evaporated to reveal a dreary, ominous day. Nonetheless, there does appear to be brighter sky behind the sparser tree line John is now gesturing toward. With renewed vigor we crash and stumble excitedly in that direction, only to discover it's a cruel mirage. Rather than an opening in the trees with a welcome clearing beyond, what we've encountered is a steep drop in the terrain, more accurately a crevasse, and an optical illusion of open space created by the precipitous falling off of the landscape. This can't be. Too disheartened to speak or even look at John, I stand at the crevasse's imposing edge, sizing up this latest and largest obstacle.

John slumps dejectedly against a rotted tree while I continue staring downhill with utter disbelief at what appears to be a geological fault line. We'd have to be Sherpas to hike in and out the deep fissure, which runs as far as the eye can see both uphill and down. In any case, there's no point attempting the descent, since nothing beyond it looks any more promising than where we just came from. Our only option is to follow the stream coursing through its deep notch, which I suppose we can track from on high, and see where it takes us. When I look over at John he stares back at me but says nothing. What's to be said? Without a word or so much as a shrug, we take a right turn and resume our hike, this time parallel to the crevasse, with no plan other than to keep walking. Dumb luck. That's all we've got left. Good or bad. Either it will save us, or it won't.

****

"I'd always dreamed I'd become a respected artist."

Here, this morning, even in these dank, impenetrable woods, I cannot escape random thoughts of Annie. With feline stealth, she's managed to slip through the door to my old life I've once again carelessly left ajar. Those were Annie's words to me while we sat staring into a fire on a winter's night. The room behind us was dark and much colder than our cozy little spot. We'd scattered some pillows on the floor in front of the brick hearth, and a half-empty bottle of wine sat between us. At the time, even the slightest erosion of our love remained unthinkable.

"But you *are* an artist," I reminded her. "Look at the remarkable work you do. You're incredibly clever."

Annie swirled the wine in her glass and gazed intently at it as if reading tea leaves. "There's a world of difference between cleverness and artistry" she finally said. "I create pop culture. Not art."

"Nonsense," I scoffed, and leaned over to kiss away this troublesome blot on our evening's happiness. Annie lightly pushed me away.

"Hear me out on this one, Jake, ok? It's healthy to open up once in a while. I'm merely stating a fact. My art is disposable. It has a shelf life. An expiration date, and a short one at that. No one will ever hang one of my posters or brochures in a gallery. And as for the few paintings I'm able to complete on my own time, hardly anybody sees them. And the people who do see them are friends, so are they ever going to offer me an honest critique of my work? Of course not. It's safe to predict that generations from now patrons of the fine arts will not be studying the creations of Annie O'Rourke. My works, if you can even call them that, inspire people to visit a zoo or an antique show, or open their wallets to whatever charity has hired me. That's all they're good for."

I didn't like the turn the conversation had taken. I'd been hoping we'd follow our usual Saturday evening progression from wine and romantic ambience to the bedroom. But Annie wasn't done. "Hundreds of years from now people will still be admiring Van Gogh or Picasso or Da Vinci," she continued. "Their paintings will always touch us deeply and profoundly, no matter how often we view them. They're alive. And through some innate magic in the artist's brushstrokes, they make *us* more alive."

I set my glass down. There was no longer any reason to keep drinking. "Are you saying you're unhappy, or unfulfilled, or something along those lines?" I asked her.

She was slow to respond. Perhaps a little too slow. "Not so much, no. Yet, you have to agree we all reach a moment in life when we realize our dreams are going to remain just that: dreams. When I was a little girl, I was certain my paintings would someday hang in a prestigious museum. Now I've grown up, and now I know they won't. Admit it, Jake, every so often we can't help looking back at what we once hoped for, comparing it to what we have, and asking ourselves if we're happy."

"And how goes the comparison these days?" I asked, outwardly casual but with a nervous fluttering in my chest.

Annie leaned toward me to caress my cheek with her hand, much like my mother did when my nighttime fears got the better of me. "Not to worry, my dear. I cannot imagine being any happier with you."

I briefly wondered how to interpret Annie's ambiguous response, then dismissed my concern. Raising my glass to offer a toast, I declared, "Here's to both of us, in love for as long and far as forever takes us. And here's to the happiness we have, which is all the happiness we need." In retrospect, how ironic it was for me to be preaching the gospel of contentment.

****

In following the downward path cut by the watery gorge for the last hour or more, we've been making a gradual descent into wet, spongy lowlands. Along with an increase in thick mosses and tall, wispy grass, we've noticed a definite thinning out of the trees, some of them having been charred and snapped by lightning strikes, producing stumps shaped like crudely amputated limbs. Even the healthier trees look more scraggly down here, and there are hardly any evergreens to speak of. In the good news department, we've also come across some human trash: a rusted tin can, a plastic water jug with some old fishing line and hooks lying next to it and, curiously, a gray and soggy pair of tighty whitey underpants dangling from a tree branch. What we haven't found are any skeletons or corpses, which means whoever abandoned this junk must've made it out alive. Unless they've been devoured by bears, which seems a far-fetched notion unless you happen to be lost and alone in the wilderness.

As the landscape flattens out and the steep gorge eases into a sloping valley, the water it's been carrying has widened and spread like a giant oil spill into grasslands and denuded trees, and even on this grey afternoon there's no mistaking a modest brightening on the nearby horizon. I'm growing more and more optimistic, but only cautiously so, my hopes having been dashed too many times already in the past thirty or more hours.

"Hey, JT," John calls to me from the rear. "What happened to the woods? And what's going on with all the mud? My feet are sinking."

"I'm hoping we're approaching a clearing. Maybe even a field with a road nearby."

"That'd be great. But until we do it's getting awfully mucky around here."

John's right. The ground beneath us is becoming more sodden with every step, and there's no mistaking the odor of dried mud in the air. Increasingly, the area is smelling like a giant beaver dam. With John still trailing behind, I steer us toward higher ground and a modest incline of chest high grass and spindly trees. As we crest the mound, what we see stretching out before us, seemingly forever, is a sight almost unbearable to process. As if we haven't seen enough already.

"Where on God's earth did this thing come from?" John cries out, almost sounding physically wounded. "How is this even possible?"

It takes a lot to render a lawyer speechless. Right now, what I'm staring at, dumbfounded, qualifies as *a lot*. Stretching out in a vast expanse before us in all directions is an honest-to-goodness, no bullshit swamp. I'm stunned. I'm baffled. Who knew such a thing even existed out here?

I hear a full blown panic in John's voice. "Ok, Jake, this is getting serious. And I mean it. We're in trouble. Deep trouble. We can't double back and we can't risk crossing this thing. Hell, we can't even see the other side. And even if we could cross somewhere, if we got soaked and didn't make it out of here by nightfall we'd be cooked."

"More like frozen," I grimly reply. "More like hypothermia. But I get what you mean."

"So what do we do?" he asks.

"I really don't know."

"That's it? That's all you've got to say?"

"At the moment, yes. Do you have any ideas?"

"None. Not a freaking one."

"Ok then. Let's not panic. Let's narrow our choices and try to figure this out."

"All right," says John. "Let's do that."

For a long while we just stand there staring over the water, each waiting for the other to speak. Finally, John turns to me and asks, "So, have you got it figured out yet?"

"No, not really," I reply. "But as I see it we have only one choice. I'd agree we can't go back uphill. That leads us nowhere.

There's no brook in sight to follow, and we certainly can't cross a swamp this big and deep. All we can do is circle this thing and hope it dries up. Or maybe we'll find a shallow spot to cross without getting too wet."

"And if neither scenario pans out?"

"Then make damn sure you keep your matches dry."

With no alternative other than to suck it up and keep moving, we grimly begin picking our way along the edges of the swamp, a living thing unto itself, something I might have enjoyed studying under different circumstances. Cattails pierce the surface of its stagnant water and tiny birds flit back and forth from one to the other, accompanied by the loud, croaking mating calls of bullfrogs the size of softballs. Miniature islands of grass and dirt, forming a kind of checker board on the swamp's surface, are separated by wide canals of water, portions of which are coated with a greenish skin, reminiscent of the crust which used to form on my mother's homemade pudding when it was left uncovered in the refrigerator for too long. Lily pads topped with bright yellow flowers bob like floating decorations at a pool party, and slender birches, permanently crippled by winter's heavy snows, bend towards the dirty water as if preparing to drink.

"One thing I can't understand," I remark to John about an hour later when we stop to drink from our communal thermos. "I've been looking at all the dead trees way out there in the water and wondering how they ever grew in the first place. I mean, they're all gray and leafless and rotten. Assuming too much water would drown a seedling, how did they get there? How did they manage to grow? Is this swamp something new?" I'm making a deliberate effort to discuss mundane topics like trees, hoping to dupe my mind into believing John and I are merely enjoying a pleasant, albeit protracted, stroll through the woods, thereby quelling my ascending fear.

John gamely does his part to keep up the fiction. "They kinda look like evil Disney characters," he suggests, "the way they're all gnarled and spooky. Take that one out there on our left. Looks like a witch's finger. You know the kind I mean? That Disney witch with the wart on the tip of her nose, beckoning to little children and cackling something like, 'Come to me, my little kiddies.'" In making the analogy he raises his voice to a shrill pitch.

"That's the lamest imitation of a witch I've ever heard. And you still haven't answered my question. How did they get there?"

"Can't say that I know," John replies, abandoning his witch's voice. "Could be the swamp wasn't always this big and they grew before the water arrived. I do know one thing. If we don't find a way out of here soon we should grab as many of those cattails as we can carry."

"The reason being?"

"The reason being simple. Don't you remember how your dad used to go on and on about them? How they can be used for fuel like torches or tinder for fires, and how they're full of starch and vitamins?"

"I never heard him say that."

"Well, let's agree that listening has never exactly been your strong suit."

"So you're saying they're edible?"

"Healthy as skinny potatoes."

****

We continue our circumnavigation of the vast swamp. Perched on dead limbs, crows with the ability to fly off whenever they like seemingly caw in laughter over our landlocked status. Fallen birches and rotting trees lean crookedly over the brackish water like crude gangplanks. Here and there, beaver dams of logs and branches appear to have been formed by some giant hand which has dumped a huge pile of pick up sticks onto the muck. And no matter where we look we face more of the same: mud and water. There's no sign of a reachable opposite bank. Heeding his own advice, John's been periodically snapping the tops off cattails and stuffing them into his backpack while we walk, in case we're forced to spend another night out here, a prospect rapidly changing from possibility to certainty.

Like an elderly driver, blinker perpetually signaling a left turn, we keep the swamp on our left and hug its periphery, hoping against hope we'll find ourselves tracing the arc of a circle as opposed to our current straight line. I don't want to think how damp and cold it will be out here when night wraps itself around us. I don't see how we'll be able to sustain a fire large enough to keep us warm.

Not freezing is probably the best we can hope for, no matter how many cattails John stuffs into his pack. I've also been keeping a vigilant eye on the darkening clouds above and trying, without success, to persuade myself rain is not imminent. I jog a few steps to catch up with John, who's forged slightly ahead of me.

"Hey, hold up a second. We've gotta talk."

John stops to wait for me. The glum look on his face tells me he too has been assessing the likelihood of precipitation.

"We have a couple of hours of daylight, if that. Let's face facts. We're not escaping before nightfall. The good news is that even though it's gonna be cold enough, there won't be a frost; the bad news is that there'll be no frost because we are most definitely going to get rained on."

John nods silently in assent.

"There's no sense hiking till dark," I add. "We need to find shelter right away, gather some dry wood if we can find it, and get prepared to wait it out. Are you with me on this?"

"I'm always with you," replies John. "Let's peel off from this water and see if we can find a drier place to hole up."

There's no time to fine tune our plan any further. Already the sky has begun spitting chilly droplets of rain.

****

Good fortune, which thus far has ignored us, at last offers up a meager crumb of sustenance. Our hasty retreat from the swamp has led us to a mass of craggy rocks rising several feet above ground level in a jagged formation. One of the larger rocks protrudes over a flatter stone directly beneath it, forming a little roof and platform about six feet in width and length. We'll be able to build a small fire and huddle there to keep dry.

By now we know the drill. John and I split up to forage for sticks and dead branches, cradling whatever is loose and dry in our arms and toting it back to our shelter. Back and forth we go, like industrious ants, until we've amassed a fairly impressive stack of wood. Despite our successful scavenging, we'll have to burn it wisely; it needs to last eight or nine hours. I can recall how Archie used to keep the thermostat at a setting low enough to make us reasonably warm, yet never quite high enough to render us comfortable. Were he with us tonight, we'd no doubt make him proud.

Dusk is turning to dark, and the evening's former chill is fast becoming nighttime's cold. Time to light the fire. John pulls a few cattails from his backpack and distributes them about the base of a modest pile of sticks. In short order we have a small fire going. Not big enough to cheer us. Not large enough to keep us very warm. Possibly not even impressive enough to scare off nocturnal predators. Just the same, it's a fire. Shoulder to shoulder we sit, staring out at the shadowy blackness, simply waiting for the rain to arrive. After several minutes John turns toward me, as if we're just two guys sitting in a theater waiting for the movie to begin. Carefully stripping away the outside of the stalk, he wordlessly offers me a piece of his cattail to snack on. It tastes like a bitter cucumber. Still, it's food and I'm famished. I choke it down and silently hold out my hand for another one, which he gives me from his stash.

****

A cold, steady rain has been falling for at least a couple of hours. Fortunately there's been no accompanying wind to blow it inward at us. Although our fire occasionally hisses and fizzles, we've managed to keep both our bodies and our precious supply of wood dry beneath our rocky rooftop. We've also decided that three cattails each is our limit. No sense risking getting sick. They tasted horrible anyway. My legs, which are bent and twisted beneath me to accommodate our small roof of stone, keep falling asleep, and the muscles in my lower back are screaming for relief. They'll just have to scream away, because there's no room to stretch out. If we try we'll get soaked. All we can do is sit in front of the fire and, every so often, stand in a low crouch to regain the feeling in our legs. No prospect of sleep tonight, and despite the fire I feel a deep chill settling in my stiffening joints.

John reaches around behind me to grab a few sticks, which he tosses onto the dwindling flame, producing extra light but no appreciable heat. "Night looks like a long one," he mutters, as much to himself as to me.

After another lengthy silence, John speaks up. "Remember those maps we used to draw for trick or treating on Halloween? We had it all figured out back then. Who had the best candy. Whose house we had to avoid cuz they'd call us inside to sit and talk, then give us crappy apples or home popped corn for the treat. Yep, we'd map out the most profitable route. Fill up our pillowcases till they were almost too heavy to carry."

"What in the world made you think of Halloween?"

"Well, first of all we're lost, which calls to mind the benefit of a good map. Mostly because I sure could use some of that candy right about now, especially a Butterfinger."

"Why a Butterfinger?"

"Cuz it sticks in your teeth long after you've finished the bar. Yessir, that's one candy that keeps on working for you. Gives you your money's worth. Course, at the moment, I wouldn't turn down a linty old Lifesaver from under a couch cushion either."

"Kind of ironic, isn't it?" I say. "On Halloween at least, we knew where to go and how to get rewarded for our planning. It's not so easy anymore."

John scowls at me. "I wasn't talking about life, JT. Just candy."

"Well, don't you ever wonder about the big picture?"

"What big picture?"

"You know, life. What it all might mean. The point of it all."

John lifts his arm and backhands the air in my direction, as though slapping me across the cheek. "Far as I can tell, nobody's figured that one out yet."

"Wouldn't you agree that it's important to –"

"Important? I'll tell you what's important!" he barks. "What's important is the smell of fried eggs and bacon on a Saturday morning when your kids are all sitting 'round the table and your wife's cooking breakfast and wearing the same ratty bathrobe she's owned ever since you got married. It's spooning up to that same woman when the day's over and the two of you are just lying there listening to one another breathe. It's watching your kids being born, watching 'em grow up, and everything that's handed your way in between. There is no big picture, Jake. None. Just days filled with moments, some of which should make even you grateful to be alive."

"I'm happy that works for you. I really am. But you know my history. I'm looking for more than what I have, or I should say more than what I had."

"Oh, I know all that, Jake," says John, clearly reaching the end of his patience. "Believe me, I know. You're like a squirrel dashing back and forth in the middle of a busy street. You don't know where to run or what side to land on. Do that long enough and the decision gets made for you, if you catch my drift."

"Yeah, I know what you mean. Still, this near death business and . . . ." My voice trails off as I run out of words. I'm too tired and hungry to try explaining things all over again, and for the moment John seems disinclined to press on with the conversation.

"And that's another thing," he finally pipes up in a voice loud enough to startle me. "You might be fooling yourself, but not me. Oh no, not me. If you wanted to hide out, if you *really* wanted to be alone and figure your way out of this self-indulgent funk of yours, you sure as hell wouldn't have come back to your home town to do it in. Not when half the people here still know you by name, or when you're living next door to your oldest friend in the world."

"Isn't that my problem and not yours?"

"Problems, problems and more problems. That's all you've got. Believe it or not, you're not the only person in the world staying up half the night worrying about shit. There's other people worried and afraid too, you know. It's just that they don't wallow in it or go 'round talking about it all the time."

Taken aback by the unexpected fury behind John's critical assessment of me, I can think of nothing to say in response. For his part, John appears disinclined to continue the dressing-down, so we let things simmer quietly for a bit. Eventually it's my turn to pile more branches on the fire, and I do so while John rests his chin on his chest and sits motionless. After a while I begin to wonder if, despite our cramped shelter, he's dropped off to sleep. Good for him. We have many uncomfortable hours to endure till dawn.

"They cut off her beautiful breasts."

Almost too soft to be heard, John's muted voice surprises me. "What did you say? I don't think I heard you right."

He slowly raises his head and turns to look at me. "You're not the only one who's ever stared down death."

"What exactly do you mean? What are you talking about?"

"Talking 'bout Meg."

"What about Meg? What is it?"

"Cancer. She has it. Or she had. Or maybe she still has it. Who really knows?"

"Wait, you're trying to tell me Meg's had cancer?"

"I'm not trying. That's exactly what I'm telling you. It's about time you looked beyond your own damn problems."

"When?"

"When what?"

"When was she diagnosed?"

"Coming up on two years, I guess."

"Breast cancer?"

"Why the hell else would they cut her breasts off?" John's voice catches when he answers, and I can tell he's close to tears."

"Why didn't you tell me?"

"You mean you couldn't pick that up on your own? You couldn't see how skinny and pale she looked? You never wondered about all the baggy tee shirts she wore?"

"No. Well, yes, I mean I did notice. I just thought she'd lost weight or maybe she was tired."

"Ever consider asking?"

That simple question cuts me. No, of course I never thought to ask. Not once. And it's too late now, yet I ask anyway. "So what are the doctors saying? What's the prognosis?"

"Favorable, they tell us. We mostly believe 'em, except when we don't."

"Reconstructive surgery?"

"Someday. Not yet. There were complications." There's a bitterness in John's voice I've never heard before.

Hunger and exhaustion have undoubtedly overwhelmed John's normal reserve. In laying naked the secret he was apparently hoping I'd discover on my own, he's finally verbalized his silent fears and, as I now comprehend, his disappointment with me. He's unmistakably weeping now. Quietly, of course, yet I can see his shoulders heaving as he leans even farther forward and buries his head in his lap.

I don't know what to say, mostly because I know there's little anyone *can* say to make cancer less terrifying and isolating. While John sits rolled up in his grief, I think back to my first dinner at his house. Could I have been a bigger jerk, or a more horrible human being? There I sat at their dining room table, condescendingly educating John and Meg about cancer's awful consequences and whining about the very same hell they'd been living through. They could've easily countered with horror stories of their own. Instead, they offered me quiet friendship and support. Meanwhile, "Mr. I'm The Only One Who Has Ever Been Sick," gave them exactly nothing in return. In a larger sense, I now see that all I've done since returning to Jackson Meadows is take from them like a selfish child. When she got good and fed up, Annie would accuse me of being a narcissist. Tonight she'd get no argument from me.

Eventually, John sits up and wipes his eyes with the dirty sleeve of his sweatshirt. “Sorry for what I said, JT. I didn’t really mean those things.”

“Listen, if you didn’t mean them then you damn well should’ve. I’m the one who needs to be apologizing. You and Meg. . . and your kids. . . I know exactly what you’ve been going through. You’re obviously a lot stronger than I am. I collapsed like a punctured balloon. But you guys . . .”

“Meg and I have each other,” counters John. “You had no one when you came back here.”

“Only because I lost or alienated everyone between there and here.”

John softly replies, “Not everyone.”

I grasp his meaning. “That’s a little ironic, wouldn’t you agree? Leaning on the two of you when you’re facing the very same issues?”

“Which, if I’m not mistaken,” he counters, “is the definition of a support group.”

John watches rain splatter on the rocks beyond our shelter, then turns to look directly at me. Given our tight proximity, our faces are a little too close for comfort. “Tell me,” he asks, “what is it that you expect – and I mean realistically – out of life, JT? What would be just enough to make you happy?”

“I wish I knew. I can’t tell you how much I wish I knew that. All I know is that life eventually breaks all the promises made to us when we were kids.”

"Such as?"

"Ok, let's start with religion and the biggest promise: the existence of a benevolent god, a shepherd too loving to abandon his flock to pain and misery. Where's the proof for that one?"

"Proof? Where's the proof that Meg will still love me twenty years from now? I take it on faith. Just like people a darn sight smarter than you and me have taken God on faith. And not *just* on faith. With some scholarship and logic behind it."

Distracted by John's supposition that Meg will live to see another twenty years, I hesitate in responding. John seizes the opportunity to wade back in. "And besides, life keeps lots of promises, JT. Tomorrow, or whenever we get out of here, the sun will feel good on your shoulders. That's a guarantee. You'll be hungry and you'll enjoy a delicious meal with people you like, or possibly even love. If you choose, you'll run however many miles you've been running each day and then reward yourself with a nap or a good book. You'll make love with a woman who attracts you for any number of reasons. Not with Annie, of course. Not anymore. Another woman though, one who swells your heart. The way I see it, every single day promises a new crack at getting some of the moments in life right. And as for the big picture, well that's nothing more than all the little pictures that fill it up. We can't live for certainty, but we *can* live for possibility."

John's unexpected eloquence has rendered me speechless. It's evident he's thought all this through, and now, out here in the cold and this rainy darkness, he's revealed a side of himself I've never witnessed in all our years together. Overcome as I am by John's passionate words, I'm fast becoming even more overwhelmed by the enveloping dampness. I'm starting to shiver uncontrollably, and because we're sitting shoulder to shoulder John can't help noticing. He reaches for a few of the larger branches and heaps them onto the fire. Then, to my astonishment, he grabs me around the shoulders and hugs me for several seconds, maybe to deliver warmth, or maybe because this is as close as he and I have felt in many years, and he cannot help himself. I do not resist. Friendship or warmth: I need whatever he's offering.

****

Day three, although it seems longer than that. My joints feel as though they've aged years overnight, and my head is throbbing from lack of food and beneficial rest. Although we managed to keep the fire burning all night, my sweatshirt and the two shirts underneath are uncomfortably clammy. Breakfast will consist of water from the thermos and the stalk of one cattail, maybe two if I can stomach it. My body's craving food, a handful of aspirin and a warm bed. What it's facing instead is another day of wandering, with no clue if our journey will take us deeper into the forest or closer to home. I considered trying to catch some fish in this swampy water and frying them up to replenish our depleted store of energy. We do, after all, still have our gear. But as much as my burning stomach endorses the idea, I reluctantly overruled it. Spending even an hour of our day stalled on the shoreline waiting for a fish to bite could mean spending another night out here, and I don't know how I could take that. Better to swallow the hunger, soldier on, and blindly hope for the best.

Thankfully the rain ended shortly before dawn, and patches of blue have begun to slice through the clouds as they disengage from one another and float away. It looks as if we'll have a sunny day. Never to be trusted, of course, but still better than rain. Neither of us has mentioned our intimate conversation from last night. Shamed by my failure to pick up on Meg's illness, I'd like to demonstrate to John, and myself, that I can be a friend capable of moving beyond his own needs, even if our rekindled intimacy ends up lasting only as long as we remain lost and dependent upon one another in these woods.

As we trudge along beside it, the swamp looks disappointingly similar to yesterday. There remains no sign of a reachable shore on the opposite side, although I'm detecting a definite curvature to the left as opposed to our previously straight path. This morning I'm also plagued by stinging blisters on each of my heels caused by wet socks which keep sinking below the backs of my sneakers, exposing my skin to rough canvas and microscopic pebbles of dirt which chafe against me like sandpaper. We've been walking at least an hour now, and I'll bet we haven't spoken more than a half dozen words. What's to say? We've run out of Plan B's.

****

Now suspended directly overhead, the sun informs us that it's already mid-day. In spite of our slow pace we're both breathing laboriously and stumbling far too often for safety. Like it or not we need to stop for a rest. Adding to our concern, we haven't happened upon a brook since yesterday and our thermos is only about one-third full. Drinking the foul swamp water is not an option, so we've been limiting ourselves to tiny sips, which we first swirl around in our mouths for several seconds before swallowing to make each one last.

"Let's stop at those rocks up ahead," I call to John, who's been running point for a while. He gives me a listless thumb up. We choose a couple of large, relatively flat boulders where the autumn sun is still powerful enough to warm us. With relief I remove my sneakers and socks to let them dry out as much as possible. John was indeed correct in what he said last night: the sun does feel good on my shoulders, despite our misery. I lie back, close my eyes, and let its rays wash over my face as well. Seconds or possibly even minutes later, I open my eyes and realize, to my amazement, that I've briefly dozed off. Looking around, I see John standing on his rock, shielding his eyes from the sun with his right hand in a type of protracted salute.

"JT, look over there," he says. "Come look across the water."

Rubbing the sleep from my eyes with dirty fingers, I at first see nothing new. Then, across the expanse of the swamp, I spot trees on the other side, closer than we've ever seen them. Even better, they're not the dead trees we've been staring at for the past twenty-four hours. They're real trees with autumn colored leaves, presumably flourishing on dry land. My spirits are buoyed by the sight, though I'm not really sure why. Who's to say reaching the opposite side of this brackish swamp will take us any closer to home?

John calls to me once more. "I have to believe this thing is getting narrower. We might even be able to cross it if we keep tracing the shore."

Rapidly donning my socks and sneakers, I do my best to sound positive. "There's only one way to find out." And off we go again.

It's soon obvious that the swamp is narrowing dramatically. After several minutes of tracing its shoreline, with John again assuming the lead, we've reached a point where it can't be more than seventy-five yards wide. Its surface has become increasingly pocked with islands of tall grass and mud, and the water itself is noticeably shallower. Problem is, there's still no dry route across it, and the afternoon is waning.

John raises his arm to signal a halt, and it takes only a few steps for me to catch up with him. "Desperate times call for desperate measures," he announces. "I heard that someplace. Anyway, I'm done with this damn swamp telling us where we can and can't go. Are you ready to be bold?"

I've heard such pronouncements from John before, the most recent one being our ill-conceived decision to "head west." At this point, however, there's nothing to lose and no reason not to listen. "What are you getting at?"

"Glad you asked." Gesturing toward the water, he says, "Take a good look out there. How deep do you figure that water is?"

"I don't know, maybe four or five feet at most."

"And you see how all those little islands are popping up out of it? Some of 'em, we could almost hop from one to the other."

"The critical word being 'some.' I see other islands a good seven or eight feet apart. We can't hop 'em all. Hell, we can't even reach the first one without getting soaked."

"Which is exactly why we'll be taking our clothes off."

"How's that again?"

"It's simple. We take off our clothes, carry them over our heads and wade from island to island. The water's shallow enough now. When we get to the other side, we dry off the best we can in the sun then get ourselves out of here."

"You're suggesting we walk buck naked and barefoot through whatever's muddy and slimy, and surely alive, under this water? Listen, we could sink up to our necks if that bottom's as gooey as I think it is. Plus, there's gotta be leeches in there just waiting to latch on to something, and I *don't* want to consider what that something might be!"

"Look, we've got no . . ."

"And what if it's too deep and we have to swim?" I interrupt. "How do we swim and hold our clothes and poles at the same time?"

"I was about to say we might have to use a modified sidestroke, but only for ten or fifteen feet at a time. Worst case, our clothes might get a little wet. Give 'em a half-hour in the sun and they should be dry enough."

John squints expectantly at me while I stare out at the swamp, assessing our options. Which are few. Either we continue walking around it for who knows how long and face another unendurable night out here, or we wade through it and hope the new route leads us to civilization. When I look back at John I know he's waiting for the inevitable response.

"Ok, but I'm keeping my underwear on. I need that much protection, at least."

"Do as you like," he replies. "Personally, I've never been a fan of soggy undergarments."

Our course of action agreed upon, we begin undressing and rolling our clothing into tight, cylindrical lengths like sleeping bags. When we're done we tie the two ends together to form a handle. I notice John has left his underwear on, too. "Second thoughts?" I inquire.

"Didn't want you to feel inadequate, if you know what I'm saying."

"Wouldn't have been a problem. Not once you hit that freezing water."

Like two swimmers poised for the starting gun, we stand crouched and motionless at the muddy shoreline, studying the topography of the swamp, trying to map out the driest route to the other side. We quickly realize it makes little difference which way we go. Wet will be wet, and once immersed our concern will be more about core body temperature than being drenched to the skin. Stepping forward, John raises his clothing and backpack over his head, dips one foot into the swamp, and without looking back resolutely commands, "Follow me."

The first steps are shocking, enough to take my breath away. I was prepared for the chill of the swamp's water. I never expected its bottom to be quite so oozy and downright frigid. It feels like squishy ice packs have been wrapped around my feet and ankles, and within seconds they've lost their flexibility. So far the water has made it only to my waist, good fortune which I doubt will last. The first tiny island, tantalizingly near, sits only about ten feet away, and in my eagerness to reach this sliver of dry land I begin thrashing toward it, overtaking John in the process. Unwise, I know, but I cannot help myself.

Arriving at our first haven, we toss our belongings ahead of us, crawl up its surprisingly steep bank and sit breathing heavily amidst the spindly grass and caked mud. "As long as this sun lasts we should be ok," John observes. "It's still high enough in the sky to warm us up."

"All the more reason to forge ahead," I tell him. Grabbing my bundle, I slide ass first into the icy murkiness once more.

We repeat this process two more times until the deepening water toward the middle makes it clear that the next leg of the journey will require swimming. "How are we going to swim without drenching our clothes?" I ask, as we sit recapturing our strength on this latest island.

"Not entirely sure about that," says John. "We only have, what, fifteen or twenty feet till the next one? Some kind of side stroke or dog paddle might work."

"Or we could float on our backs and paddle that way."

"Won't know till we try."

From the swimming hole I frequented as a kid to my reckless drives to the hoop, to the cases I could've settled for a safe figure yet gambled on and took to trial, my life, until recently, has been a series of icy plunges, consequences be damned. I doubt leaving Annie to hide out in Jackson Meadows qualifies for the bold risk category. It's never a risk when there's nothing left to lose. Such are the thoughts which flash through my head before I push off from the bank with my oldest friend, to invent a method of swimming one-handed through a swamp.

John and I both top six feet in height. The water has us beaten by at least a foot. My side stroke instantly proves useless, and I begin sinking like a torpedoed battleship. It's time to improvise, necessity being the mother of invention. So I turn onto my belly and commence a furious one-handed dog paddle, simultaneously kicking my legs like pistons, never looking left or right to see how John's faring. At the moment, it's every man for himself. After a minute or two of frenzied splashing and spitting out gulps of foul-tasting water, I arrive at the postage stamp of dry land I've been aiming for. Grabbing hold of a tiny sapling, I pull myself onto its bank and lie motionless on my back, lungs burning from exertion, feeling sweaty and chilled to the bone at the same time. It's not until I hear splashing from the direction of my feet that I think to look for John. His wet hair is plastered to his scalp; clearly he went under. He looks as spent as I feel.

Once he's caught his breath John inquires, "How'd your clothes make out?"

Taking a moment to inspect them, I tell him, "Not too bad. Little wet around the edges, but not bad. You?"

"Damp. Like a heavy sweat . . . a really heavy sweat."

Rising to one knee, I assess the next stretch of water we're going to have to cover. "How many more times do you think we'll have to swim?"

John stands to better surveil the landscape. I see that he's shivering, his middle age belly hanging over his wet and sagging underwear. "One more. I guarantee it. The paddling will take a bit longer, but one more's gonna do it."

"You sure about that?"

"Yes I am, because one more is all I can take."

And with that we grab our gear for what we hope is our last big plunge. I need to believe we're swimming toward the comfort and safety of home, which for me and for the time being anyway, appears to be Jackson Meadows.

****

Our plan when we made it to shore was to dry off in the sun before donning our clothes, even build a fire if absolutely necessary. When at last we reach the other side of the swamp I'm much too chilled to sit naked in the feeble sun or wait for a fire. Instead, I perform as many jumping jacks as I have energy for, in order to get my blood pumping, then hurriedly dress. My clothing is moist but not soaked. John follows my lead. Relatively dry, we're ready to proceed. The question is where.

"Can we agree on west?" John asks. "It will take us in the opposite direction of the swamp and, as I said before . . ."

Before he can finish I interrupt him. "I know. I know. We drove out east. Home must be west."

"True. But think it through, Jake. East takes us back into the water. North and south leave us following the swamp again. West's the only one way to go, as I see it."

"Fair enough, if we can agree there'll be no detours. It's easy to see which way the sun is sinking. Come hell or high water we follow it wherever it takes us. No doubling back, no second guessing ourselves. A straight line. Agreed?"

"You'll get no argument from me."

For a few miles our route takes us on a slight incline until it eventually flattens out. The forest is dense – what else is new – and twice we come upon small brooks which we cross by hopping from one exposed rock to the next. On the bank of one brook we spy a discarded Styrofoam container which once held worms, offering hope that we're nearing civilization, or a dirt road which might be used by logging trucks or, better yet, might lead us to a hunting or fishing camp.

From the position of the sun, the time appears to be about 4:00 p.m. That's when John suddenly stops dead in his tracks and grabs my right arm. "Shhh. Do you hear that?' he asks. "Hear that rustling?"

I cock my head to listen. "No, nothing, I don't . . ."

"Quiet!" he commands. Still gripping my arm like a vice, he stands poised and motionless.

And then I do hear it. From about thirty yards away, a heavy thrashing is emanating from the underbrush, accompanied by the unmistakable sounds of panting and loud snorting. Even more alarming, whatever's making those noises is undeniably heading our way, and quickly.

"Bears? Do you think they're bears?" I exclaim to John, desperately hoping he'll tell me I'm wrong.

"What else can it be?"

"Coming for us?"

"What do *you* think?"

"But why? What do they want with us?"

"Why? Why doesn't matter."

John has now removed his backpack and begun swinging it wildly above his head. "Start making noise. Loud noise! Lots of it. And for God's sake don't stop."

We begin screaming at the top of our lungs. All I can think to say is, "Get out of here. Get lost," as if these particular bears somehow comprehend the English language. Although the oncoming sounds slow down momentarily, they do not stop. It's clear we're in for a confrontation.

John suddenly turns to me and says, "Run. Take off as fast as you can. I'll distract 'em."

"Are you nuts?" I exclaim. "No way I'm leaving you here."

"Listen to me, Jake. I'm bigger than you and I can swing this backpack. If I yell loud enough and don't back down they're gonna feel threatened enough to turn around."

"You sure about that?"

"Of course not. Go. Just freakin' go!"

The coward in me momentarily considers turning tail and running. Yet when I look over at the harmless, good-natured John striving to make himself appear menacing, and when I understand how, instinctively, he's chosen to save me, risking bodily harm and perhaps his life, my only choice, come what may, is to stand shoulder to shoulder beside him. Kind of like The Alamo. Kind of like brothers.

Despite my decision to stand and fight, my actions at the moment of attack are not exactly heroic. Certain that our enemies are about to breach the tree line, I shut my eyes like tight fists to await the unimaginable pain soon to be inflicted. Not only do these bears outweigh and outnumber us, they possess razor-sharp claws and teeth. There's no way they'll be scared off by John's soggy backpack and our desperate screeching. Just when I swear I can feel their hot, hungry breath in my face, that's when I also hear their loud barking and yelping. Barking? Bears? What have I missed here? Do bears also bark? Something doesn't add up, especially when I hear John call out in a happy, singsong voice, "Well hello there, fellas. What brings you way out here?"

At last summoning the courage to open my eyes, I'm shocked to discover John down on both knees petting three black Labrador retrievers, who in turn are jumping on him delightedly and licking his dirty face. It's all too much to process. Seconds ago we were facing a certain mauling, possibly death. Now it's doggie playtime.

"Dogs?" is all I can say to John. "No bears? Those were *dogs* coming after us?"

"Safe to say we spooked ourselves just a bit," John laughs, still enjoying the company of his newfound friends.

"But where did they come from?" I ask.

"Tucker, Sam, Bear. There you are! Are you bothering these nice gentlemen?" From the same dense tree line an old woman emerges. She's wearing a flannel shirt, jeans and hiking boots, and kind of a do-rag thing on her head, iron grey hair spilling out in thin strands beneath it. In her left hand she's carrying a walking stick which appears to have been hand-carved. Her face tells me she's at least thirty years older than us; the rest of her is in remarkable physical shape. Whatever her age or condition, I'm grateful beyond speech to see another human, and I have to stifle the urge to rush up and hug her. We must be near home. Maybe not ours, but somebody's home just the same. Right here and now, this old woman is as close as I've ever come to meeting the guardian angel my mother used to swear existed for my protection.

John rises to offer a handshake to the woman, and when he does the dogs trot obediently back to her. "I'm John Caldwell," he says, "and this is Jake Taylor. We've gotten ourselves turned around a little in these woods. Do you mind telling us where we are?"

"Nice to meet you, boys. I'm Hilda Plunkett. My husband and I own the farm about half a mile from here. Well, not so much a farm anymore. We're too old for any big enterprise. Nowadays we're down to some chickens and a veggie stand."

It's my turn to talk. "And where's your farm located?"

"We're on Lost Valley Road, about three miles east of its intersection with Route 2. Where are you boys coming from, if I might inquire?"

John fields this one. "Well, that's a good question. The best I can do is tell you where our truck's parked. It's been sitting on the side of Garland Road for longer than we'd like, right next to the bridge near the lumber mill."

"Gracious me," Hilda exclaims. "That a good seven or eight mile drive from here."

"Longer than that, I suspect, if you take the route through the woods," responds John dryly.

Second-guessing is pointless. Nevertheless, I have to ask. "Hilda, if one were to follow the big swamp back there in the woods for as far north as it extends, where would that lead, exactly?"

"Lordy, let me think. You mean Butler Swamp? It would take you nowhere, really, other than deeper into the National Forest."

"Are there any houses or roads in that area?" I ask.

"No, not a one. Just fishermen and . . . uh . . . campers like you passing through." I can see her scanning our immediate vicinity for any sign of camping gear. Nothing to see, of course. Just two filthy wanderers inappropriately dressed for an extended stay in the woods. Before she can follow up with the obvious – and embarrassing – question, I pose another of my own.

"Do you suppose we could follow you back to your farm, maybe hitch a ride to our truck?"

"Absolutely," she replies. "More than happy to help." She turns back toward the tree line, waves us along, then pauses. I can tell she's deciding whether or not to bite her tongue. Candor wins out. "Pardon me for saying so. You boys look like you could use a hot meal," she observes in a motherly tone.

"And a shower," adds John.

"Oh yes, for sure. But that would've been extremely rude of me to mention."

CHAPTER THIRTY-SEVEN

Let's just label it a sheepish reunion for two inept woodsmen and leave it at that. There were plenty of joyful tears from John's wife and kids, robust hugs all around, and much good-natured scolding from friends and family, who begged John to promise he'd never venture that deep into the woods again. John was the center of attention; I merely hung about the periphery taking it all in, at times shouldered aside by people needing access to him in order to wrap him up in one more bear hug.

As I understand events, when John hadn't arrived home by late evening of our first night in the woods Meg tried reaching him on his cellphone. Unable to contact him, she assumed he was out of range, not an unusual occurrence up in these mountains. She knew there was no way a search party, if one was even necessary, would be able to look for her absentee husband until morning. As a result, she sat alone and worried her way through the night, peering out windows for any sign of John's noisy truck.

When morning arrived and John remained missing and unreachable, Meg called Arthur Marcoux, the county's only game warden. She informed him where we'd been planning to fish and how long we'd been gone. Always ready to help, Arthur assured Meg he'd take a run out there right away and see what he could dig up, unquestionably a poor choice of words on Arthur's part. When Meg asked Arthur if he owned a tracking dog, preferably a bloodhound, Arthur told her, sorry, all he had was an unreliable old beagle named Molly. And besides, he informed her, there was too much water out there for any dog to nose us out.

Eager as Arthur might have been to help, Meg also knew he was pushing seventy and walked with a pronounced limp. His glasses, lenses thick as prisms, did not inspire confidence in his tracking ability either. It took only a couple of phone calls from Meg to set into motion an extensive phone chain soliciting volunteers, and thus, within a few hours, more than two dozen hardy and determined men had taken to the woods in search of their friend. If found, I would be a collateral beneficiary of their hunt. In fact, had they come upon just me, wandering alone in the woods, none of them would've even known who I was. Of course, they never found us. Who could ever have traced or logically guessed at our crazy, circuitous route to safety?

****

One person who would've been glad to see me, if only he could recognize my face, lies semi-conscious in the hospital bed next to where I now sit. It's Archie, so frail he hardly dents the mattress, mouth agape, his snoring interrupted by disjointed mutterings. I foresee the end approaching and I'm not sure, exactly, how I feel about that. Should I be relieved that his long ordeal, mine too I'd say, is nearly over? Should I be readying myself to mourn the loss of a father who's been leaving me in stages for years?

Exhausted from our nightmare in the woods, I never thought to check my phone before collapsing into bed upon returning home. Why would I? Nobody ever calls. It wasn't until the next morning that I retrieved a voice message telling me Archie had been unexpectedly transferred from Meadows Retreat to the local hospital. Mention was made of a "sudden deterioration" in his condition, which turned out to be a gross understatement. I knew, of course, he'd been failing incrementally for a long while. Despite that, I was not prepared to discover how near he'd crept toward the edge of life's precipice in such a brief time.

I've been sitting here watching him for the last couple of hours. On any other day I might be growing antsy rooted to the sticky plastic cushion of this hospital chair. This afternoon though, still spent from three grueling days in the forest, I'm content to sit here idly and mull over Archie's life, and by extension my own. I've resisted the impulse to talk to him. He'd more or less clammed up toward the end of our rides together, so what would be the use in trying to reach him now? Instead, I'm acting as a stand-in for the role he played during the happiest of our recent trips around town, mentally jumping from era to era in our history, retracing the path of our life together which, at its start, stretched out indefinitely. Now, our journey seems to have been heartbreakingly brief.

I've been picturing myself as a small boy, no more than five or six, playing trucks with Archie. Like me, he's on all fours on the living room carpet, pushing a dump truck across its thick fabric and mimicking the roaring and grinding of the gears as they shift. We called ourselves "Sam and George the Working Guys," never deciding which one of us was Sam and who was George. And years later, there he is at my college basketball game, ensconced in his customary spot half-way up the bleachers when I sneak a glance his way during a time-out. He won't send me a thumbs up in return. He won't even crack a smile. Even so, I know he's scrutinizing my every move, and after the game he'll be supremely prepared to critique my performance. I also know he's carrying a large stash of pennies in his jacket pocket, and that he'll transfer a penny from one pocket to the other with every point I score, just to be sure he's keeping an accurate count. And now, together with my mother, he's visiting my office in downtown Philly, one of his infrequent appearances there. I'd expected to find him relaxing in the waiting room, perhaps browsing through a newspaper. Instead, when I hurry there after finishing up with a long-winded client, he's on his feet, his back to me, studying a magazine cover with my picture on it, framed and hung a couple of years earlier after that publication had run a feature story on Philadelphia's trial lawyers. Approaching from behind, I call out my hello. Slowly, almost solemnly, he turns to me, gives both my shoulders a hard, protracted squeeze, then says, "Let's go, boy. Your mother's waiting in the car." The squeeze meant he was proud of me; the strength of it told me how much. Such memories of the years and the man I've lost stab at my heart. With those days gone forever, I'm now left alone to visit whatever moments I can still recall, and to accept the pain which accompanies those nostalgic trips as being a necessary part of the deal.

****

It's not quite October, and already the feel of the northern New England landscape is palpably changing. In the dusky quiet before dawn and late at night beneath a glowing moon, I can smell and feel winter in the air. The daily temperature is now quick to drop and slow to rise, and trees have begun shedding their brightly colored leaves. As my dear mother loved to say, "There's going to be a big change in the air."

For the time being I've discontinued my morning runs. Surprisingly, after a spring and summer of mostly empty days, I suddenly have things to do, decisions to make. Remaining true to his nature to the very last, Archie still clings stubbornly to life, if one can label it so. I've been spending the bulk of my days and evenings sitting in his room, waiting for something, anything, to happen. Every once in a while he'll come to, peer groggily at me, then drop off to sleep again. On rare occasions he's spoken *of* me, as if to a third person, rather than *to* me, sounding as though his tongue is too thick and heavy for his mouth, "It's Jake. He's home" or words to that effect. Each time it's happened I've leapt from my seat and leaned over the bed to address him directly, although when I grasp his skeleton hand and speak, he never responds. It seems that even now, at the end, I'm asking for more than he has the capacity to give.

The nurses who breeze busily in and out assure me they can tell from years of experience when a patient is about to go. Actually, the word they most often use is "expire," which to me sounds too much like food that's gone bad. So I've been sticking with "go," which implies Archie's heading somewhere else, perhaps better. These nurses have been exhorting me to take some time for myself, cut out for a few hours or, better yet, the entire day. They have my number, they say. They'll call me if it's time. I tell them I don't doubt their skill or perceptiveness, not one bit. I try explaining how I have to stick around for the entirety of the process, not just the ending, how it's something I need to absorb and remember. I tell them I'm hoping a long goodbye will make the end easier to accept. They smile kindly at me and say they understand, only to repeat their suggestion that I take a break.

John and Meg have been stopping by to keep me company, as has Sarah, of course. During Meg's first visit I offered up a lame and tardy apology for missing the signs of her illness. She brushed it off like lint from a shirtsleeve, a little too brusquely to assuage my conscience. Surprisingly, in the several hours we've sat together in

Archie's private room, John and I have only infrequently spoken of our misadventure, maybe due to embarrassment over our locally publicized display of ineptitude, or possibly because we revealed more to one another in those woods than is now comfortable for either of us to acknowledge. I did ask him why he tried to shoo me away to face the oncoming bears by himself. Scowling darkly, he replied, "And they say there's no stupid questions." He then excused himself to visit the rest room, leaving me to contemplate his affection and loyalty.

****

It's now grown late on a Saturday afternoon. Archie's been lying still as death all day, and I'm feeling lonely and hungry. Sarah left me a voicemail this morning offering a home-cooked meal and a brief respite from my vigil. No advance notice necessary, she said. Just show up. She'll be there regardless. Consequently, when Archie's evening nurse pops in to adjust some monitor that's been beeping annoyingly, I inform her I'm taking a chance and will be gone until morning. I of course ask her to notify me immediately if anything changes, and she of course assures me with a "you don't need to remind me" smile that the entire staff knows how to reach me.

After she departs I rise with cracking joints from the chair to which I've been glued, lean close to Archie's face and then, for some inexplicable reason, like a kid dutifully informing a parent where he can be found, I tell him I'm going to Sarah's for the evening. Without opening his eyes, and hardly moving his dry, cracked lips, Archie hoarsely responds. "Be a good boy. I love you," he rasps.

Dumbfounded by his unexpected response, I bend even closer, near enough to smell and feel his sour breath on my face. "Archie, what did you say? Can you hear me? Are you there?" No response. No sound. No movement. Not even the tiniest flutter of an eyelid.

Scarcely able to breathe, I hover motionless above him for several minutes, hands clenching the bedrail, pulling so hard for something more out of Archie that my chest begins to ache. When something more doesn't arrive I impulsively grasp his right hand, not to hold, but to shake. In his lifetime, Archie prized few things more than a firm handshake. This time ours will be one-sided. I squeeze his limp hand as strongly as I dare and tell him what I have no recollection of ever verbalizing before: "I love you too, Archie. I love you too." Memory alone guides me to the door of his room, as I cannot see through the tears.

CHAPTER THIRTY-EIGHT

"Oh, Jake. That's one of the saddest and most touching stories I've ever heard," says Sarah, pulling me to her chest for a hug and refusing to let go, as if attempting to absorb a portion of my sadness. Tiny droplets of water spill onto my neck as she sniffles noisily in my ear.

Standing there, eyes burning from tears and a lack of sleep, it hits me – again – that I have but two people in this world who truly care for me. There's John, who loves me like a brother and has made it clear he needs me to be a part of his life. And there's Sarah, who might someday grow to love me, notwithstanding the risks I pose. To this day, I wonder how much I might offer either of them in return.

"Come, let's sit down," she tells me, disengaging from our embrace and leading me to the couch. "Do you suppose Archie actually knew you were there and understood what you were saying? Do you think it's possible?"

"I really can't say, Sarah. I'd like to believe he found his way back to me for a moment, I truly would. But the skeptical part of me wonders if such a belief isn't just magical thinking. It's more likely his words were a reflexive response by his brain to the type of statement he'd heard many times before – kind of like when he stuck his elbow out the window when I opened it on our first trip around town. Maybe it was just some random synapse firing in a surprisingly appropriate manner."

"Yet from what you've told me, he didn't say he loved you, or order you to be a good boy, all that often. So it's unlikely that those specific words, those incredible words, would've been an automatic reply to whatever registered in his brain, right?"

"Right. Or possibly not right. I want to believe he needed to speak those words before dying. I want to believe he was just strong and stubborn enough to momentarily fend off dementia and death in order to speak his final piece."

"Whatever the reason, you have to admit those sentiments were there inside him."

"Deep, deep inside him," I say, "and often too far removed to sustain the journey to his tongue."

Sarah stands, bends to kiss me lightly on the forehead, and moves off to the kitchen, where she's thrown together a pasta dish mixed with vegetables and oil, together with a side salad. After days of foraging from the snack machine at the hospital, it all tastes delicious. Still, like a brewing storm, Archie's imminent death hovers low and ominous over our table. I tell Sarah, "Tonight I want to remember how it feels to enjoy a meal when he's still alive, before the time arrives when I can speak of him only in the past tense. I know how it was with my mother. As soon as she died it felt as if she'd been gone for years. One day or one year, it's all the same when the loss is forever."

****

Only a fool trusts a sunny day. And here's something else I've learned: nurses, no matter how perceptive they pride themselves on being, can't always tell when their patient is about to expire, as they say. As promised, one of them reached me by phone, waking me around 3:00 a.m. from my slumber next to Sarah. Offering an apology and her deepest sympathy, she informed me that Archie had slipped from this life, unnoticed and alone, about twenty minutes ago. I saw no point in asking why, with the end so near, I hadn't been called. I simply thanked her for letting me know and said I'd be at the hospital within the hour. After hanging up, it immediately struck me that death represents our ultimate physical weakness. I hoped it was Archie's choice to surrender to it in private. I hoped he'd been stubbornly waiting for me to leave his bedside, to abandon my vigil, so he could end the struggle on his own terms. I'd feel better believing that to be true.

Sarah rode with me to the hospital. Rushing together through its eerily quiet hallways, we passed darkened rooms housing sleeping patients until we reached Archie's. When we got there his door was entirely closed. It reminded me of my first visit to Meadows Retreat. And so, here I now stand, once more pausing outside Archie's door, still apprehensive about what I might encounter.

"You go in alone, Jake," Sarah whispers, giving my arm a squeeze. "Go say your goodbye."

No reason to knock. And thus, for the final time, I enter Archie's room.

His death, I'm relieved to discover, could first be mistaken for sleep. I hadn't said anything to Sarah on the way to the hospital, but I was worried his eyes would be open or his mouth open, evidence of some ghastly death throe. I dreaded having to close his eyes or force his jaw upward, and worried that even if I did, something might unexpectedly pop open again. I wanted to find him at peace, or at least seemingly so.

In some respects, except for the absence of IV tubes and the whirring and beeping of the machines that once monitored his failing vital signs, this could be mistaken for just another of my visits. Archie lies there, motionless and silent, while I study his features for the final time. Already he looks paler, to the point of ghostly, and I fear that if I touch his hands or face they will feel unnaturally cold. And so I don't touch him. I'd prefer the one-sided handshake from yesterday to be our last physical contact. Although nonresponsive, at least his limp hand did not carry with it the chill of death.

Standing there alone, I wait for tears which do not come. Instead I feel the need to speak to him, as if, from some universal distance he may now have traveled, Archie might hear what would've been inaudible and unintelligible to him only an hour before. I still have important things to tell him, words and sentiments I once assumed there'd be time for. Such is the fallacy of the human mind: we trust we'll have plenty of time, until of course we don't.

"So long, Arch," I say to him. "For once, I'm getting the last word. It's sad how callous life's evolution can be. Parents and children: we commence our journey together joined at the heart and hip, sharing each day, never imagining life will be any different. Then the child moves away – moves on as he's supposed to do – and all that remains are the occasional phone calls, birthday cards, and visits around the holidays. I now understand that children let go of parents too readily, and with only an occasional backward glance turn their attention elsewhere. I now see how, all along, you and I were alike, Archie. Each of us was Sam. Each of us was George. I'm trusting we both understood those things we never found the time or the words to express. I'm glad we finished up by taking our rides around town. It was good seeing life through your eyes, revisiting the old days. I'll never forget our final months together, and from now on whatever I can remember will have to be enough. So, Archie," and here I pause to raise both palms in surrender, as the tears have now arrived in full force . . . "enough."

****

On Election Day in Jackson Meadows people cast their ballots at the Town Hall, which has anchored the corner of Main and Mechanic Streets for over a century. The majority of voters tend to show up after work to carry out their civic duty, which means the waiting line at that time of day stretches out the door and around the corner of the old brick edifice. And so it's gone with Archie Taylor's wake. A different building, of course, but the same long line snaking all the way out to the street. Hundreds of mourners have shown up to pay their respects to Archie, and in doing so have confirmed my lifelong assessment of the man: he could be endearing and irritating, often simultaneously. But never, ever, could he be ignored.

In one respect, the large turnout is gratifying and surprisingly comforting. On the downside, Archie has no surviving spouse or siblings, and because I'm an only child it's been left to me alone to stand by the urn holding his ashes and greet everyone. Most of the conversations run about the same, commencing with a handshake from the men and a hug from the women.

"Hi, Jake. I'm (fill in the name). Sorry for your loss." (*Thank you. It was good of you to come.*)

Followed by the platitudes, served up to make both of us feel better:

"He's in a better place now." (*Yes, he certainly is.*)

"He's been reunited with Mary. Never seen a happier couple." (*Nor have I.*)

"Archie was quite a man." (*Indeed he was.*)

"I remember the time (fill in the event)." (*Oh yes, Archie lived life to its fullest.*)

"Archie would go on about you all the time. He was extremely proud of you." (*I hope so. I was proud of him too.*)

Right now, after nearly four hours of such exhausting back and forth, my mind and body are numb with fatigue. All I want is to retreat to the empty house on High Street and sit by myself in the quiet. Thankfully, the line has now dwindled to a few straggling mourners with, no surprise, John and Meg bringing up the rear. Meg hugs me but says nothing. Perhaps, like me, she's veered closely enough to death to understand how ineffectual words of support and sympathy can be. For a change it's John who does all the talking.

"Well, JT, looks like we're a couple of orphans now. Feels strange, doesn't it, when both parents have passed on. 'Course, you'll always have a family. You'll always have us."

Coming from John, notwithstanding our recent interactions in the forest, that's quite a speech, and this time, possibly for the first time, I'm the one who initiates a hug. Just when I'm afraid I might start crying he adds, "We know you haven't eaten in a while. Come on back to the house for some food."

"That's really nice of you," I say, "however. . ."

"I took the liberty of inviting Sarah," he adds with the barest trace of a grin.

I reply with a shrug of acceptance. When have I ever said no to John?

CHAPTER THIRTY-NINE

"There's always a demand for brick and mortar book stores in Pennsylvania. Lots of folks down there enjoy reading, you know."

"And there are plenty of jobs for lawyers in New Hampshire. Believe it or not, we have courts and judges and people up here who avail themselves of the law, just like in the big cities."

That was the gist of the conversation between Sarah and me when I suggested she consider moving back to the Philadelphia area with me. We were lying in her darkened bedroom, the sheets twisted around us.

"I realize it's only been a few months. Even so, I feel like we already have something special between us," I told her, pleading my case.

"Jake, I'm flattered, if that's the right word, and I don't necessarily disagree. I'd say what we have is something promising, a budding relationship that could very well blossom someday. You've needed comfort and intimacy. And I admit, for different reasons, so have I. But we shouldn't forget that need, be it physical or emotional, can be mistaken for love. Wouldn't you agree? And also, let's not forget that I have a son. I can't just uproot him from the town where he was raised based on a blind hope that, in the long run, you and I will prove right for each other."

"Listen, Sarah, I understand it's a lot to ask. And even more to trust. We haven't lived together. We haven't slogged through a difficult day at work and come home to one another exhausted and cranky. We haven't had to juggle finances or make any tough decisions, at least until now. And other than dinners and a couple of movies, we haven't even had what you'd call real dates. I get all that. I honestly do."

"Then what makes you believe we could ever work?"

"Well, we do have a history, a passionate history, one that goes back a long way." As soon the words escaped my mouth I realized it was a feeble response, smacking of desperation. I'd been in this situation before, arguing a motion or a case I knew I couldn't win, unable to offer the judge anything compelling or persuasive to advance my position. What I might've said to her was, "Come with me because I love you." Perhaps she would've professed her love as well, although I doubt it, for she too would've recognized the danger in verbalizing a simple hope masquerading as the strongest of emotions.

"Do you remember the kids we hung out with when we were young," she asked, "and how friendships were largely a product of geography? When those kids lived in our neighborhood or were in the same classes with us in school we were fast friends, or so we believed. Then, when one of us moved away the friendship petered out."

"Your point being?" I don't know why I said that; I knew where she was going.

"These past months you and I have had fun and, I'll grant you, a great deal more than that. But what we've had isn't real life, not by a longshot. It's more like we've been teenagers again. Despite your ordeal with Archie and all the other stuff clanging around in your brain, your first responsibility has been to yourself. You've been living in your boyhood home, exercising daily, and occasionally playing basketball. Every so often you eat with John's family, and more frequently with me. You have no job and enough money not to need one, at least not for now. You have no ties or commitments to anything or anybody."

"Wait, that's not fair. I do have . . . ."

"Oh, I know what you're going to say. Yes, I agree there's a renewed bond with John, not to mention whatever it is we've started. Believe me, I'm not pointing a finger at you alone. In some respects I've been living the life of a teenager too. My son stayed with his father most of the summer, and even now that he's back home he's always at a party or a school event or sleeping at a friend's house. Except for the bookstore, which of course I love running, my time is my own. Plus, as much as I hate to say it, thanks to his father my son has a college fund, my house is paid for and I have no financial worries. I've been free to throw myself headlong into the thrill of a new romance. It's been exhilarating to feel young and alluring again, to pretend I'm not a middle-aged mother. The question is, what happens if new becomes old and the fantasy's exposed for what it truly is?"

She had me there. I saw no point in protesting. "I know, Sarah. I wish I didn't, but I know you're right. I never told you this, but the second night we were lost in the woods John opened up about home and how much he loved it. He called Jackson Meadows his "intimate piece of the infinite sky." That phrase has stuck with me, especially coming from John. He's perfectly content living here in his tiny sliver of the world. He lives in Jackson Meadows because he was born here. That's all the reason he needs. I'm different. You and I both know Jackson Meadows isn't right for me, at least not at the moment. Archie's house goes on the market next week; I've already signed the listing agreement with Elaine Richards. Remember her from high school? Anyway, she thinks it'll sell quickly based on the location."

"I already knew that, Jake. News travels fast and doesn't have far to go in a small town."

"So I'm guessing you were anticipating this conversation?"

"I've been rehearsing my answer for a week," she replied, her eyes offering me the hint of a smile. "Some of my early drafts had an entirely different ending."

"When I'm gone will you visit me in Pennsylvania?"

"I will – just as often as you come back to Jackson Meadows to see me."

"We'll be keeping score then?"

"Oh, I do hope so."

"And why is that?"

Kissing me lightly on the tip of my nose she said, "Because, Jake Taylor, you've always played to win.

****

That conversation with Sarah took place three days ago. Today, on a bright and crisp Saturday morning, John and I are busy clearing the last of the stuff out of the house before it's officially listed for sale on Tuesday. Other than a couple of pieces of Archie's bedroom furniture, which John promised he could put to good use, everything else is destined for the town landfill or the local Goodwill Store. Except for Archie's old mercury thermometer. I'm keeping that. The urn containing his ashes, which seem equally worthless and precious, sits conspicuously on the kitchen counter. The ashes will be scattered into the water of Archie's favorite fishing hole, the one we always left for him, to be taken wherever water goes. The urn, merely junk without its contents, will eventually get tossed.

Despite the cool fall temperature we're both sweating from exertion. We've been at this for a few hours, and though it's barely noontime we're already fatigued and hungry. "What do you say we grab ourselves a piece of the floor and eat lunch?" suggests John. "I've got beer and sandwiches in the cooler I left downstairs."

"Let's see, the last time we sat down for sandwiches and alcohol we got ourselves into a bit of a predicament. I don't suppose there's much chance of that happening this time."

"No, I don't suppose," says John brusquely, sounding surprisingly peeved by my meager attempt at humor. "Stay here. I'll grab the cooler."

Side by side we wolf down our sandwiches, our backs resting against my parents' bedroom wall with its outdated paper of flowers and curling vines. "You know," I remark, "Archie and my mother bought this house when they learned she was pregnant with me. That's nearly half a century of memories. After Archie died, I briefly considered keeping it. I figured if I hired someone to look after it I might use it as a place to get away. It took me all of two days to conclude it's too painful here. Too many ghosts."

John replies, "I understand how you might feel that way, especially living alone. For me, it's different. I like to think of myself as the caretaker of my family's history. These days it's my turn to shoulder the load. Somewhere down the line, hopefully *way* down, I'll pass it on to my children, if they want it. There's a comfort in that type of continuity, even if I won't be around to witness it."

"It sure as hell took you long enough to start spewing out all these profound thoughts. For months after I came back you barely said anything beyond what was necessary."

"That's because I knew you wouldn't listen."

"And now?"

"And now, I think you're figuring stuff out. Not everything. No one ever does. But enough to realize you could be happy someday."

"And how about you? Are you happy? I mean truly happy?"

John rubs his chin thoughtfully. "I'll say this: each day I'm open to the *possibility* of happiness. And if I look hard enough for it, if I think on what I have rather than what I don't, or what I'm afraid of losing, I can usually find it."

"I'm not sure I understand you."

"Ok, look at it this way. Life's all about losses and gains. Would you agree with me on that? Sometimes I wish my kids could be little again. I wish I could sit them on my lap and read to them, or leave milk and cookies with them for Santa Claus. How I loved Christmas Eve back then. But as my own father used to say, 'That ain't gonna happen.' I've accepted the notion that change isn't the worst thing in the world. I share new experiences with my family now. Different, of course, but no less rewarding. I'm trying to treasure what I do have and not beat myself up over what's missing or already gone. Granted, it's not a foolproof formula, and sometimes I do get all balled up in the past, like when I'm with you. But it works well enough for me, I guess."

"And what about Meg and her health? Doesn't that weigh on you?"

"Only every day. Sometimes I'm so fearful of what might happen to her I can hardly draw a breath. That's when I scold myself for worrying about the future instead of enjoying whatever I can of the here and now. Of course, I don't always heed my own advice, which is when . . . ." He leaves his sentence unfinished, his voice trailing off.

"Enough said. I know how hard it is to turn off the voices in your head."

“I was going to say,” John corrects me, “that’s when I force myself to get good and busy. So how about we haul the dresser and bureau out of here and into my house?”

****

We choose the easier task first, which is moving the dresser. Once its drawers are removed, it’s light enough for one man to carry, albeit too bulky for a solo job. It takes us no time to haul it out of the house. The bureau we’re now eyeing with great apprehension is another story entirely. With its chipped finish and a few drawers that won’t cleanly close, it’s never matched the rest of the bedroom furnishings. I suspect Archie acquired it at an estate sale, unable to pass on his notion of a bargain, while my mother, too sweet and patient to say no, resigned herself to co-existing with it. The bureau is fashioned from solid oak, and lifting it will surely sap whatever remains of our energy for the day, in part because two deliciously stuffed sandwiches and two beers apiece have rendered us drowsy and unambitious.

Having first removed the drawers, which proved almost as difficult to pull out as to push in, we step back to reassess the hulking monstrosity. “Are you absolutely certain you want this old thing?” I ask.

“It sure ain’t pretty, I’ll grant you that. Trust me though, I’ve got a perfect place for it in one of the spare bedrooms. The rest of the furniture there's pretty beat up. This old thing will blend right in."

"Ok, if you say so. Staring at it won't make it any lighter. Let's move it away from the wall, then figure out the best way to get it through the doorway."

Girding myself for what I anticipate will be a brutal lift, I bend like a weightlifter from the knees and, from its side, grab two of the bureau's stubby legs, front and back. John squats down to do the same, and as he does I tell him, "We'll do it on my count of three, ok?"

"Ready when you are," he grunts.

"All right then. Grab hold. Here we go. One, two . . . ."

"Hold up a second," he exclaims. "What the heck is this?"

"What's what? Forget about it. Just lift."

"No, I can't. Set your end down. There's something stuck to the bottom of the rear leg. Come around here and lift the back higher so I can pry this thing off."

When I reach John's side of the bureau I find him on all fours, scratching and picking at a dusty black square beneath the leg. "It looks like a book, or part of one anyway. Your dad must've used it as a shim. I didn't realize how uneven the floor is back here. It drops off like a cliff."

"Well, whatever it is, just peel it off so we can finish this job."

I tilt the bureau forward onto its two front legs while John gives the square a good yank. “There,” he exclaims. “Got it. You can let it down now.”

Much more impatient than interested, I remain standing over him while he inspects it. “What is it?” I ask.

No response from John.

“What is it?” I ask again.

More silence.

“Ok, you want me to guess, is that it?”

“No, what I really want is for you to sit down beside me.” Puzzled by the unexpectedly somber tone of John’s voice, I obediently plop down next to him.

Without another word John hands over his discovery, which looks to be a leather bound journal, its front cover worn and cracked, the back one missing. Some of the pages have been ripped out, while many of the ones remaining are partially torn. It’s a mystery to me why the ever resourceful Archie would’ve utilized a book rather than wood as a shim. When I take a closer look at its contents my surprise turns to astonishment. Every single word on every page is written in the impeccable penmanship Archie was so proud of, and each entry is dated. His calendars, I’ve now discovered, were not the only records he kept.

“This is a diary!” I exclaim to John. “Why on earth would he wedge a diary under the leg of a bureau? Why not keep it in a drawer? Or destroy it if he wanted to? I don’t understand.”

"It's a damn curious spot for it, that's for sure. When he stuck it here, maybe by then he didn't understand either. Remember, he lived alone with that dementia for quite a while."

"But a diary? Why a diary? That rear leg must've been wobbly for years. Surely there was already wood or cardboard underneath it. Right?"

"One would think so. I agree. He must've torn some pages out, plus the back cover, to make the shim fit properly. Why else would he destroy some of them but leave others?"

"Let me check the dates. At least they'll tell us when he wrote this stuff."

"Good idea."

While John sits patiently next to me, I leaf through the thirty or more pages still attached to the binding. I'm tempted to read every word. One revelation at a time though, and so I concentrate only on the dates, which doesn't take long. Afterwards, looking up at John, I declare, "These are all from after my mother's accident."

"And most of what we've found is from the front of the diary, right?"

"Correct. Safe to say he began writing it after her death."

"And probably kept doing so until his mind wouldn't cooperate anymore."

"And then, for God knows what reason, it became a shim."

"More than a shim," John says. "Much more. It's a gift, Jake. It's a final conversation with your dad, or as close as you can get to one anyway." He pauses before adding, "Tell you what, I'm gonna leave you two alone. No rush. This old bureau will still be here tomorrow." With that he gives me his usual light punch to the shoulder, rises stiffly to his feet, and leaves me alone on the bare floor with Archie's diary. It seems that, once again and as always, Archie will have the last word.

CHAPTER FORTY

I consider moving to a more comfortable spot to pore over the diary, until I remember there are no chairs left in the house. No matter, it's more intimate sitting here in his bedroom next to this ugly bureau. My heart is thudding in my ears as I open the damaged cover and begin reading the first entry, written one month to the day after my mother's untimely death.

I'm sitting at the kitchen table staring at a tuna sandwich I have no appetite to eat. Since you left me, Mary, silence seems even more silent than before. Does that even make sense? I can actually hear the emptiness in my life. I visited your grave this morning. Walked all the way there. What reason had I to hurry? Why not kill time when, after all, time without you is killing me? I'll be back to see you this evening. For now, I'll sit here alone and listen to our grandfather clock in the living room tick away the minutes. I can hear it all the way from the kitchen, like a heart in the distance I can no longer feel beating. No lunch today. I'll wrap this sandwich up in tin foil, maybe eat it for dinner. How I wish you were here to scold me for skipping a meal.

For the moment anyway, one entry is enough to read. Too much, in fact. Already I'm blinking back tears. Is it Archie's gut-wrenching sorrow that makes me so emotional, or have his words, a curious blend of practicality and naked pain, dragged me back to the familiar grief over my own losses? I *am* sure of one thing. The tough as nails Archie rarely, if ever, bared this emotional side of himself to me. He and I loved one another from a distance, much as one stands at least an arm's length away from a painting in order to fully appreciate it. Too late now to be sad or resentful. That's just how it was.

Subsequent entries, penned on random dates spaced weeks apart, continue in the same vein, with Archie recounting the mundane events of his day to his beloved wife, never neglecting to include how desperately he misses her. Many of them are quite brief, just a paragraph or two. Short or long, they're all equally sad, with Archie pining for the intimacy and comfort he'd never again enjoy. Reading along, I'm reminded how Annie and I would lie in the darkness after retiring to bed, and how she'd rest her head on my chest and we'd talk while sleep crept slowly up on us. Now that she's lying next to someone else, I wonder if she ever thumbs through the pages of her memory and thinks of me, or if for her I'm better off forgotten.

Roughly two-thirds of the way through the journal, chronologically almost two years out from her death, Archie's handwriting becomes noticeably sloppier, his command of the language less precise, his loneliness increasingly mixed with frustration and outright anger: *I fear I'm losing you, Mary. I still see you everywhere. Sometimes I can't recall the sound of your voice. How can that be? It frightens me. To help me remember I look at pictures of you. Sometimes I forget where they were taken, or when.*

Among his final entries, before the remaining pages were torn and apparently discarded, Archie pens one of his saddest letters to my mother: *I can't throw away your clothes. They're still in the drawers and hanging in the closet. I touch them and try to feel you again. They don't smell like you anymore. I spray your perfume on them. When I did it last night I fell asleep holding your red sweater. Or maybe it was the blue one. What good is loving someone if we don't even get to keep our memories of them? Where's the sense in caring when it all gets taken away?*

****

Archie's bureau is gone. John and I lugged it out this morning, leaving the house on High Street broom clean, as my overzealous realtor likes to describe it. Tomorrow I'll be gone too, bound for Philadelphia to confront, if I'm able, what I foolishly attempted to escape. First on my list is Annie. She might be married by now. I don't know. I do know it no longer matters. The love that once flamed brightly between us died long ago. Dead is dead. Nothing, and no one, gets a return ticket. I won't knock on her door or call her. That's too direct. In much the same manner that I waited for her in that high school gym decades ago, I'll try to find a way to run into her on the street, maybe when she's leaving her job. She doesn't drink coffee, of that I'm certain, but perhaps she'll sit with me in a booth somewhere, ideally a shabby little café which she finds quaint. It would be a fitting spot to bid a final goodbye and, this time, to apologize to her and really mean it. And if we do speak, I hope we'll discover that a mutual fondness has replaced our love. I hope we can smile and laugh when recalling some of our best moments. I hope we can be grateful for them. I hope we'll always remember them. Having lost too much and too many, I'm learning that memories, for as long as they endure, can be of comfort as well.

I've also decided it's a bad idea to return to high-stakes legal poker in the city. For me, it would be too much like an alcoholic tending bar. The temptation to make my life all about wins and losses at the possible expense of everything else would be dangerously seductive, and after all that's transpired I cannot risk backsliding in that direction. I'm better off setting up a one-man shop in the suburbs, hiring someone with computer skills who can also answer the phone, and taking on only those cases with true merit. I'm hoping that by keeping things simple I'll be freed to fill my days with more rewarding endeavors. I'm not entirely sure what those endeavors will be. I do, however, finally have some rough ideas.

Before departing in the morning, I'll be staying at Sarah's tonight. There's no reason not to. We haven't ended anything. In fact, now that we've agreed to allow our relationship to develop as it will rather than where we might unnaturally force it to go, both of us are relieved and, I dare say, even optimistic. I've had all I can take of trying to fashion life into something it cannot become. It doesn't work. I realize that now. These days I'm more inclined to wait things out, accept what I've been given, and try to appreciate each day's imperfect offerings. I learned the hard way that it's a waste of precious time to do otherwise.

With my car mostly packed and Sarah minding her store, I have time for a final drive around Jackson Meadows. In my mind, while doing so, I'm chauffeuring the ghost of Archie in his baggy windbreaker and Red Sox cap, right elbow poking out the window, surveying the landscape with quizzical interest. As I wend my way through the quiet village streets, the stark emptiness of the seat to my right calls to mind one of the notes from Archie's sad journal and the lesson it imparted: there's nothing worse than loneliness and regret. Granted, there may be no point to all our striving and our suffering. We're doomed to lose what we love, and even the recollections we cherish most dearly will grow duller as the years fade into one another and the arc of our life curves downward to its inescapable conclusion. Yet there's no sense, no benefit I can identify, in going it alone. We can grow old and bitter waiting in vain for something better than what we already have. Or, as John, in his own quirky way has explained, we can try to set regret and doubt aside, share this mystery ride with people we love, and hope like hell for a happy trip. Although I'll never trust a sunny day, I might learn to enjoy one.

****

My goodbye with Sarah was wrapped in hugs and promises, both of us wondering aloud if this was the end, even as we prophesied that the distance I'd be putting between us would pertain only to the miles and not to our affections. Until she fell like soothing rain into the feverish summer of my life, I'd nearly forgotten how badly I missed intimacy and easy companionship, and how such things help ward off dark thoughts which can blind a person to any happiness life might offer. Even if Sarah and I don't survive, I've no desire to end up like poor Archie, alone with my sandwich, listening to time tick slowly by.

I promised John I'd stop by his house before leaving today. It's Sunday and he said he'd be around. When I arrive, Meg greets me with her usual warm hug at the front door, wishes me luck and happiness, then informs me that John's waiting for me in the barn. Puzzled as to what on earth he could be doing there, I cross his scraggly lawn, climb the familiar steps, and find him sitting on the floor beneath the hoop, back against the wall, arms crossed over raised knees. There's no ball in sight, no immediate hello from him, just a brief upward glance to acknowledge my presence.

"Hiding from something?" I ask.

"We're all hiding from one thing or another," he replies glumly, speaking more to the floor than to me.

"Like we did in that treehouse we built in your front yard when we were kids. We'd sit up there for hours spying on the world. Nobody could see us."

Still declining direct eye contact, John mutters, "Nothing could touch us up there in those branches. We were safe."

"And this old barn, this was another refuge," I add, hoping to draw him out. "An even better one."

"That was a long time ago."

I take a seat on the floor next to John, and for a while we sit side by side in silence. When at last John rubs his chin reflectively, I know he's about to say something. "I hope whoever buys your place will have a kid who plays basketball," he tells me. "Be good to hear a ball bouncing up here once in a while."

"I suppose it would."

He studies the floor some more. "You know, revisiting memories can be more satisfying than trying to relive them," he says to me, almost in a whisper.

I know exactly what's gnawing at him. He's trying to apologize for dragging me too deep into the woods, for getting us lost, and even more so, for failing us over the past several months. He's telling me he's worried that whatever he tried to do for me – and for him – wasn't sufficient to restore our friendship and rouse me from my funk, as he once called it. As much as I once would've loved to extract a rare apology from my oldest friend and watch him struggle to say he was sorry without ever using the word, I cannot let his pain continue. Nowadays my heart goes out to him for caring so much and trying so hard.

"Hold it right there," I tell him. "Don't ask me why, but getting lost with you in those woods, being cut off from everything in my world except you, might've been the best thing that could've happened to me. To us. It clarified some things, and that's all I'm ever going to say about it. So let's not get all gushy or morose, ok? You hear me? Let's just say I truly appreciate all that you and Meg have done. Trust me on this one. We have more happy memories to be made. I'll be back. I promise."

Almost instantaneously, John brightens up. "Or else we can visit you sometimes," he adds eagerly. "I'd really enjoy a tour of Philadelphia. Maybe bring the clubs and take up golf again. Does that sound like a new adventure?"

"Certainly a safer one," I reply. "Why don't we call it our new Plan B. And assuming I can find a large enough place to live, there will always be a key under the mat for you and Meg. Speaking of whom, how's she doing? Things still ok?"

"At least for today," John replies.

"I suppose today is all we ever have."

"Exactly what I've been trying to tell you all along, JT," he exclaims, applying the palm of his hand to my forehead for final emphasis.

CHAPTER FORTY-ONE

Before leaving the barn John surprised me with a colorfully wrapped gift, accompanied by strict instructions not to open it until I'd reached Pennsylvania. I held out only as far as the scenic overlook just outside Jackson Meadows before the temptation to see what he'd given me proved too powerful to resist. I've parked my car facing north before turning the engine off, affording me one last view of the town I'm leaving behind once again. Mine is the only car in the small lot, and except for the whoosh of an occasional vehicle rushing past on Route 3, all is quiet on this frosty Sunday morning in early November. The gift's meticulous wrapping job is unmistakably Meg's doing. Whatever's inside is undoubtedly John's.

I carefully remove the paper from the box it covers, as if I intend to re-use it. I want to make this moment last, to hang on a few moments longer to John and Meg, to Sarah and Archie, and to the town that began to feel like home. Having placed the wrapping on the seat next to me, I begin opening the box, only to find it's been taped on all four sides. Leave it to John to overdo things. I rip off the tape, open the top, and pull out something wrapped – and again securely taped – in a large mound of tissue paper. Shredding the covering, I'm surprised and a little disappointed to pull out only a grey tee shirt. It hardly seems like an inspired gift, until I hold it up before me and discover a photo of a large, menacing black bear on its front, with the word "Bear" spelled out in block letters beneath the image. Turning the shirt around, I find that its reverse side sports a photo of a happy dog, tongue out, eyes eager to please, with the words "Black Lab" spelled out in block letters. And toward the bottom, way down low on the back of the shirt, I spy a hand-written inscription in black magic marker: "If there's ever a next time, we'll know the difference."

****

John's gift having been tucked back into its box, I've been sitting here staring at the village of Jackson Meadows for quite a while. It looks the same as when I arrived in May, yet somehow feels different. It changed for me, subtly, the way life often does. Down in that river valley, I found the friend I wasn't looking for and a woman who offered hope for new love when I'd believed such a thing lay beyond my grasp. And I buried a father there. Archie spent years struggling to teach his hard-headed son at least a few good lessons. Ironically, he imparted some of the most valuable ones during the worst of his dementia and after his death. Whatever I might have done for him in the months before his passing, I hope he sensed that by my actions I was trying to say “I love you” without, of course, ever using the words.

November’s chill has now seeped into my car. Time to turn it back on. I need the warmth and I need to leave. I have nowhere to go and everywhere to go. Either way, I’ll be there soon.

Acknowledgments

My thanks to Christine for her patience in answering my many questions early on about the publishing process, and for the direction given. I owe an immense debt of gratitude to Mia for her careful editing, astute suggestions, and ultimately the confidence she gave me to share the fictional world I fondly created. Thanks to Kate for her design talents, among several others. Thanks also to Brian and to Kaitlin Mary for believing their old man could actually pull this feat off, and for regularly telling him so. And thanks to Judy for understanding.

It almost goes without saying that writing can be a lonely, grueling and frustrating process, and if not for the encouragement of my patient and loving wife Bev, who maintained her enthusiasm for the manuscript even when mine sometimes waned, I might not have finished what I optimistically began years ago.

Lastly, thanks to the lifelong friendship that inspired it all.

Further Acknowledgments

The reference in Chapter 13 to a burned house for which only the chimney remained standing is to a poem by Robert Frost entitled, *The Need of Being Versed in Country Things*.

The reference in Chapter 13 to the expression on Archie's face resembling the distance on the look of death is to a poem by Emily Dickinson entitled, *There's a Certain Slant of Light*.

The trial over the kicking horse in Chapter 28 was inspired by a newspaper account in the "Backward Glance" section of the *Coos County Democrat*, which I clipped out, and then lost, a number of years ago.

About the Author

David Hartshorn grew up in Lancaster, New Hampshire, and is an honors graduate of Middlebury College with a degree in American Literature. He currently lives in Burlington, Connecticut where he is practicing trial attorney. *More Than Halfway There* is his first novel.

Made in the USA
Middletown, DE
04 July 2021